Constance Santego

Healing of a Soul

Constance Santego has been practicing and teaching *The Nine Spiritual Gifts, Granted from Spirit,* for over twenty-four years. She lives in British Columbia, Canada, with her husband.

www.constancesantego.ca

ALSO BY CONSTANCE SANTEGO

FICTION
The Nine Spiritual Gifts Series:
Journey of a Soul – (Vol. 1 Michael)
Language of a Soul – (Vol. 2 Gabriel)
Prophecy of a Soul – (Vol. 3 Bath Kol)

NON-FICTION
The Intuitive Life, The Gift of Prophecy, Third
Edition
Fairy Tales, Dreams and Reality… Where Are You
On Your Path? Second Edition
Your Persona… The Mask You Wear
Angelic Lifestyle, A Vibrant Lifestyle
Angelic Lifestyle 42-Day Energy Cleanse
Archangel Michael's Soul Retrieval Guide
SECRETS OF A HEALER, SERIES:
Magic of Aromatherapy (Vol. I)
Magic of Reflexology (Vol. II)
Magic of The Gifts (Vol. III)
Magic of Muscle Testing (Vol. IV)
Magic of Iridology (Vol. V)
Magic of Massage (Vol. VI)
Magic of Hypnotherapy (Vol. VII)
Magic of Reiki (Vol. VIII)
Magic of Advanced Aromatherapy (Vol. IX)
Magic of Esthetics (Vol. X)

FOR CHILDREN
I am big tonight. I don't need the light!

Published by: Maximillian Enterprises
Editor: Ana Joldes
Interior Layout: Constance Santego
Book Layout: ©2017 BookDesignTemplates.com
Cover Design: Jennifer Louie
Soft Cover ISBN: 978-1-990062-08-7
eBook ISBN: 978-1-990062-09-4
Created and published in Canada. Printed and bound in the United States of America
Ordering Information: csantego@gmail.com

Cast of Characters

**Some of the Residents of New York City, USA,
and other places.**

Alexandra (Lexi) Elizabeth Constantine:
Fashion designer in Upper East Side Manhattan.
Daughter of Olivia and Marcus Constantine
(Italian). Fiancée to Reverend Edward Julien
Hawthorne. Her boss is Sebastian. Friends with
co-worker Southern belle, Sherie.

Susannah Grace Constantine:
Lexi's belated sister and now guardian angel.
Lived in Dumbo (Down Under the Manhattan
Bridge Overpass). She was an antique collector
for Aryeh Jacob Kofman and dated Billy
Randazzo.

**Olivia Sarah Constantine (Maiden name,
Austin):** Mother to Lexi and Susannah.
Widowed housewife. Parents were from
England. She lives in Dyker Heights, Brooklyn,
NY.

Reverend Edward Julien Hawthorne:
Mortician and minister of a funeral home in

Brooklyn. Fiancé to Alexandra (Lexi). Casandra is his secretary.

Tamara Reeve: Psychic medium and teacher of many of the Spiritual Gifts. Fiancée to Greg Masones. Now owns her grandmother's brownstone in Brooklyn Heights.

Detective Ferguson "Red" Redington: 1st-grade homicide investigator, Manhattan Bureau – Midtown South Precinct, Shield number 1323, NYPD. Lives in Far Rockaway Beach, Queens, on Long Island, NY. His family comes from England.

Greg Masones (AKA Julian D'Angelo): At large. Accountant for the Genovese crime family. Italian immigrant. Son of Serena D'Angelo. Was Tamara's fiancé.

Isabella Jackson: Famous actress. She moved around to wherever her next movie was being filmed. Friends with Lexi, Edward, and Redington. Girlfriend of belated Hans (now Erland, an Elf) and mother to Aias.

Hans Magnusson (Erland): Lawyer. He lived in Switzerland but was from Sweden. He inherited his family's fortune, and his grandfather was Olof. After he died, he became a walk-in soul to Erland in the Elemental Realm of Alfheim, Still communicates with Isabella.

Aias Jackson Olof Magnusson: Son of Isabella and Erland. He was a half-elf with many gifts, the main one being able to heal.

Kesia Bango: Gypsy tarot card reader. Daughter of Florence. Ancestral Granddaughter of Tatiana Masones and Clementina (Tatiana's mother). Related to Greg, he is her uncle.

Main Angel of each Novel

Book 1 – Archangel Michael
"Warrior"
Companion Book – Archangel Michael's Soul Retrieval Guide.
Book 2 – Archangel Gabriel
"Messenger"
Companion Book – Your Persona... The Mask You Wear.
Book 3 – Bath Kol
"Daughter of the Voice," the Holy Ghost, and Gabriel
Companion Book – The Gift of Prophecy.
Book 4 – Archangel Raphael
"God Has Healed"
Companion Books – Secrets of a Healer Series.

Healing of a Soul
The Gift of Healing

A Novel
4th in the series, The Nine Spiritual Gifts
"The Gift of Healing"

Constance Santego

Vol. 4

Dedicated

to all the healers and

doctors of the world!

Healing of a Soul

The Nine Spiritual Gifts

In the New Testament, my favorite story is
"The Gifts."
Corinthians 1, Chapter 12, Verse 4-11
*(Maybe a little differently worded
depending on which Bible you have).*

The variety and the unity of gifts

There are many different gifts, but it is always
the same Spirit; there are many different ways of
serving, but it is always the same Lord. There
are many different forms of activity, but in
everybody, it is the same God who is at work in
them all. The particular manifestation of the
Spirit granted to each one is to be used for the
general good.

To one is given from the Spirit the gift of
utterance expressing **wisdom**; to another the gift
of utterance expressing **knowledge**; in
accordance with the same spirit, to another,
faith, from the same Spirit; and to another, the
gifts of **healing**, through the same Spirit; to
another, the working of **miracles**; to another
prophecy; to another, the power of
distinguishing spirits; to one, the gift of
different tongues; and to another, the
interpretation of tongues. But at work in all
these is one and the same Spirit, distributing
them at will to each individual.

The New Jerusalem Bible

*A*waken to the spirit world, for there lie your gifts granted by Spirit.

~ Constance Santego

"*T*he doctor of the future will give no medication but will interest his patients in the care of the human frame, diet, and in the cause and prevention of disease."

~ Thomas A. Edison

Fact:

All biblical references, science, legends, and myths are real *(slightly changed to fit the character)*. This novel was written as a story inspired by Spirit to give you, the reader, a new perspective, a new way to learn, and a new opportunity to empower your life.

All characters are fictional, but the locations are based on reality.

Prologue

The Hippocratic Oath, in Greek, from the 1923 Loeb edition, and then followed by the English translation:

ὄμνυμι Ἀπόλλωνα ἰητρὸν καὶ Ἀσκληπιὸν καὶ Ὑγείαν καὶ Πανάκειαν καὶ θεοὺς πάντας τε καὶ πάσας, ἵστορας ποιεύμενος, ἐπιτελέα ποιήσειν κατὰ δύναμιν καὶ κρίσιν ἐμὴν ὅρκον τόνδε καὶ συγγραφὴν τήνδε:

ἡγήσεσθαι μὲν τὸν διδάξαντά με τὴν τέχνην ταύτην ἴσα γενέτῃσιν ἐμοῖς, καὶ βίου κοινώσεσθαι, καὶ χρεῶν χρηΐζοντι μετάδοσιν ποιήσεσθαι, καὶ γένος τὸ ἐξ αὑτοῦ ἀδελφοῖς ἴσον ἐπικρινεῖν ἄρρεσι, καὶ διδάξειν τὴν τέχνην ταύτην, ἢν χρηΐζωσι μανθάνειν, ἄνευ μισθοῦ καὶ συγγραφῆς, παραγγελίης τε καὶ ἀκροήσιος καὶ τῆς λοίπης ἁπάσης μαθήσιος μετάδοσιν ποιήσεσθαι υἱοῖς τε ἐμοῖς καὶ τοῖς τοῦ ἐμὲ διδάξαντος, καὶ μαθητῇσι συγγεγραμμένοις τε καὶ ὡρκισμένοις νόμῳ ἰητρικῷ, ἄλλῳ δὲ οὐδενί.

διαιτήμασί τε χρήσομαι ἐπ' ὠφελείῃ καμνόντων κατὰ δύναμιν καὶ κρίσιν ἐμήν, ἐπὶ δηλήσει δὲ καὶ ἀδικίῃ εἴρξειν.

οὐ δώσω δὲ οὐδὲ φάρμακον οὐδενὶ αἰτηθεὶς θανάσιμον, οὐδὲ ὑφηγήσομαι συμβουλίην τοιήνδε: ὁμοίως δὲ οὐδὲ γυναικὶ πεσσὸν φθόριον δώσω.

ἁγνῶς δὲ καὶ ὁσίως διατηρήσω βίον τὸν ἐμὸν καὶ τέχνην τὴν ἐμήν.

οὐ τεμέω δὲ οὐδὲ μὴν λιθιῶντας, ἐκχωρήσω δὲ ἐργάτῃσιν ἀνδράσι πρήξιος τῆσδε.

ἐς οἰκίας δὲ ὁκόσας ἂν ἐσίω, ἐσελεύσομαι ἐπ' ὠφελείῃ καμνόντων, ἐκτὸς ἐὼν πάσης ἀδικίης ἑκουσίης καὶ φθορίης, τῆς τε ἄλλης καὶ ἀφροδισίων ἔργων ἐπί τε γυναικείων σωμάτων καὶ ἀνδρῴων, ἐλευθέρων τε καὶ δούλων.

ἃ δ' ἂν ἐνθεραπείῃ ἴδω ἢ ἀκούσω, ἢ καὶ ἄνευ θεραπείης κατὰ βίον ἀνθρώπων, ἃ μὴ χρή ποτε ἐκλαλεῖσθαι ἔξω, σιγήσομαι, ἄρρητα ἡγεύμενος εἶναι τὰ τοιαῦτα.

ὅρκον μὲν οὖν μοι τόνδε ἐπιτελέα ποιέοντι, καὶ μὴ συγχέοντι, εἴη ἐπαύρασθαι καὶ βίου καὶ τέχνης δοξαζομένῳ παρὰ πᾶσιν ἀνθρώποις ἐς τὸν αἰεὶ χρόνον: παραβαίνοντι δὲ καὶ ἐπιορκέοντι, τἀναντία τούτων.

I swear by Apollo Healer, by Asclepius, by Hygieia, by Panacea, and by all the gods and goddesses, making them my witnesses, that I will carry out, according to my ability and judgment, this oath and this indenture.

To hold my teacher in this art equal to my own parents; to make him partner in my livelihood; when he is in need of money to share mine with him; to consider his family as my own brothers, and to teach them this art, if they want to learn it, without fee or indenture; to impart precept, oral instruction, and all other instruction to my own sons, the sons of my teacher, and to indentured pupils who have taken the Healer's oath, but to nobody else.

I will use those dietary regimens, which will benefit my patients according to my greatest ability and judgment, and I will do no harm or injustice to them. Neither will I administer a poison to anybody when asked to do so, nor will I suggest such a course. Similarly, I will not give to a woman a pessary to cause abortion. But I will keep pure and holy both my life and my art. I will not use the knife, not even, verily, on sufferers from stone, but I will give place to such as are craftsmen therein.

Into whatsoever houses I enter, I will enter to help the sick, and I will abstain from all intentional wrong-doing and harm, especially from abusing the bodies of man or woman, bond or free. And whatsoever I shall see or hear in the course of my profession, as well as outside my profession in my intercourse with men, if it be what should not be published abroad, I will never divulge, holding such things to be holy secrets.

Now, if I carry out this oath and break it not, may I gain forever reputation among all men for my life and for my art; but if I break it and forswear myself, may the opposite befall me. – Translation by W.H.S. Jones.

William Henry Samuel Jones (1876–1963) was a British author, translator, and academic. He was known as **Malaria Jones** because of his theory that malaria was instrumental in the downfall of the classical civilizations of Greece and Rome.

~

Archangel Raphael, the saint of healing. His name means "God has healed."

In the Old Testament of the Bible, there is a book called Tobit (Tb). Archangel Raphael acts as a companion to Tobit's son, Tobias, who journeys to Media from Nineveh and heals Tobias's fiancée and father. It is only at the end of the journey that Raphael reveals himself by name as "one of the seven holy angels of the Apocalypse" that attend the throne of God.

Raphael is the regent of the sun, chief of the order of virtues, governor of the south, guardian of the west, ruling prince of the 2nd Heaven, overseer of the evening winds, guardian of the Tree of Life in the Garden of Eden, one of the six angels of repentance, and an angel of prayer, love, joy, and light. But above all, he is, as his name denotes, the angel of healing.

Raphael is the angel who heals the soul by bringing the "blind" back to "believers."

6   Constance Santego

Chapter 1

July 10th – Wedding Day
Lexi

"I hear wedding bells," Sherie said in her cute Southern belle accent as she came into a small room that Lexi was using at the front of Edward's church.

As Olivia watched Isabella place the headpiece on her daughter, she wiped a tear from her eye and said, "I am so glad that you and Edward made up. I was a little worried that you would become an old spinster."

"Mother, a spinster? Really? I'm not that old."

"Well, you are thirty-six."

"Mom, you know my career took priority, and besides that, most of the men I work with are gay."

Wiping another tear, Olivia said, "Well, I have no need to fret about it now. You're getting married. I just wish your sister and dad could have been here."

Looking in the mirror at Olivia, Lexi responded, "Mom, you're going to wreck your make-up. Maybe go and be seated. We're almost ready."

Olivia kissed her daughter's head, thinking, *Thank God Isabella could sub in for Tamara,* but whispered, "Your dad would have been so proud."

Lexi smiled awkwardly at her bridesmaids as her mom left the room. To shift the room's vibe, she said, "You all look so beautiful."

Lexi had designed the teal floor-length, V-neck silk dresses to match her wedding gown. She loved how the matching tulle showed off the intricate aquamarine gemstones hand-sewn throughout the netting. The ladies looked stunning in their very chic gowns.

Looking at herself in the mirror, Lexi looked like a Greek goddess in her one-of-a-kind backless wedding dress. The V-neck gave way to a cinched waist. The flow of the floor-length gown was spellbinding. As she moved, the light silver tulle fabric shimmered and glittered like stardust overtop of the white silk lining. It reminded her of beautiful ice crystals that shimmered brilliantly in the sun. And instead of a veil, Lexi wore a sparkling crystal tiara with matching earrings that dangled from her ear lobes.

She had also designed the men's attire. Edward's silver and gray tux matched her dress. Little Aias, who now looked five, was the ring-bearer and looked adorable in his dark gray suspender shorts, matching vest, and teal bowtie. The best man and the groomsmen were wearing identical outfits but with pants, not shorts.

The minister performing the ceremony was a good friend of Edward's dad, Reverend O'Malley. The ladies were waiting patiently for one of the ushers to come and tell them when he was ready to start the ceremony.

Lexi looked at the clock on the wall. *Fifteen minutes late, really?* "I thought it was supposed to be the bride who was running late. What is taking them so long?" Lexi said, getting antsy.

"I am sure they are just waiting for stragglers to come in and get seated. Edward probably thinks that it is you who is late," chuckled Isabella.

Lexi looked at the clock again. Five more minutes had gone by. "Okay, something is wrong. Kesia, please go and find out what is taking so long."

Kesia quickly went out the door.

A few moments later, the door opened.

While looking at her make-up in the mirror, Lexi said, "So, what is taking so long?"

"Alexandra."

That wasn't Kesia's voice. Turning, she saw Detective Redington staring at her. Startled, she asked, "What are you doing here?"

"Lexi, I am so sorry. I just came from a crime scene. It's Edward. He was there. He's—"

Not being able to finish his sentence before she fainted, Redington barely heard her say, "Oh my God, the prophecy is coming true!"

"What prophecy?" asked Isabella as she went to catch Lexi.

"The prophecy that Mukesh read in Lexi's Vedic Astrology Chart while we were in India. He predicted that there was going to be a misfortune concerning her marriage," answered Kesia.

Chapter 2

July 10ᵗʰ – Wedding Day
Crime Scene

Sirens screaming.

"Hey, I found another one over here," Edward heard a man yelling to someone.

"Is he alive?"

"I don't think so."

Then came a familiar voice. "How long do you think they have been like this?"

"Maybe an hour or two," a female voice answered.

"Did you find any identification?" the familiar voice asked again.

This time a man answered. "No. But I did find this in the guy's pocket."

"It looks like a wedding ring."

I'm alive! I'm alive! Edward thought. *Why aren't you helping me?*

Edward was past the point of feeling any pain. Most of the time, he imagined time like in a dream. All noises were magnified and intensified. He felt strange and lost at times, but he felt safer when he heard that familiar voice. *I recognize that voice but from where?*

"I'm done with my initial examination of the bodies, Detective. I won't be able to tell you more until I get them back to the morgue," the female coroner replied.

That's it! That's where I know the voice from. It's Redington. Red! It's me, Edward. Red, can you hear me? Yes, take me to my morgue.

"Take him to the emergency room," Redington said, getting a weird vibe.

No. I just need to go home. I'm okay.

To the coroner's surprise, the EMT found a heartbeat, faint, but there was one.

"How did you know?" the coroner asked.

"Just a hunch," the familiar voice said. "Hey, wait. I'm coming with you."

An ambulance carried the bodies to the hospital. Edward's head looked like a football when he was admitted into the emergency room. Someone had smashed his head in with a bat. His eyes were so swollen that only his dental records confirmed who he really was.

Edward was drifting in and out of consciousness.

Mom, Dad, how have you been? Sorry I haven't talked to you lately. Nobody would give me the phone number at the hotel you were staying in. So, how's the trip been? Is dad spending time with you or just golfing? How he loves his golf. Oh, this is so nice. I miss you, guys.

Within minutes of arriving at the hospital, the doctor had ordered a CT scan that revealed acute subdural hematoma. Edward's score on the Glasgow Coma Scale—a neurological scale that measures a person's conscious state—was dropping quickly. The highest score is fifteen, indicating that the person is fully awake and alert. The lowest score possible is a three, indicating that the person "does not open their eyes," "makes no sound," and "makes no movements." Edward's score was a four.

The last thing Edward heard was someone telling another person, "The police don't suspect that it was a robbery, but that leaves me trying to figure out the reason why these three people had to die. Let's hope this fella's luckier and isn't number four."

As a nurse came in with the dental records, the doctor read the patient's name out loud.

"His name is what?" Redington asked.

"Reverend Edward Hawthorne."

"Alexandra! The wedding! I have to go!"

Chapter 3

July 10th – Wedding Day
Edward

My ears pop at the sound of the people speaking as they touch me. I could hear them normally before. Why do they sound so weird now?

It is unclear to me if there is something in my nose. My body feels mushy, and my limbs feel like they weigh a hundred pounds, but I can't move my arms to check. I feel detached from my body. I know it's mine, but I am not fully connected to it.

I hear the doctor tell someone to give me a sedative. No! I scream, but all I hear is a distorted whine and realize that a machine, not I, made the sound.

Thinking back to this morning, my mind grows groggy as I go to sleep from the drugs.

\#

Waking up unrested, Edward got out of bed. Still sleepy, he wobbled over to the shower. Taking off his housecoat, he stepped in and turned on the water. Putting his hands up to his face, he splashed some on to wake up and then realized that he would be married today.

Instantly waking up, he finished washing and dried himself quickly. *I still have to get the ring.*

Calling an Uber to pick him up, he headed toward the front doors.

His secretary and good friend, Casandra, met him just before reaching it. "Everything is ready for you in the cathedral. Alexandra's favorite flowers have just arrived, and someone is placing them there now. Edward, it looks beautiful. Where are you headed?"

"I need to pick up her ring. The guy just finished it."

Casandra looked at her watch. "Hurry back. You still have to get into your tux. You wouldn't want to miss your own wedding."

Edward nodded as he rushed out, hopped into the waiting car, and gave the driver the address.

"Are you sure you want to go there?" the driver asked.

"Yes."

"It's your coin," the driver replied but said it with a tone insinuating that it was his *life* that was at stake, not his money.

The drive wasn't too long, but Edward now understood the driver's tone of voice. The address was in Brownsville, notorious for being one of the top ten most dangerous areas in New York City.

"Are you sure this is the address?" Edward asked.

"It's the one you gave me," the guy answered.

Edward nervously paid the guy and got out of the car.

"Sorry, pal, but I am not waiting for you," he said and drove off almost before Edward shut the door.

Initially, Brownsville, a residential neighborhood located in East Brooklyn in New York City, was used by the Dutch for farming and manufacturing stone slabs and other construction items. Then, its residents shifted to mostly Jewish factory workers. But in the 1930s, the neighborhood changed to a majority of African-American and Latino residents. That is when it achieved notoriety as the birthplace of "Murder, Inc.," an organized crime group that acted as the enforcement arm of the Italian-American Mafia, the Jewish Mob, and other closely connected organized crime groups.

Walking toward the street access of the commercial building, Edward opened the door cautiously. It wasn't 10:00 am, so he thought it shouldn't be too busy in there.

He was mistaken. Two guys were waiting for the storekeeper to bring them their items. The storekeeper brought out a small box for Edward as he passed another to a guy with biceps as big as tree trunks. Edward couldn't help but watch as the guy with the big biceps struggled to do up the heavy gold chain around his neck. His buddy, laughing, finally helped him put it on.

Having never been to this store before since the jeweler had met him at his funeral home, Edward was happy that a friend of his had forwarded his phone number. Opening the box to look inside, Edward took out the ring he had the jeweler design for him… even happier now since he was extremely impressed with the quality of his craftsmanship and the even better price tag. *What a deal. Alexandra is going to love this!*

Another man came into the shop wearing a long trench coat even though it was almost 75° Fahrenheit.

"Give me what you owe," Edward heard him say to the storekeeper.

"Take your sorry ass somewhere else. He's busy," said the guy with the biceps.

Not even looking at the guy, the man in the trench coat revealed a concealed bat and started swinging, knocking him out.

The sound was horrifying.

As if in slow motion, Edward watched as the big bicep guy stood there dazed, took a few wobbly steps backward, then fell to the floor with blood pouring out of his head like a faucet.

The bat didn't stop moving. Within seconds, the storekeeper and the friend were down. The guy in the trench coat just kept beating them.

As he turned toward the door, he spotted Edward.

Edward backed up slowly, putting the wedding ring into his pocket, raising his hands to signify surrender. Just as the bat connected with his skull, a bright white light exploded somewhere behind his eyes. The pain came from all directions. Unable to make any intelligible noise, Edward passed out.

That was the moment Edward knew why he was in the hospital. He remembered the terror, fear, and pain. It was as if he had been struck by lightning, white-hot pain.

The monitor connected to Edward sent out a piercing noise, and the heart monitor on the screen started flat-lining.

"Doctor, he's crashing and going into cardiac arrest!" yelled the nurse.

Doctor Singh instantly turned around and came back into the room.

The nurse placed the mouthpiece over Edward's mouth and started pumping a handheld bag valve mask.

She would have started cardiopulmonary resuscitation, better known as CPR if the doctor wasn't right there.

Before Edward stopped breathing altogether, Singh took hold of the two paddles connected to a much larger machine. The paddles he was using had metal plating on one side and plastic handles with buttons on the other side. Singh watched as one of the nurses turned the green button on the defibrillator.

The nurse using the bag valve mask stopped and removed the unit.

"CLEAR!" Singh shouted as he placed the paddles on Edward's chest and pushed the buttons.

The machine was set to deliver a high voltage of three hundred joules of electrical energy that would surge through Edward's body, stopping his heart long enough to allow the contractions to reset.

In that instant, Singh remembered his professor say, *"Many people don't know that the heart is dependent upon a small amount of electricity that comes from a person's sinoatrial node—the natural pacemaker that sets and maintains the heartbeat. This electric current is transmitted from a group of cells located in the right atrium wall in the heart, causing it to contract and send oxygen-deprived blood to the lungs. Without this natural electricity produced in our body, we would die."*

After watching the monitor, Singh told the nurse to increase the joules to see if Edward's heartbeat returned to normal.

"CLEAR!" he shouted again.

The sound on the monitor started to beep in the rhythm of a normal heartbeat.

Edward was unconscious, but at least his breathing seemed normal.

Singh let out the breath of air he was holding and hoped Edward wasn't in a coma.

Chapter 4

It had been many weeks since that dreaded day, her wedding day. The day Detective Redington was coincidently on the scene when they identified Edward, beaten and unconscious in some rough part of town. The why of it all had not yet been discussed with Lexi.

"What did you have to do to become a doctor?" Lexi asked.

Standing beside Edward's hospital bed, checking his vitals, Doctor Neo Singh replied, "Do you mean all the steps I had to take to become a neurosurgeon?"

"Yes."

"Do you have your phone with you?"

"Yes."

"Look up the definition."

Lexi was offended that he didn't actually answer her question.

As he was leaving the room, he said, "And in case you meant my pre-med major, I received my bachelor's degree in neuroscience."

Lexi googled neuroscience first. Neuroscience integrates psychology, cell biology, genetics, biochemistry, physiology, anatomy, and other branches of the life sciences to provide comprehensive insights into the structure and function of the brain.

Then she searched the requirements needed to become a neurosurgeon. A neurosurgeon is a physician who specializes in the diagnosis and surgical treatment of disorders of the central and peripheral nervous system, including congenital anomalies, trauma, tumors, vascular conditions, infections of the brain or spine, stroke, or degenerative diseases of the spine.

Lexi looked at Edward. *Trauma. You definitely had trauma.* Lexi continued to read.

The education and training to become a neurosurgeon are rigorous and extensive and include the completion of:

- Four years of pre-medical education at a college or university.
- Four years of medical school, resulting in an M.D. or D.O. degree.
- One year internship in general surgery.
- Five to seven years in a neurosurgery residency program.

- Some neurosurgeons complete a fellowship after residency to specialize in a particular area.
- Continuing education—annual meetings, conferences, scientific journals, research—to keep up with advances made in the complex field of neurosurgery.

Speaking to Edward, even though he was in a coma, Lexi said, "At least you have a doctor who seems to be finely educated."

"What did he answer? I didn't hear it," Redington said as he came in and kissed Lexi on her forehead.

"Funny."

Red had been coming in every day since he found Edward. He couldn't get the look on Lexi's face out of his mind when he told her the news—absolute fear; then she went white as a ghost. He hadn't been able to catch her as she fell to the ground from fainting. He still remembered how she had banged her head on a table and the blood that stained her wedding gown.

"How are you doing?" He was getting worried about how thin she was getting.

Lexi nodded. "Fine."

"Here, I brought you a latte and a muffin. I thought you might be hungry."

Taking the coffee, she said, "Thanks. I could use a good cup of coffee right now."

Redington placed the wrapped muffin on the portable table beside Edward's hospital bed and said, "Make sure you eat this later, will ya?"

Lexi nodded but stared at Edward. "It's been four months. Why hasn't he woken up yet?"

"I am just grateful to know that he has insurance. This place must be costing a pretty penny."

"I wish Tamara was here. She would have known what to do." Now thinking about Tamara, Lexi asked, "You still haven't heard anything about her in Nepal?"

"No."

"It's just my luck that I couldn't go and find her," Lexi said sadly.

"Alexandra, maybe she doesn't want to be found."

"I doubt that. Tamara probably thinks Julian is still out there and is hiding from him."

A group of interns came into Edward's room.

"What are the two main healing purposes for a coma patient?" the attending asked the interns.

One of the new interns said, "To help the patient wake up from a coma and to prevent secondary complications."

"That is correct."

A pretty little Asian physical therapist, with biceps like a bodybuilder, came in just as the group was leaving and said, "Hi, Lexi. Time for his daily stimulation."

Redington hadn't been there before to witness this part of Edward's treatment.

"What are you doing?" he asked.

The therapist answered, "I provide structured and organized sensory stimulation."

"Oh. I thought your only job was to move him."

"Yes, most people do think my only job is to preserve the patient's physical condition through flexibility and range-of-motion exercises, but we are trained to work on all five senses, including touch, vision, sound, movement, and smell."

Redington's curiosity was heightened, and he asked, "You're telling me that a person in a coma can smell?"

"Aromatherapy is more than just for smelling. It has many healing benefits. It can penetrate the skin and enter the bloodstream. Stimulating the nervous system is just one of the benefits."

Based on Dr. Singh's neurological assessment, Edward's rehabilitation team was next to come into the room. These nurses provided oximetry monitoring, tracheostomy care, suctioning, psychological services, and nutritional intervention.

And lastly, for the morning routine, another nurse came in and provided the medications to help stimulate Edward's brain.

"Wow, Alexandra, no need to worry about Edward's care. I would say this is first-class."

"The doctor calls it Edward's neuro-recovery coma program. Care is provided round-the-clock, with all of the necessary adaptive support and stimulation that he requires and needs," Lexi said as she lovingly squeezed Edward's hand.

"Now, all we need is a miracle," Redington said as he kissed Lexi on the forehead again and left.

Chapter 5

Sitting at his desk staring down at Edward's chart, Neo Singh drifted into a memory of standing with his classmates when they had passed their final boards to practice independently as physicians. His Greek mother, Naida, and East Indian father, Paal, were watching with pride. Then, with his hand over his heart, he repeated the modern version of the Hippocratic Oath. *I swear to fulfill, to the best of my ability and judgment, this covenant…*

Coming back to the present moment, he thought to himself, *Edward's chance of recovery is dwindling with each day.* Neo knew all too well the continuing debate about the potential for recovery of patients in a vegetative state is not very likely. The longer a patient remains in a coma, the poorer their chance of recovery. Most doctors know that almost half of the patients who have not recovered consciousness are forever left in a vegetative state by the end of the first week. Unfortunately, Edward had been in a vegetative state for weeks. *I hate that I must tell Miss Constantine the truth that Edward's chance for a full recovery is almost nil, but not today, maybe in the next day or two.*

It was his parents' 40th anniversary, and he was going to their place for dinner.

Upon entering their house, he was greeted by the familiar aroma of curry. His younger sister, Evangeline, had prepared a traditional Indian meal: salad, naan bread, raita—yogurt thinned out with a bit of water, salt, and roasted cumin powder—pickles, and Indian pickled onions. The main course consisted of corn kadai masala, potato, eggplant in pickling spices, and chicken biryani—a juicy chicken mixed with basmati rice, topped with a spicy buttery sauce. For dessert, there was an Indian cheesecake.

Neo and his sister had grown up within both cultures and enjoyed the benefits of each.

As Neo came into the kitchen, he said, "Namaste, sis, smells delicious."

"Yiasoo," she greeted him in Greek, then kissed him on the cheek.

Evangeline's ten-year-old son, Todd, asked Neo, "How was your day at the hospital, uncle? Anything interesting that I would think was lit? Like, did you perform any brain surgery today?"

"Ya, you'll like this one, Todd. I had to cut into…"

Teasing, Evangeline yelled, "Stop! Don't tell him that. We are going to be eating in a few minutes."

"Awe, mom. I can handle it."

"Well, I can't. Now get out of here, you two."

As they left the room, Neo grabbed Todd and gave him a fake noogie on the top of the boy's head.

Evangeline came out of the kitchen and said, "Okay, everyone, have a seat. We're ready to eat."

Neo's father, Paal, said grace in Sanskrit:
Brahmārpañam Brahma Havir
BrahmāgnauBrahmañāhutaṃ,
Brahmaiva Tena Gantavyam
BrahmakarmāSamādhinah.
Translation—
The act of offering is God.
The oblation is God.
By God, it is offered into the Fire of God.
God is that which is to be attained by he who performs action pertaining to God.

After dinner, Neo watched his mom bow her head and mouth the Greek Orthodox Thanksgiving After-Dinner Prayer.

He knew it well. *Glory to the Father and to the Son and to the Holy Spirit, now and forever and to the ages of ages. Amen. Lord, have mercy. Lord, have mercy. Lord, have mercy. Lord, you have gladdened our hearts in your creation, and we have rejoiced in the work of your hands. The light of your countenance has shined upon us, Lord. You have gladdened our hearts. We have been satisfied with the good things of the earth. We shall sleep in peace and repose in you, for you alone, Lord, have sustained us in hope.*

Before the plates were removed from the table, Todd shared what had happened at school that day, "A girl at school was using a pendulum during lunch and showing us how blessing your food changes the vibration of the food to a higher state of energy."

Neo commented, "There is no science to prove that blessing your food actually works. Food is broken down into chemicals by your body's digestive system and administered, stored, or dispelled as needed."

"I know, but I thought it was cool. It gave tangible evidence to a ritual."

"Neo, you take science so literally. Have you forgotten your religious upbringing?" Evangeline said, defending her son's excitement.

Neo lifted his eyebrows to say, sure, whatever, or I guess, while looking at his sister. *I see death every day. It has become hard for me to believe that there even is a God.*

Getting up so he wouldn't ruin the evening, he said, "I have to go back to the hospital. Thanks for dinner." Kissing his mom and dad goodnight, he said, "Love you both," then headed to the door.

Chapter 6

Placing the last crystal in the center of the Star of David, Luna bowed her head and prayed to the Horned God and Mother Goddess.

She had been working on this spell for days. The sacred geometry of the crystal grid was perfect for enhancing this specific spell.

She had been practicing Wicca for about two years now, and even though her friends joked about her being a pagan witch and practicing dark magic, she knew better. All of her spells and rituals were for protection, healing, abundance, and love. She had once practiced a shark magic spell to ward off evil but never had she practiced spells for vengeance or black magic.

The spell she was working on was for a friend, Kesia. They had known each other since kindergarten.

A few days ago, at school in Jersey Shore, Luna was at her locker as Kesia walked up to open her own, which was right next to Luna's. She still remembered what Kesia had said, *"Long before modern medicine existed, it was common for people to look to pagan witches, despite their nefarious reputations."*

Shocked and unsure of how to take Kesia's words, Luna responded, *"We're a particularly powerful source of healing."*

It seemed that was all Kesia needed to hear, for from that moment on, she was "attached to the hip" to Luna.

Luna heard a knock at the front door downstairs and her mom saying hi to Kesia.

"I'm almost ready," Luna said as Kesia walked into her bedroom.

The look on Kesia's face was awestruck. Luna's room looked like it was from a medieval fantasy. There was a wooden moon on one wall with crystals and gemstones sitting on tiny shelves. A dreamcatcher with feathers and tasseled beads hanging from a deer horn was on another. Many lit candles, antique potion bottles, herbs, plants, and wands were on tables and shelves. On the wooden floor was a two-foot circle, the crystal grid Luna had created for this spell.

Sitting on the floor and crossing her legs into a lotus position, Kesia said, "Tell me about the pattern."

"Galileo once said, 'Mathematics is the alphabet with which God has written the universe.'"

"The pattern is math?"

"Of sorts, yes. Artists, musicians, and philosophers have long evoked the power of sacred geometry in their work, from Da Vinci to Pythagoras."

"Geometry?"

Luna traced the "Star of David" pattern with her finger. "Sacred sequences are inherent in everything from a simple pinecone to a snail shell, to the human body, to the Great Pyramids at Giza."

"It looks like a six-sided star."

"It is. Two triangles, one overlays the other. The hexagon shape symbolizes the union of opposites that creates life itself: the fusing of male and female, of heaven and earth, lightness and darkness."

"Opposites, like yin and yang."

"Similar. The Jews adopted the spiritual symbol Anahata, the heart chakra symbol from the Hindus."

"Fascinating. Who knew that geometry could be so interesting? Math class just took on a whole new meaning for me."

"I am using this symbol today as the 'Merkaba Vehicle.' The divine light vehicle used by ascended masters to connect with and reach those in tune with the higher realms."

"How does that help the spell?"

"The Star of David is a multidimensional vehicle used to strengthen our connection with the Source. I will be calling down the power to heal. We need a powerful source of magic to do that. Who better than a god?"

"I guess nobody. Hey, what are the candles and other stuff for?"

Luna had placed bamboo sticks to create the star and, for the circle, a circular row of olive leaves to build the crystal grid, after cleansing the space by smudging it using the smoke of white sage and sweetgrass. Almost touching end to end, encircling the star was an outer ring of quartz point crystals—cleansed previously by moonlight. Placed between the gemstones were two large white candles and two very large raw selenite rocks. Placed evenly outside the gem circle were five different colored flowers to signify the five elements, earth, air, water, fire, and spirit.

"All of this is needed to attract the energy we require for this spell to work," Luna shared as she passed Kesia a piece of paper and a quill pen. "Here, write down the person's name that you want to do the spell for."

Kesia took the pen and paper and wrote down Rev. Edward Hawthorne.

Taking the piece of paper, Luna folded it and placed it under the crystal in the star's center.

"Does the pink stone resting on the paper mean anything?" Kesia asked.

"It is rose quartz. It purifies and opens the heart at all levels to promote love, self-love, friendship, deep inner healing, and feelings of peace."

Kesia watched as Luna lit the candles, picked up a handheld wand made of tanzanite, and started tracing the geometric-shaped pattern on the floor.

Not understanding what Luna was saying, Kesia asked, "What language is that?"

"It is a special purpose magical language that is whispered during the incantation."

"Like Abracadabra?"

"Sort of. Language has power. People use words to hurt, conceal, soothe, and evoke emotions in others. The right words affect real change."

"As in, 'You're grounded.' My mom likes those words," Kesia joked.

Luna laughed, then said, "Or, I now pronounce you husband and wife. Words are powerful. This specialized linguistic form is one common ingredient of magic. The power is in words themselves."

"What words are you saying?"

"Words to produce a desired transformational outcome. In this case, healing."

"Is it similar to a mantra?"

"Similar. The earliest mantras were composed in Vedic Sanskrit in India. The words I am using are English and Latin, though."

"Are they easy to learn?"

"Spells have two distinct phases, the first one concentrating on gathering in power, the second one on releasing it. It takes a bit of time to learn how to perform a spell. For now, I will say it for both of us. Your job is to think about Edward being healthy. I'll do the rest."

She didn't want to spook Kesia and tell her everything. *She wouldn't understand who the Horned God and Mother Goddess are.*

Chapter 7

On the other side of the Atlantic Ocean, Isabella's doctor's assistant had called to schedule Aias's routine check-up.

"Ah, I am not sure that we will be in town."

"Madame, your son needs his check-up and immunization."

"Ah, yes. I guess he does."

The assistant made an appointment for the next day and told Isabella the time.

Looking at Aias, Isabella thought, *This should be interesting.*

The next day, Doctor Zutter was very surprised at Aias's growth. "There is not much we can do for gigantism. I will order a scan of his brain just in case he may have an adenoma."

"Adenoma?"

"Yes, a benign tumor on his pituitary gland. The pituitary is responsible for producing growth hormones. If your son has a tumor, that will explain his fast growth."

"Doctor, I have researched most of the growth syndromes, and most talk about deformities and slow learning, which he has neither. In fact, he is very proportionate for a boy of five."

"Yes, I was there when you gave birth, but your son isn't even a year old."

"I believe he is a child prodigy," Isabella said, trying to shift the doctor's thinking. "It is defined in psychology as a person under the age of ten who produces meaningful output in some domain to the level of an adult expert."

"Yes, I know what a prodigy is, Ms. Jackson. And yes, he shows the language and cognitive milestones of a five-year-old, which I agree would be odd for a person diagnosed with gigantism. Wait here, will you please?"

A few minutes later, the doctor came back with another doctor. "Ms. Jackson, this is Doctor Reynolds. He is also from America. He would like to assess Aias."

"Is that necessary?" Isabella asked, trying to figure out a way to get Aias out of there without causing a scene. "Aias is doing great, and now that he has his shots, it's all good."

"Ms. Jackson, is it?"

"Yes."

"You look familiar to me. Have we met before?"

"No. I don't believe so." *But I am sure you have seen me on TV or at the movies.*

Doctor Reynolds shook his head. "I will only be a few minutes with your son. You can stay if you like."

Isabella didn't have much choice. Nodding, she followed him and Aias into another room.

As they were walking, Aias laughed and touched an old lady passing him by in the hallway.

"Hallo, da Kleiner (Hi, there little one)," she said in German.

"Hallo Frau. Wie geht es dir? (Hello, lady. How are you doing?)," Aias replied in perfect German.

"Besser jetzt, danke (Better now, thank you)."

Reynolds looked at Isabella. "How old is he?"

"Technically, not even one."

"Astonishing."

"That was nothing. Aias also knows how to speak English, Swiss, and Swedish. After we spent some time in India, his Hindi became pretty good, too."

Dr. Zutter came into the room. "What just happened? Old Mrs. Hunkler's blood pressure is normal. She said a little boy touched her, and like magic, she felt better."

Isabella grabbed Aias and held him to her. "Ah, about that."

Dr. Reynolds spoke up, "Doctor, Mrs. Hunkler is old. Her blood pressure can't just magically fix itself. However, she must be having a good day and obviously remembered to take her pills."

Doctor Zutter looked at Aias and then at Isabella. "Humph," he mumbled and walked out of the room.

"Has he been able to do that for long?" Dr. Reynolds asked.

Isabella acted like she had no idea what he was talking about.

"His healing abilities?" Dr. Reynolds clarified.

Isabella took a deep breath. "Since he was about a month old."

"Remarkable. I have a friend I want you to meet."

Chapter 8

$\mathcal{L}$exi had quit her job as a fashion designer.

She needed to spend as much time with Edward as possible. Sebastian told her that there would still be a place for her when she was ready to come back. She also gave up her Fifth Avenue apartment and moved back in with her mom in Brooklyn.

Lying in her bed, not being able to sleep, she was staring at the ceiling. Doctor Singh had sent her home and told her that she needed a good night's rest and that he would call her if there were any changes.

Hey sis, how are you doing?

Susannah? Wow, I haven't heard from you in such a long time. I thought you abandoned me.

Never.

I am so worried, Susannah. Edward is not waking up.

I know. I've been watching when you are there.

Can you please help him? Can you wake him up?

Sorry, it doesn't work like that. I am not allowed to interfere.

Lexi started to cry.

I wish I could, Lex, but God knows what he is doing, and only he can wake Edward up if that is what is supposed to be.

But it isn't fair. I was supposed to be married and living a wonderful life as his wife.

I know better than you think.

Ah, right, of course, you do. How selfish of me.

Lexi, you have to start eating. You are getting too thin. It is not part of your life's path to becoming anorexic.

I don't feel hungry. Actually, I don't feel anything. I think I am numb.

Lexi, you have to eat. So, starting tomorrow, you will begin juicing.

That sounds like an order.

It is.

You'll have to show me how.

I will.

Susannah?

Ya.

Where does a soul go when the body is in a coma?

Lexi, there are three parts to a soul, the vegetative, sentient, and the intellectual. If you imagine a plant, it only has a vegetative soul. It only has the power that allows for the basics of existence—nourishment, growth, and reproduction. Its only purpose is for the survival of higher life forms, as in the production of oxygen, absorption of carbon dioxide, medicines, and wood.

I forgot how important plants are.

The sentient or sensitive soul is inherent in all animals, as both can be irrational or rational. Many qualities are similar. They encompass sensation, perception, and movement. But the difference between an animal and a human is the intellectual or rational soul. This is specific to human beings only and is part of the soul's responsibility—reason and thought. Right now, Edward's vegetative soul is in control of his body.

So, is his soul still in his body?

Sometimes, Edward's astral body or soul may be hovering in and out of his physical body.

Without an intellectual soul, will he live? Lexi asked.

From the esoteric point of view, death happens when the astral cord or silver cord, which connects the soul to the physical body, is finally severed or broken. Until that happens, a person is technically still alive.

Scared, Lexi asked, *Is he going to wake up?*

Because of the drugs they are giving him, there will be moments that he may open his eyes and even move a little. He won't be able to see the people around him, but he can still hear them.

Are you saying he can hear me?

Lexi, it is vital that you talk to him as if he were alive. Your voice may be what awakes him.

Susannah? So, does that mean Edward's soul is with his body and not in one of the levels on its way to Heaven?

Yes. All parts of his soul are hovering near him. He had a traumatic experience, and his soul left his body. You would want this. So that he feels no pain while his physical body heals. It will be his emotional body that we may have to worry about.

His what?

Oh, Lexi, I said too much. I am being called back.

Susannah! You can't just leave me. I have more questions.

Chapter 9

It was hot, and Edward was sweating. As he looked down, his feet and legs were black as night. He was also naked, running through the African rain forest near the Congo River with a crossbow. Something in his subconscious said that the arrows would be poisonous. He wasn't sure if he was being chased from all the screaming and singing or if he was chasing something.

To his astonishment, a duiker, better known as an antelope, emerged from nowhere and ran right past him. Soon after, he figured out that he was part of a Pygmie hunting tribe, and all their screaming was to keep the lowland gorillas, forest elephants, and chimpanzees away.

Running in the same direction as the other men, Edward jumped out of the way when one of the men pounced suddenly on an anteater, capturing it.

A few moments later, he heard a squeal from a slain duiker and then an excited cheer. They would feast tonight.

Edward was following behind the other men, trying not to get noticed. His eyes went wide as he came into their village. It was like going back in time. Among the lush tropical plants and trees were primitive straw huts with large leaves covering the tops. Some naked women with their faces tattooed and their breasts hanging flat, from never wearing a bra, were mending nets that the men used to catch the duiker and fish, while others were cooking monkey heads in a pot over a fire.

To Edward's surprise, today's kill would be prepared to eat for another day. Tonight's supper consisted of wild yams, fruit, mushrooms, termites, and caterpillars. All were served on a large leaf, substituting for a bowl.

Edward was amazed that there were still humans living equivalent to one of the earliest stages of human culture. He remembered the Greek meaning for Pygmy was "dwarf." Looking at them, he could understand why, when the tallest man was only four-foot-eleven. He was part of the Twa rainforest people of Africa, also called Batwa. Twa meant "hunter-gatherer or bushpeople."

As a holy man, Edward had mixed feelings about their religious beliefs. The Twa believed in Animism—natural physical entities such as animals and plants possess a spiritual essence—meaning they were atheists. They believe that the forest spirits provide abundance. Another contrast to the Christian belief is that the snake represents the devil, but to the African people, the serpent represents eternal life, regeneration, power, protection, and wisdom.

In Edward's coma state, his dreams seemed so lucid, and he was surprised when he teleported to Ireland as a "wee folk." He was now part of the Leprechaun Myth.

In reality, the Twa migrated to Ireland. Even though the Irish called the Twa "Leprechaun," they called themselves Akan. The name "Leprechaun" (Lepr-Akans) comes from the Old Irish *luchorpán*, a compound of the roots lú (small) and corp (body). The Twa were also known by another name, "Wild Irishmen." In Gaelic, *Dubh Eireannach*, means "a black Irishman."

Edward teleported to a small clay country home with a straw roof, and instead of wood fencing in the field, there were straight rows of three-foot-high piled rocks that created a square barricade that contained a donkey and a pig. He was part of the Ekuoba Irish kinship group, and at the time of his arrival, he heard a newborn baby's cry.

Heading in the direction of the noise, Edward heard one of the tribesmen say, "It's a boy. His name is Kofi."

Edward knew that the Akan people named their children after the day of the week that they were born. It had to be a Friday.

Edward was impressed with the advancements that the Twa people had made while living in Ireland. They now had knowledge of modern medicine, metallurgy, material science and engineering, clothing manufacturing, and shoe-making, which the Irish thought was magical.

The day after he had arrived, a man came around preaching about the "Holy Trinity" by showing people the shamrock, a three-leafed plant, using it to illustrate the Christian teaching of three persons in one God.

The leader of this small Twa kingship told the man that they believed in the power of the snake and didn't need his shamrock, that the snake was the holder of knowledge, strength, and renewal.

Edward knew that the Twa believed that a rainbow was the shadow that arises from the body of the great snake. And with Ireland's rainy weather, the Twa felt very blessed to be amongst so many rainbows.

Unfortunately, Saint Patrick was mortified and rallied a group to help him banish all the "snakes" from Ireland into the sea. He told the townspeople that if they could catch a Leprechaun, they would be granted a wish—

mostly, he knew the townspeople would want to be paid in gold.

Edward remembered a class in seminary school teaching about how the pineal, pituitary, and hypothalamus were three glands in your brain, that when spiritually activated, were said to bestow the power to grant your wishes and that these glands were also known as the three Wise Men who came to visit Christ, bearing gifts.

Edward had a flash memory of Tamara. She was teaching that the colors of the rainbow were a symbol for the chakras, and chasing the rainbow to find the pot of gold at the end of it represents a spiritual journey for the seeker on the path to enlightenment. Edward found it coincidental that the Leprechauns' primary color was green, which was considered the heart chakra. Coincidently, it was the gateway to the God-consciousness, which had also been linked to finding "gold."

Edward's lucid dream dissolved as he heard the nurse's voice checking in on him. Still in an alpha state and remembering his lucid dream, Edward had mixed feelings about Saint Patrick. *If a man of God could not turn the non-believers into believers, then his only option was to banish them.* He understood back in the day that was the way, but in today's world, even an atheist has rights. He couldn't believe that he had never heard the truth about what kind of snakes Saint

Patrick banished, that it was actually the Twa people who were banished to the Irish Sea Shore.

Edward's thoughts became worrisome as he contemplated the soul of the non-believer—thanks to the first adventure with Lexi, he knew what would happen to the soul once the body died. *Would the Twa people go to Heaven if they believed in a snake instead of believing in the same God that I do?*

Chapter 10

Standing outside waiting for his next patient to be admitted into the emergency room, Neo was staring at the blue "Star of Life" on the side of an ambulance. *Not sure why they called it a star when it looks more like an X with a line through it.* He had learned in med school that the six branches of the star signify the six main tasks performed by rescuers: detection, reporting, response, on-scene care, care in transit, and transfer to definitive care.

The doctor beside him said, "When I was in the US Military Medical Corp, our army's hospital steward's badge had the caduceus symbol on them."

Neo looked over at the doctor and said, "The symbol with the two snakes intertwined around a winged rod?"

"Ya." The guy pointed to the "Star of Life" on the ambulance and said, "This is the Rod of Asclepius. Do you know the difference?"

Neo looked at the blue cross with the snake winding around a staff and said, "I know it is named after the Greek god Asclepius, who was a deity associated with healing and medicine."

As the men were talking, a nurse came out and said, "Doctor Singh, your patient will be a few minutes late. The ambulance is caught in a traffic jam."

Neo nodded and was about to head back in when the other doctor said, "Did you notice the symbol on her nameplate? It was the caduceus with two snakes, not the Rod of Asclepius with one. Years ago, the American Medical Association used this symbol but eventually switched. The nurse's union never did."

"So, what is your point?" Neo asked.

The doctor smiled and said, "The majority of people believe that the two snakes with a winged staff is the symbol for medicine and don't know that it actually is a symbol of professionalism and craft. The caduceus with two snakes and wings is considered alchemy and associated with the Greek god, Hermes, or the Roman god, Mercury."

Neo looked at the doctor and said, "Even though alchemy was foolish, it helped advance the medical field, and nurses should be proud to wear a symbol that represents the highest honor of professionalism."

The doctor was about to say something, but his ambulance arrived, saving Neo from hearing any more of his story.

As Neo waited patiently for his patient to arrive, he remembered a story he'd heard about a wizard who carried a magical staff when he visited the sick. This magical rod was made from an upside-down sapling branch so that a gemmed vial could be intertwined in the roots. The wizard would then fill the vial with a blend of frankincense, pine, lavender, and camphor oils.

Thinking how naive people could be, Neo chuckled at the thought of this wizard's magic.

One of Neo's university assignments was a report on aromatherapy, and he knew the science behind the wizard's so-called magic. The vial on the staff was the perfect height—nose height—and acted as the wizard's personal antiseptic when he visited any contagious cases.

This thought reminded Neo of a report he did in med school—he had used a timeline for the advancement in herbal medicine. Symbols carbon-dated on a French cave suggested that plants were used for healing as far back as eighteen thousand years ago. Neo was fascinated with the history of healing and that the ancient Sumerians, the Yellow Emperor of China, and even the Egyptians used essential oils and herbs for medicine.

Neo had written in his report of how essential oils were recorded in the Christian Bible, the Jewish Torah. For centuries, the magic of herbs was used by healers, priests, wise men, and women worldwide, right up until the 1800s, when a new concept was born, the "pharmaceutical" industry.

As a modern Western medicine doctor, Neo knew that American physicians today healed using only evidence-based medicine, which he was about to practice since the sirens were nearing and his newest patient was arriving.

Chapter 11

Neo's patient had arrived. The man brought in by ambulance was in his early twenties and was hit by a car while riding his motorcycle.

Even though the guy had been wearing leather and a helmet, his boots had flown off during impact, creating road rash to his feet. Neo hoped that most of the dirt and rocks could be removed so that infection would not set in.

That was not the seriousness of the accident. Neo wasn't sure if the man's vertebrae were fractured, dislocated, crushed, or compressed.

Unfortunately, the X-ray revealed that this young man needed an operation on the spine. Neo knew better than anyone that there was always the possibility that this guy might never walk again.

#

A couple of new male interns were watching Neo operate on this young man. The intern on the right said to his buddy, "I have this as an exam on Monday. Is it okay if I tell you about the spinal cord?"

"Sure."

"The spinal cord, known as the 'central nervous system,' is a column of nerves that connects the brain with the rest of the body. It is the main pathway for information connecting the brain to the peripheral nervous system."

"Tell me what the PNS controls," his friend said.

"Everything else, movement, breathing, eating, eliminating waste, lovemaking…"

"Really, lovemaking? I am sure with that answer you will get an 'A' on your exam."

"Hey, you might be able to get it up, but without your peripheral nervous system, you wouldn't be able to move."

The buddy shook his head. "Go on."

"The nerve fibers in the spinal cord branch off to form pairs of nerve roots that travel through the vertebrae."

"So, why is the spinal column so important?

"Because damaged spinal nerves can cause paralysis."

Both interns looked at the clock on the wall.

"The amount of time Dr. Singh has spent operating… It doesn't look good for this dude."

#

Of all the specialties he could have chosen, Neo chose neurosurgery. A few of the conditions he dealt with included working on people with brain tumors, aneurysms, epilepsy, seizures, coma patients, and of course, spinal issues.

Neo knew the guy's chances before going into today's surgery, but even with a ten percent chance of recovery, the family had requested the surgery be done.

Neo knew everything a person could learn about the brain and spinal column. He knew the brain was the most protected part of the body, and without a brain, a person could not function. He knew that the brain only used sugar as energy. He knew that different parts of the brain controlled the five senses, touch, sight, hearing, smell, and taste.

Neo looked up and saw the two smiling interns watching him from the observation room. Frustrated, because he knew they were smiling because they were eager to learn his craft, but they wouldn't be smiling long. His patient had just died on the operating table.

Even though Neo was brought up in two religions, Greek Orthodox and Hinduism, he knew how he became an atheist. *If there was a God, how could he let young people die?*

Death was not new to him, and he knew that it came with the job. Heart disease, diabetes, and cancer were also high on the list of mortality patients.

If people only realized that doctors are not gods, they would look after their bodies better. Unfortunately, thinking this only made his mood worse, and now he had to go and tell the parents that their son didn't make it.

Chapter 12

Lexi happened to be coming to visit Edward when she coincidently walked by Doctor Singh, who obviously was giving bad news due to the couple's reaction.

It saddened her to see a lovely woman crumble into her husband's arms, crying.

Oh God, please let Edward live. I don't think I could handle him dying.

Lexi hurried to Edward's room. Even with the IV drip attached to his wrist, the oxygen tubes in his nose, and the monitors beeping every so often, one would never know that Edward was in a coma. He just looked like he was in a deep sleep.

As Lexi touched Edward's forehead with her lips, she heard someone lightly knock on the open door and say, "May I come in?"

Looking at the door to see who was speaking, Lexi said, "Yes, please do, Kesia. Edward would be happy to know that you came to visit. It is so nice of you to come all this way."

"It was no problem. Mom wanted to see my aunt, and so I caught a ride with her. Has he woken up yet?"

"No. He's still in a coma."

Kesia looked surprised and said, "Really? Not even a flinch?" *That's weird. Luna's spell should have worked.*

"No, nothing. I pray every day that he will wake up, but my prayers have not been answered yet."

Trying to figure out what went wrong with the spell, Kesia asked, "Does the doctor think he will wake up?"

"From what I can gather, every day that he doesn't wake up, he is closer to the doctor saying that he won't."

"Don't give up, Lexi. I am sure he is just enjoying his time off work," Kesia said with a slight laugh, trying to keep the mood light.

Lexi smiled politely and looked at Edward.

Thinking of other ways to wake Edward up, Kesia questioned, "Did you ask your sister for help?"

Lexi looked at Kesia, answering, "Ya, but she can't help. Susannah says that he can hear us, though."

"Well, in that case… Edward, now you listen to me, you old fart. It is time to wake up from whatever dream you are having and get back to this world."

"Kesia, I don't think that is the tone of voice Susannah meant to speak in."

"Have you tried it yet?"

"No."

"Then how do you know it won't work? He should be awake by now. We ..."

Lexi tensed up. "We? What did you do, Kesia?"

"Nothing."

"Kesia, what did you do?"

"Well, I asked a friend of mine to do a spell to wake him up."

"You didn't."

"It's okay. It was white magic."

"Kesia, what if it makes him worse?"

"No. Luna had me think of Edward being healthy. He should be awake by now."

"He is healthy, just not awake. The doctor said that all his internal and external injuries have healed."

"Then, why isn't he waking up? Hey, wait! I said healthy. Not awake. I've got to go."

"Wait! He moved."

Edward's eyelids started to twitch. Then he started to choke on the tube in his throat.

Lexi pushed the button to call the nurse as she yelled, "Help! Someone, help him!"

Kesia backed up as the nurse came in and rang a different button that sounded an alarm.

In moments, there were many medical staff in Edward's room.

Doctor Singh came in and instantly removed the tube that Edward was choking on, then said, "Give him a sedative. He needs to come out of his coma slowly."

Once the commotion had settled down a bit, Lexi asked Dr. Singh, "Is he going to wake up?"

Neo looked at Lexi. "He has a better chance now. But Lexi, don't get your hopes up just yet. There is a good chance that he will fall into a coma again. Even if he does wake up, he has a long road ahead of him. He may need therapy to relearn basic things like tying his shoes, eating with a fork, or even learning how to walk again. In the worst-case scenario, he may have problems with speaking or remembering things."

"But he could wake up for good, right?"

"There is a very good chance that he will. Lexi, I need you to go home. We need to do a few more tests. Someone will call you soon."

"I can't leave. I need to be here when Edward wakes up."

"Lexi, it could be days."

"I don't care."

Frustrated with her, Neo said, "Then go wait in the waiting room."

Seeing that Lexi was hesitant about leaving, Kesia grabbed her arm and pulled her out of the room, saying, "It's okay, Lexi. He is going to be okay now. The spell did work. I just had the wrong word. I needed to use the word awake, not healthy. Man, Spirit is literal!"

Chapter 13

After returning to Jersey Shore from New York City, Kesia instantly went to Luna's. Running up the stairs to her bedroom, Kesia excitedly danced around and said, "For a few moments, he woke up."

Disappointed, Luna said, "Only for a few moments?"

Kesia stopped dancing and looked at her friend. "I thought you would be happy."

"No. The spell was supposed to wake Edward up for good. We'll have to try another one."

Luna started searching through a leather-bound book that resembled one you would imagine a warlock using. Quickly thumbing through the pages, she looked for a different spell.

Luna placed another strand of Edward's hair into a large shell, along with some dried citrus, a bloodstone crystal, some dried coffee grounds, and a sprinkle of mugwort.

Holding the shell up to the sky, Luna chanted, "Mother Goddess, strengthen what's weak, mend what is broken, and heal what is sick," then placed the shell on the ledge of her windowsill. "After the next full moon, Edward will wake up for good."

"When is that?" Kesia asked.

"September twentieth. It is called the harvest moon."

Kesia did the math. "I have to wait for ten more days?"

"If you want him to wake up, you do."

"Isn't there something faster we can do?"

"True magic isn't like TV, where a person can wiggle their nose or finger, and *poof*, something manifests or disappears."

"I was hoping it was."

Sitting back down, Luna asked, "Kesia, what do you think Wicca means?"

"I imagine it is the use of spells."

"It means to bend or shape nature to your service."

"Isn't it a cult?"

"It is a religion that is based on 'hidden knowledge' about the universe and its mysterious forces."

"But it's a cult, right?"

"So is any other religion. Kesia, a cult is a social group that is defined by its unusual religious, spiritual, or philosophical beliefs."

"Are you telling me that Edward is part of a cult? It's hard to believe that a Christian man like him would be part of a cult."

"If any type of ritual or ceremony is performed, any religion is considered a cult."

"But then why do Christians say bad things about occults?"

"Now, if you say the word 'occult,' a person is talking about a category
of supernatural beliefs and practices that generally fall outside the scope
of religion and science."

"What does that mean?"

"Anything that has to do with mysticism, spirituality, divination, and magic. It can also refer to extra-sensory perception or parapsychology. At one point in history, even astrology and alchemy were considered part of the occult."

"But wouldn't any religion be an occult? They all preach about making contact with the supernatural?"

"I'm not following you. What do you mean, Kesia?"

"Most religions pray to a God. Science can't prove that God exists, and so it must be a practice of occultism."

Luna raised an eyebrow. "Interesting, early Christianity used to be considered an occult by both the Jews and Romans, but since they believe and pray to a man, not God, they are not considered an occult."

"In my family, gypsies don't follow any one religion, but some have adopted the beliefs of black Saint Sarah, or some call her Kali Sara."

"Why?"

"To the Romani, she was known as Notre Dame de Ratis, Our Lady of the Raft. The legend goes something like this… One day, Sarah had a vision that the Saints who had been present at the death of Jesus would come and that she had to help them. So, as the waters were merciless that day, Sarah borrowed the cloak of one of the Three Marys and used it as a raft. She floated toward the Saints and helped them reach land."

"But why do you pray to her?"

"Kali Sara is the protectress who will cure sickness, bring good luck and fertility, and grant success in business ventures. It was a tradition in my family that we would lay the clothes of the sick out and ask her to heal them. There is even a statue in Saintes-Maries-de-la-Mer in France where people still bring flowers and clothing, then light a candle and request her help."

"So, you believe it because it is a tradition in your family?"

"I guess. I never thought of it like that."

"Most of our primary beliefs are formed by our parents, ministers, and teachers. Luckily, I just so happen to have teachers that believe in the casting of spells," Luna said as she lit a candle for Edward's incantation.

Chapter 14

$\mathcal{L}$exi walked into the Catholic church that she had grown up attending. To the side of the main altar, there was a tiered rack holding many votive candles. She knew that the term "votive" came from the Latin word *votum*, which meant a vow, pledge, religious undertaking, or promise. It could also mean a prayer.

Taking a long thin piece of wood from a container, she ignited it from touching the flame of one of the other candles, then lit an available candle.

Kneeling on the cushion provided, she silently said a prayer for Edward. "The saint of healing, Archangel Raphael, whose name means God has healed, please help Edward recover from his injuries and return him to me."

She had been practicing this candle lighting prayer ritual since she was a young girl. Over the years, she had prayed for deceased loved ones, the sick, for the health and welfare of family and friends, and the intentions and needs of all in the world.

She loved that a lit candle signified her prayer offered in faith, and that the smoke of the burning candle represented her prayers going upward to heaven. She also loved that while it was burning, her prayer was being looked after by Christ's healing light energy, and she could return to her regular activities.

Before getting up to leave, she silently recited a couple of passages from the Bible that she was taught when she was in catechism, *"I am the light of the world. No follower of Mine shall ever walk in darkness; no, he shall possess the light of life" (Jn 8:12) and "I have come to the world as its light, to keep anyone who believes in Me from remaining in the dark" (Jn 12:46).*

Hi, Lexi.

Susannah.

Did you know that Archangel Raphael is the angel who heals the soul by bringing the "blind" back to "seeing?"

I knew that he was the angel of healing.

He is. But I meant bringing a person who doesn't believe back to believing.

Do you mean as in an atheist becoming a Christian?

Yes. That is Archangel Raphael's primary goal.

I thought that he healed the physical body.

He can do that also, but his main job is to "heal the soul." Do you remember the story of Tobias in the Old Testament?

Kind of... Is he the one whose father and soon-to-be wife Archangel Raphael healed?

Yes.

Do you remember what a lament is?

No.

Here, I will recite a prayer of lamentation.

> *You are just, O Lord,*
> *and just are all your works.*
> *All your ways are grace and truth,*
> *and you are the Judge of the world.*
> *Therefore, Lord,*
> *remember me, look on me.*
> *Do not punish me for my sins*
> *or for my needless faults*
> *or those of my ancestors.*
> *For we have sinned against you*
> *and broken your commandments,*
> *and you have given us over to be*
> *plundered,*
> *to captivity and death,*
> *to be the talk, the laughing-stock, and*
> *scorn of all the nations among whom you*
> *have dispersed us.*
> *And now all your decrees are true*
> *when you deal with me as my faults*
> *deserve, and those of my ancestors.*
> *For we have neither kept your*
> *commandments*

nor walked in truth before you.
So now, do with me as you will;
be pleased to take my life from me;
so that I may be delivered from earth
and become earth again.
Better death than life for me,
for I have endured groundless insult
and am in deepest sorrow.
Lord, be pleased
To deliver me from this affliction.
Let me go away to my everlasting home;
do not turn your face from me, O Lord.
Better death for me than life prolonged
in the face of unrelenting misery:
I can no longer bear to listen to insults.

What are you trying to tell me, Susannah?
A lament is a tool that God's people use to navigate pain and suffering. A lament is a way to cry out to God when in the midst of distress. Lexi, the Bible is filled with many songs of sorrow. Over one-third—fifty or so—of the Psalms are laments. In the Bible, one whole book, Lamentations, expresses the confusion and suffering felt after the destruction of Jerusalem by the Babylonians.

I'm glad that you reminded me of these stories in the Bible, Susannah. To be honest, I always thought the people in these stories were whining.

Lexi, when a person hurts physically, they cry out in pain; when they hurt religiously, they cry out in lament. According to the Oxford

Dictionary, the definition of lament is "a passionate expression of grief or sorrow."

What does all of this have to do with me, Susannah?

Lexi, you need to bring Edward's faith back. He was conflicted between his religious upbringing and what otherworldly adventures he was experiencing with you. He is in spiritual pain.

How do I do that?

Pray. The "Four Elements of Lament" are:
> *Turn to God.*
> *Bring your complaint.*
> *Ask boldly for help.*
> *Choose to trust.*

You just want me to pray?

Yes, but in a specific way. Here is a lament from Psalm 130:1, "Out of the depths I cry to you, O Lord; Lord, hear my voice!"

I will have to read up on lament in the Bible. I have forgotten what they are, Lexi thought honestly.

Lexi, the most common form of prayer in the Bible, is not praise. Instead, it's a lament, and Edward will need your help to regain his faith.

Chapter 15

Doctor Singh was attending a mandatory conference and going through the list of speakers. Finally, he decided to listen to an Ayurvedic doctor speaking on pain.

"Pain is a message sent by the body to the brain, signaling that disease, injury, or strenuous activity has caused trouble in some area," the speaker was saying.

Neo was listening with interest. So many of his patients complained about being in pain.

"There are four main occurrences of pain: *referred pain*, which originates from the skin, muscle, ligaments, joints, or organs. *Functional or psychological pain*, which originates from a person's emotions. *Cutaneous pain*, which originates from superficial tissue, and lastly, *neuropathic pain*, which originates from any nerve in your brain, spinal cord, legs, or arms."

Next, the speaker showed a diagram explaining the symptoms of pain in different parts of the body.

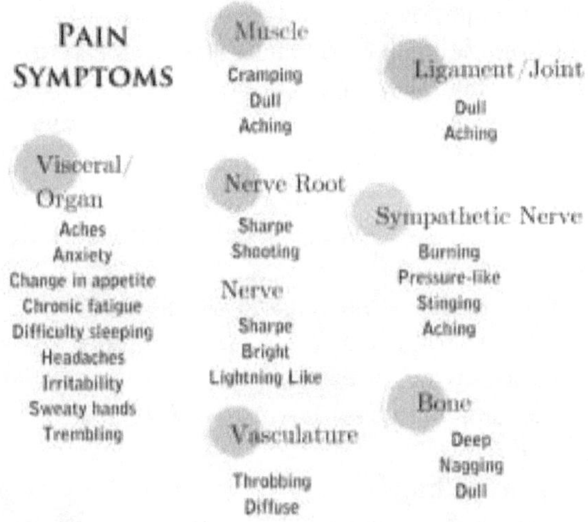

He then explained why delta sleep of at least two hours a day is needed for the body, mind, and soul to heal, "A person moves through stages of sleep, from light sleep, which typically begins shortly after you get into bed and lasting roughly one to ten minutes then moves into theta, which encompasses about fifty percent of your night's sleep. Stage three, REM—your dream state—and stage four is considered deep sleep, also known as delta."

Neo started taking a few notes down as the speaker talked.

"It is imperative that a person gets a deep sleep because it reduces negative emotions and increases incidents of positive emotions. In addition, delta sleep enhances the restorative physical healing powers of your body. This type of deep sleep is considered quality sleep and enhances your ability to concentrate and focus effectively. It also boosts your memory power. Do you know what causes a person not to wake up rested?"

Neo put down his pen and listened.

"Stress. Stress causes a sleepless night. Do you know what cures stress?"

Neo chuckled. *Not having a full load of patients?*

"Yoga nidra."

Neo remembered what that was. His father had mentioned it many times when Neo was a child.

The speaker confirmed his thought. "It is commonly known as yogic sleep." Jokingly, the speaker said, "You may be wondering if a yogi sleeps any differently than you do."

Neo waited for his answer.

"No. Though, it is a powerful meditation technique."

Neo sat back disappointed. *Great. Like I have time to teach that to my patients.*

As if reading his mind, the speaker said, "Yoga nidra is a practice that everyone, from children to seniors, can do."

Neo looked at the speaker.

"You cannot practice yoga nidra incorrectly."

I am sure I can. Just ask my dad. He tried teaching me his ways.

"All you have to do is follow the voice that is guiding you."

That I could do.

"Yoga nidra encourages deep rest and relaxation. The body scan and breath awareness alone can calm the nervous system, leading to less stress and better health."

This seems promising.

"Here is a sample meditation that encompasses removing negative energy and pain. Sit back in your chair and listen to my words. Let them be your words. If you believe in asking for extra help from your guides or angels, go ahead and ask now. Get yourself comfortable and close your eyes."

Neo had nothing to lose, so he closed his eyes.

The speaker continued the meditation by saying, "Scan your body and take a mental note if there is any pain, discomfort, or issue.

When you are ready, take three deep breaths. Try to breathe with your mouth open.

Breathe all the way down to your feet and
toes. Imagine your muscles relaxing.
As you breathe, your legs start to relax.
As you listen to my voice and take another
deep breath, all outside noises diminish.

Focus now on your stomach and tummy area.
All of the muscles and organs are now
relaxing.

Your circulation is flowing. Your lymphatic
and immune systems are cleansing and
healing whatever and wherever as needed.

Taking another deep breath, your shoulders,
arms, and hands relax, and you start to feel
lighter, or some people may imagine feeling
heavier. Choose whichever one you prefer.

Breathing in and out.

Your neck and head are relaxing, even your
eyebrows, ears, and chin. Every muscle in
your body is relaxing as you breathe.
Now focus on any area in your body where
there is pain, discomfort, or an issue. If you
have more than one area, start with one and
come back to the next one right after or later,
when you have time.

Acknowledge any sensations, thoughts, or
feelings that you are having.

Now put a color to this first area. Imagine that there is a color to the pain, discomfort, or issue. Focus on that color.

Next, imagine breathing in a crystal-clear sparkly color through the top of your head (the baby's soft spot or crown chakra).

Now, create an opening from the area of pain, discomfort, or issue and allow the color you initially imagined going into a garbage can or being vacuumed up. Do this until all the color is gone and only the crystal-clear sparkly color is left.

Take a few nice deep breaths.

Once the color is gone and the crystal-clear sparkly color is left, create a new color, a healing color. Maybe it is your favorite color or any new color that comes to your mind.

Now with that new color, fill that pain area until all the crystal-clear sparkly color is gone. So much so that some of this new color is being pulled or sucked into the garbage or vacuum.

Say to yourself three times, "I am healed. I am healed. I am healed."

Next, think of some positive affirmations or positive words to put into this new colored area and place them in this healing area.

You will be able to repeat this meditation any time you need to. Some people only have to do it once, and the pain or issue is cleared for good, whereas others need to repeat the meditation due to recreating the pain or problem in their daily life.

Later, when you practice this at home, you can do the same meditation to any other pain area that you may have.

Now take a breath, wiggle your toes and open your eyes, feeling wonderful.

I have a tape available for each of you to use for yourself or your patients. It is a gift from me."

Neo opened his eyes and moved his right shoulder. *Amazing. It actually worked.* It felt good. It had been achy this morning due to sleeping on it wrong.

Chapter 16

Arising from the ashes came the most brilliant of colored birds, blazing like sunlight. A fiery red phoenix soared into the night's sky. Its head resembled that of an eagle's. Its wingspan tipped with golden feathers was eight feet across, larger than most birds on earth. Its tail, long like a peacock, with blue, green, and purple hues, trailed behind like a kite's ribbon flying in the wind.

He was magnificent.

This is incredible! I feel free, empowered, and so alive! Edward thought as he did a spiral spin while flying through the midnight sky.

The phoenix symbolizes rebirth, eternity, and hope. According to legend, it obtains new life by arising from the ashes of its predecessor.

Blinking, Edward came out of the lucid dream of being a phoenix and opened his eyes.

Why are all the colors I'm seeing so muted? And why do my ears feel like they need to pop?

Opening his mouth and yawning, Edward popped his ears.

He could hear a beep that started to quicken.

Seeing a nurse, Edward groggily said, "Where am I?"

Pushing a button, the nurse replied, "Brooklyn Neurocritical Care. The doctor will be with you in a moment to answer any questions you may have."

A few moments later, Doctor Singh came into the room. "So, you have decided to wake up. How are you feeling? Any pain?"

"Why am I here?"

Doctor Singh stopped what he was doing and looked at Edward. "Do you know your name?"

Edward tried to remember, but it was blank. "No."

"What day do you think it is?"

"I have no idea."

"Can you move your toes?"

Edward tried.

"Good," Neo said, ticking off the box that recorded that Edward could.

"Can you squeeze my hand?"

Doctor Singh placed his hand into Edward's. "Good."

"Can you move your legs?"

Edward tried.

"Hmm, we'll work on that. How about your arms?"

Edward tried again.

"That is not a problem yet. Don't worry. Many patients regain full movement within a few days."

"Why am I here?"

"You were banged on the head pretty hard."

"How long have I been here?"

"Over two months."

Edward closed his eyes and took a breath. "It must have been pretty bad."

Not lying, Neo said, "It was, but the good news is all your internal organs have healed. You will have a couple of scars, though."

"So, Doctor. What is my name?"

"Reverend Edward Julien Hawthorne."

"I'm a reverend?"

"That is what your fiancée says."

"I have a girlfriend?"

Neo padded Edward on the forearm for reassurance and said, "Many of my patients recover their memory. The best thing that you can do is get some rest."

"Doc, I think I have had almost a lifetime of rest, don't you think?"

Neo smiled. "It seemed you needed it."

Lexi came rushing into the room, hugging Edward. "Oh, thank God!"

Not recognizing her, he moved his head away from hers and said, "You must be the fiancée."

Lexi slowly removed herself from Edward. "Pardon me?"

Edward looked at the doctor for help.

"Miss Constantine, Edward has amnesia. At this moment, he does not even remember who he is, let alone you."

Lexi put her hand to her mouth and gasped. "Is it permanent?"

Looking at Edward, he said, "I will escort Miss Constantine out into the hallway. I will be back later to check in on you. Push the button if you get hungry or need anything. The nurses will be in regularly to check on you." Then turning to Lexi, he said, "Miss Constantine, please follow me."

Chapter 17

"His name is Acharya Shri Sharma," Doctor Reynolds told Isabella. "Here is his card."

Reading the card, Isabella asked, "He is in India?"

"Yes, I know it is far but well worth the trip."

Isabella looked at the card again. "He lives in Puttaparthi?"

"Yes."

Not sure if she really needed to go there, she said hesitantly, "You believe that Aias needs a teacher?"

"Your son's gifts are none that I have witnessed here in Switzerland, nor in North America. He needs a teacher, a guru, a Vedic sage, someone who understands his gifts and can educate and train him on how to use them safely."

Isabella looked at the doctor. "You're sure?"

"Yes, I will contact Acharya Shri Sharma ahead of time and tell him that you and your son will be arriving shortly. And Miss Jackson, once you are in Puttaparthi, you must go to the ashram of Sathya Sai Baba. Acharya Shri Sharma's assistant will only meet you there."

#

The nearest international airport to Isabella's destination was the Kempegowda International Airport in Devanahalli, a suburb of Bangalore, about one hundred and nineteen kilometers from Puttaparthi.

At least I have been to Bangalore before. I must find the time to connect with Zeenat while we are here. Waiting for the flight over, Isabella researched on her phone what an ashram was—an active monastery. "I wonder what wonders we will discover in Puttaparthi?" Isabella said out loud to Aias.

The flight over to India was quicker than Isabella thought it would have been. *Thank goodness I can afford a private jet.*

Shortly after arriving, and just before 9:30 AM the next day, Isabella and Aias were met outside of Sathya Sai Baba's ashram by a very nice-looking younger Indian man. He was wearing a navy blue and print silk dhoti kurta—a mix of a shirt, vest, and fitted suit jacket. It was done up to his neck by buttons that were off to the side. The bottom edge was cut diagonally, and the long side almost touched his left knee. The pattern on the print was a beautiful design of many colors. The cuffs, neck edge, and pocket trim matched the vest design. The cream-colored pants he was wearing billowed out at the sides and tapered down to fit tightly around his ankles. His cotton-fitted shoes were the color of gold, and to Isabella's delight, the tips curled up almost like one would imagine Aladdin's did, though these were sewn back onto themselves and used as a tab.

In a thick accent, he said, "Namaste. I am Dilesh Chakladar, one of Acharya Shri Sharma's devotees. He has asked that I give you a tour of the Sathya Sai Baba's ashram before going to his. Before we enter, please put these on." Delish handed Isabella a peach-colored choli—a short-armed shirt that would partly bare her midriff—matching loose-fitting pants, and edged in gold was a long sheer silk saree—scarf—that was worn wrapped around the waist at one end and draped over the shoulder at the other.

Aias, who now looked almost twelve, was given a plainer version of Dilesh's outfit to wear.

After changing, they entered the ashram, and Isabella could hear singing.

Noticing, Delish said, "It is being sung in Sanskrit. In your language, the first verse translates to:

All praise to You, Lord of the Worlds
Swami Sathya Sai, our Lord
You protect devotees who cling to You
Show Your mercy to us who sing to You
Knowing You are God in human form
All praise to You, Lord of the Worlds."

As they started to walk, Isabella could smell camphor.

Being very intuitive to Isabella's body language, Delish said, "Arathi is a Hindu ritual in which a camphor flame is waved in a slow circle, facing Bhagawan—God. The flame is offered to the Lord after the prayer is said or the bhajan session—devotional singing. Here in Prasanthi Nilayam, the Arathi is sung, and the ritual is performed at the end of each darshan, which is the act of beholding a deity, divine person, sacred object, or natural spectacle."

"It is very enchanting."

"The first time Sri Sathya Sai Baba explained the significance of this ritual was in 1966. The waving of the camphor flame at the end of the bhajan sessions is to remind you that your sensual cravings must be burned away without leaving any trace behind. You must offer yourself to God to merge with His Glory."

"Sai Baba believes in God?"

"Sai Baba said the basic truth in all religions… is one and the same. The philosophical ideas or practices and methods of approach may vary, but the final objective and goal are only one. All religions proclaim the 'Oneness of Divinity' and preach the cultivation of universal love without regard to caste, creed, country, or color."

"He sounds like a wise man."

"He was."

"Was?"

"Yes, he died on the 24th of April 2011."

"Oh, I am so sorry to hear that."

"Not to worry, he has reincarnated."

"He has reincarnated?"

"Yes, this will be his third reincarnation. He was known as Shirdi Sai Baba during his first life."

"Is that what is so special about him? That he reincarnated?"

Delish stopped and looked at Isabella. "No. He not only established free specialty and general hospitals and clinics, but he also provided drinking-water projects, ashrams, auditoriums, schools, and even a university. But what made Sai Baba special was his abilities. He could bilocate, materialize Vibhuti—holy ash— and other small objects such as rings, necklaces, and watches. He could perform miraculous healings and resurrections. He was also clairvoyant, omnipotent, and omniscient."

"Oh, now I understand why Doctor Reynolds wanted Aias to train here in India," Isabella said

after hearing about all the spiritual gifts Sai
Baba possessed.

Chapter 18

Delish finished his tour of the Prasanthi Nilayam ashram in front of the temple of Lord Ganesha. Aias turned and looked at the statue of Lord Ganesha. "Mama, look at this elephant."

Isabella turned and walked a couple of feet over to where he was standing.

Delish said as he walked over to them, "Prayer starts here every morning. He is one of the best-known and most worshiped deities."

"It is funny-looking," Aias said.

"The story behind how Lord Ganesha received that funny elephant head is this: It is said that Devi—heavenly—Parvati, who is the Hindu goddess of love, beauty, purity, fertility, devotion, and divine power, wanted a private bath. And since her firstborn son was not there to guard the door, she carved an idol of a boy out of turmeric powder and breathed life into it, unbeknownst to her husband, Lord Shiva, the Great God. The story proclaims that the clay boy, named Ganesha, did his job and guarded the door, denying Lord Shiva entry into his abode. Shiva tried to reason with the boy, saying that he was Parvati's husband. The boy stood his ground, determined not to let Lord Shiva enter until his mother had finished her bath. So, in Lord Shiva's divine fury, he severed the boy's head clear off with his trisula—trident—thereby killing him instantly.

"Goddess Parvati was so mad that she vowed to destroy all of creation. Lord Brahma, being the Creator, could not have this and pleaded with Goddess Parvati not to kill all beings. She said she wouldn't, but only if two conditions were met. One, that the boy is brought back to life, and two, that he be forever worshiped before all the other gods.

"According to this legend, an elephant head was the first head found and brought back to replace the cute little chubby boy's. Honoring her request, it was Lord Brahma who breathed new life into the boy and announced that the boy was the first deity to be praised each day."

Aias touched his head and looked at his mother, saying, "Mom, you will have to lock the bathroom door if you don't want any intruders. I'm not getting an elephant's head."

Isabella laughed and patted her son's head.

Delish asked, "Aias, did you know that Lord Ganesha's huge belly symbolizes the created universe?"

"No, but he does have a big belly."

Delish smiled. "Lord Ganesha is also known for his ability to clear obstacles and pave the way for us to move forward in life."

"Elephants are big. Mama, they can do that, you know, clear a path through the forest."

Also adding, Delish said, "His large elephant head symbolizes wisdom, understanding, and discriminating intellect."

"He does have a large head to fit a big brain."

Delish nodded. "His trunk is magical. It can hold anything and everything that exists in the universe."

"Wow."

Delish smiled and added, "The trishul—weapon of Shiva, similar to a trident—over Ganesha's forehead symbolizes time: past, present, and future."

"Mama, he can tell the future like Aunty Lexi."

"Do you see the mouse?" Delish asked.

Aias pointed. "There it is."

"The mouse symbolizes uncontrolled desires and ego. Like Lord Ganesha, the mouse can live in the world without being tempted," Delish said, trying to instill morals into his story.

"Like chocolate?"

Smiling at the young boy's innocence, Delish asked, "Did you notice his four arms?"

"Yes."

"His four arms represent the four inner attributes of the subtle body, *Manas*—the mind, *Buddhi*—the intellect, *Ahamkara*—the ego, and *Chitta*—the conditioned conscience."

"Mind, intellect, ego, and what?"

"The conditioned conscience."

"What is that?"

"It represents the space behind the forehead, which is the seat of visualization that links man with the conscious, subconscious, and super-conscious mind."

Being polite, Aias said as if he understood, "Oh."

"Do you know what super-consciousness is?"

"Like the powers of the superheroes?"

"Well, in a way, yes. They would need to use it to use their superpowers. Super-consciousness is the ability to control the highest consciousness above that within the normal range of attention. Did you know that is why you are here, Aias?"

Aias looked at his mother. "Is that why we are here, mama?"

"Yes," Isabella replied to her blessed son. "So that you can learn to use your super-consciousness." *No need to stroke his ego and tell him that he was born with a superpower.*

Chapter 19

"Lexi, what is wrong?" Detective Redington asked as he saw her crying in the waiting room.

Between sobs, Lexi answered, "He doesn't recognize me."

"Who?"

"Edward."

"He woke up?" asked Redington, surprised.

"Yes."

Redington looked up to see if he could see Edward but couldn't. "What did the doctor say?"

"That I should go home, that it might take Edward days before he is well enough to leave. Redington, he doesn't know who I am." Placing her face into her hands, she started to weep again.

"Alexandra, does he have amnesia?"

"That is what the doctor thinks."

"What else did the doctor say?"

Crying harder, she said between sobs, "To go home."

"What else? Come on, Alexandra, pull yourself together. What else did the doctor say?"

Lexi looked up and tried to gain control of her emotions, saying, "That he may never remember who I am and to go home." Her emotions won, and she began crying uncontrollably.

Redington took Lexi into his arms and patted her back. "I am sure he will regain his memory. Let me go find out what I can."

Redington got up and went to the nurse's station. Showing his badge, he said, "I am the detective on Mr. Hawthorne's case. How is he?"

The nurse put up a finger to insinuate, "just a moment," and called someone. "Someone will be here in a moment to speak with you."

One of Doctor Singh's assistants came walking down the hall and stopped at the nurse's desk, then walked over to Redington. "Detective, we have not found a next of kin. However, we need to so that we can inform them of the reverend's situation. Do you know how we can contact his family?"

Looking over to Lexi, he said, "She is the closest to a family member that you are going to find."

"I see. That does present a problem."

"How so?" Red asked.

"Mr. Hawthorne does not know who he is," the assistant answered.

"Like nothing?"

"No. Edward doesn't even remember his childhood."

"It's good he remembered his name," Red said.

As the assistant was about to say something, Neo walked up and said, "He didn't. He is just trusting me that it is his name."

Looking at Dr. Singh, Redington replied, "I see. So, what do we do now?"

"We can only release him to family or an authoritative figure, like yourself," Neo answered.

"What? Wait. I can't look after him," Redington said, panicking.

"Then we do have a problem," Neo said disappointedly.

Redington looked at Lexi. "What if I take him, but she looks after him?"

"I am sure we can make that work."

"When will he be ready to leave?" Redington asked, worried that it might be right this moment.

"If everything goes as we expect, in three days."

"Fine, get the paperwork together, and I will be back in three days."

"Perfect. We'll call you if there are any changes."

Redington left his contact info with the assistant and walked back to Lexi, saying, "Come on, Alexandra, let me take you home."

"Not without Edward."

"Alexandra, the doctor said we could come and get him in three days."

Coming in and out of reality, she said, "Really?"

"Yes."

Lexi got up and let Redington walk her out of the hospital.

Helping her into the front seat of his car, he said, "We are going to have to figure out a schedule."

"For what?"

"For you and me to look after Edward."

"Oh…" Lexi answered without emotion.

"I am not sure where the best place for him to stay is. Your place, mine, or his?"

Wiping away her tears, Lexi started to feel like herself again. "His place might be too overwhelming, and I don't have a place right now."

Redington looked at her. "Right, I forgot you were living at your mom's. I guess that only leaves my place."

"The beach will be nice to walk along. He will like that," Lexi said, remembering Redington lived by the ocean.

"Little cold this time of year, but I guess we can make it work."

Redington drove Lexi to her mom's, and as she got out, he said, "I will pick you up in three days unless the doctor tells us differently."

"Thank you, Red."

"Don't thank me yet. You haven't lived with me."

Chapter 20

Isabella and Aias followed Delish down the streets of Puttaparthi to Acharya Shri Sharma's much smaller ashram.

Upon entering, Isabella was surprised to see a man with long dark hair and beard sitting cross-legged on a red mat underneath a giant banyan tree, speaking to many young boys. The boys were dressed in sunflower yellow uniforms that resembled a robe, and across their foreheads, they had three white lines painted. "What is this place?" she asked.

"It is a *gurukula,* a Sanskrit word that translates to guru—'teacher' or 'master'—and *kula,* 'family' or 'home' or as you would call it in the USA, a spiritual school," Delish answered.

"Is this where Aias will train?" Isabella asked, surprised at the modesty of the school.

"Yes, he will live here with us."

"Live here?"

"Yes. All students must stay here, but don't worry, you may visit."

"I may visit? I think you are mistaken. I am not leaving Aias here alone."

"As you can see, he will not be alone."

"This is not what I had agreed to."

"I was informed that you agreed that he must develop his gifts. We have a value-based system where the focus will be placed on the uniqueness of the child so that they can excel in their abilities."

"His uniqueness is very special, but I do not think this is the right place for him," Isabella said, not wanting to leave her son.

"Come with me, please. I will show you more."

As Aias listened to the guru speaking to the students, Isabella took hold of Aias's shoulder and guided him to follow her.

"But mama, I like it here."

"Come, Aias."

Delish moved along to another classroom and then stood in front of a window, opening a curtain to the side so they could peek in.

To Isabella's astonishment, a cup sitting on a table, as if by magic, lifted off the table and over about five inches before returning to the tabletop. "How did he do that?"

"He is learning how to develop telekinesis."

The boy who used telekinesis to move the cup couldn't have been ten years old. Astonished,

Isabella said, "I wouldn't have believed that unless I saw it with my own eyes."

"Your son will not only be safe here to develop his gifts, but he will also learn languages, science, and mathematics through group discussions and self-learning. And he will be required to help with chores."

"Please, mama, I want to go to school here," Aias begged.

"Well…" Isabella thought about it. She did just get an offer to play the leading role in another movie. "How much does it cost?"

"There is no cost."

"No cost? What is the catch?" Isabella said, knowing that there was always a catch to something free.

"I guess there is one catch. When he is finished training here, a traditional gesture of acknowledgment, respect, and thanks to the guru is required. It may be monetary, but it may also be a special task the teacher wants the student to accomplish. In Aias's case, it will be a special task."

Looking at Aias's pleading face and knowing that she could pay any fees if the special task wasn't accomplished, she asked, "When are you expecting him to start?"

"Today."

Isabella followed Aias to a room with many beds where he was given a uniform like the other boys. "Will this be where he sleeps?"

"Yes. All the students are considered equal, no matter what financial position in society he comes from."

Aias quickly changed into his new attire.

Isabella followed Delish and Aias back to where the other children were, then asked, "What are they learning today?" as Aias took a seat beside one of the other students.

"It is from the oldest of Hinduism sacred scriptures, the Vedas—written in Vedic Sanskrit. The guru talks about the four Vedas, the Rigveda, the Yajurveda, the Samaveda, and the Atharvaveda. Aias will also learn about *Samhitas*—mantras and benedictions, the *Aranyakas*—text on rituals, ceremonies, sacrifices, and symbolic-sacrifices, and the *Brahmanas*—commentaries on rituals, ceremonies, and sacrifices."

Not wanting to disturb Aias, Isabella said to Delish, "Can you tell him that I will see him tomorrow?"

"Oh, that will not be permitted."

"But it is the weekend. I was going to take him sightseeing."

"Going out of the *gurukula* is strictly prohibited for students."

"Okay, then I will pop by sometime tomorrow."

"Miss Jackson, now that he is a student here, he will have to follow our rules. A student cannot talk to parents, guests, or visitors without permission. You will also need prior notice and confirmation to be able to come and visit the *gurukula* and meet with your son, but he will call you occasionally."

"So, you are saying I just placed my son into jail?"

"No, spiritual school. If you want your son to develop his gifts, he will need the sanctuary we provide. The vibration of the outside world disrupts the student's concentration."

Delish escorted Isabella out of the ashram. "He is in God's hands now. Trust in his path of enlightenment."

"How will I contact my son?"

"He will contact you."

"When will that be?" Isabella asked as Delish shut and locked the gate.

"When he is allowed. Trust in God, Miss Jackson. Your son is in good hands."

Isabella could see Aias from the gate. He turned to her and waved.

Turning around to walk away, she couldn't, so she sat down on a bench outside the gate.

Isabella, you are not alone. I am still with you, Erland said.

Hans? I mean Erland. How do I leave our son with strangers? He is only a baby. I know to the outside world he seems twelve, but he isn't a year old yet.

Isabella, elf years are strange to a mortal. First, he will grow at the speed of one month, equaling a year, until he is one. Then, he will grow at one month, equaling two years until he is twenty-one. Then time slows down, and he will grow at ten years, equaling one month, meaning that he will only age one month for every ten of your years.

You are telling me that he will look twenty-one next year on his birthday when he should be two?

Yes.

And when I am eighty, he will still look twenty-one?

Yes.

If only I could be so lucky to age that slowly.

You will be beautiful at any age, Isabella.

You are too kind.

I mean it.

I miss you, Erland.

I am always near you.

I know, but I can't touch you.

True.

I am going to miss him.

One year will go very fast, Isabella. Just pretend he is at boarding school.

I can do that, but my heart aches already, and I haven't even left the property.

Technically you have. You are outside of the gates.

Elves are so logical.

True.

How do I leave him?

This might help. In ancient Rome, the god Jupiter is known in Vedic astrology as a guru or Lord Brihaspati, the teacher and guru of the gods and devas. He is equivalent to the Greek god Zeus and is the god of the sky and thunder. Jupiter obtains the heavens.

Is Jupiter a god?

Yes, and in Vedic astrology, Jupiter is the planet of luck and fortune. Another attribute of Jupiter is its rulership of religion, philosophy, and spiritual affairs. Jupiter also controls the outcome of parents' relationships with their children. Isabella, since you have given the care of our son to the Hindu belief system, pray to Jupiter for our son's welfare.

Do you want me to pray to Jupiter, the god, or Jupiter, the planet?

It doesn't matter. It is all the same. You could also wear yellow sapphire or topaz. It will achieve the same outcome.

I do like sapphires.

As Isabella sat there talking to Erland, a young boy ran over to her.

"Don't worry. I will look after your son. I'm not supposed to tell you, but he will be calling you in three days with amazing news," he said in pretty good English and then quickly ran back into the *gurukula.*

See? Jupiter is looking out for you already.

Chapter 21

*I*sabella didn't leave Puttaparthi. For the last three days, hoping to get a glimpse of Aias, she walked to the *gurukula* and sat on the bench outside the gates, just waiting. *He hasn't even missed me enough to call me.*

She had to be in New York City by Thursday. She had accepted the role to play the mother of a young girl in an upcoming film that promised to be next year's box-office hit. But she couldn't get herself to leave without knowing that Aias was going to be alright. So, that left her three days to decide to pull Aias from this school or leave him alone in India for months at a time, possibly for a year. *I don't know if I can go without hearing from my son. I can't even handle a couple of days, let alone months.*

As she sat there contemplating her dilemma, an old blind man came and sat down beside her on the bench. She scooted over a bit to give him more room.

"Your perfume smells like lilacs in the spring. It reminds me of my belated wife, Jyotika. So many years ago, our son had brought some of this perfume from the Americas. She loved it so."

Surprised by his command of the English language and only a slight accent, Isabella said, "Thank you, it is the soap from the hotel I am staying at."

Coughing from old age, he said, "Ah, the gods have shone on me today. It is so nice when they have blessed me with such a lucid dream of my loving wife. I am truly a lucky man."

Isabella looked at him. *From the looks of you, you don't have many days left here on Earth.* "I am happy that I could partake in your happiness."

"Why are you waiting here? Are you sick?" he asked her.

"Me? Sick? Oh, no, I am healthy as a horse."

"I never did understand that saying, healthy as a horse."

Isabella tried Kesia's trick and googled the saying. "It says here that horses have four to five times more white blood cells in their blood and have a higher body temperature than humans, so they do not catch human diseases."

"Ah. Now I know. Thank you."

"My pleasure."

"So, why do you sit here on the bench for people waiting to be healed?"

Isabella touched the bench and shifted her body, not sure if she should get up. "This bench is for people waiting to be healed?"

"Yes. I am here for my session. I hear that I am in for a treat today. That God has brought us an extraordinary healer."

"Oh, how very nice for you."

Just as he was about to say something else, Delish came over to retrieve him. "Sri Pandya, please take my arm, and I will lead you in." As the old man took Delish's arm, Delish said, "Miss Jackson, it is a pleasure to see you again."

Before she could say anything, Aias called out from just inside the gate, "Mama, I am going to heal that man you are with. Did you come to watch?"

Standing beside him was the young boy who said that her son would call her in three days. *Oh my, he literally meant to call out, not to call me on the phone.*

Isabella looked at Delish to see if she could follow them inside, but he shook his head.

"I am afraid I have to watch from here, but I love you. Are you doing well?"

An older man came up to Aias and said something to him to make him turn away from her, but as the old man and Delish came into the compound, Aias snuck a peek and waved at her, nodding his head up and down.

Even though she could not go inside, she was divinely granted a view from where she sat on the bench as the old man was seated by the banyan tree and Aias came up to him, placing his small hands over the man's eyes. Not five minutes had passed before Aias removed his hands.

"भगवान की जय हो! मैं देख सकता," the man yelled in Hindi and then again in English, "Glory be to God! I can see."

A tear escaped Isabella's eye as the man got up and walked without his cane. She watched as he hugged her son. The smile she saw on Aias's face said everything. He was happy and in God's hands. She could leave.

Chapter 22

Wrapped in a towel from just having a shower, Isabella walked into the kitchen of her New York hotel suite.

"Hi, mama," Aias said.

Almost jumping out of her skin, Isabella screamed. Not sure how he got in, since the door automatically locks, she backed up a step and pinched herself, saying, "I'm not dreaming."

"Of course not."

"Aias, how did you get in here? I wasn't informed that they let you out of the *gurukula*." Still startled from seeing him, she continued, "Actually, how did you get here from India?"

"I just popped in for a quick visit. I can't stay long. I don't want to get into trouble, but I want you to know that I am doing well and not to worry about me."

"Thank you, but who let you into the hotel room? It was locked."

"That's funny. Nobody, silly, I let myself in."

"Come here, you, and hug me. I miss you."

Since he didn't move, she went to him.

"You grew…" She hugged him, but her arms went through him as if he was vapor. "Aias! What is going on?"

Laughing, he said, "Gotcha. I knew that I could do it."

"Do what?"

"Yesterday, one of the older boys was bragging about how he could do bilocation and that it would take me many years, if ever, to learn. I proved him wrong."

"Aias, what is bilocation?"

"Oops, gotta go, mama. Love you."

"Aias!" she shouted, but he had already disappeared.

Isabella quickly looked up "bilocation" on her laptop. *The ability or fact of being in two places at once. The existence or the ability to exist simultaneously in two places.* "Wow. Now that is amazing."

Isabella read a website that mentioned that many saints could bilocate. Saint Padre Pio was the main person written about. He was a Catholic priest who served the parish in San Giovanni Rotondo, Italy, and could do many miracles. Bilocation was just one of them.

"Wow! Catholic priests."

She kept reading about other saints who could bilocate. Saint Maria Faustina Kowalska appeared in multiple places at once to spread the message of Divine Mercy. Saint Martin de Porres, Saint Francis Xavier, and Saint Joseph of Cupertino could also bilocate.

Isabella's phone rang.

"Hello?"

"Miss Jackson, this is Delish in India."

"So, it is true?"

"Pardon? What is true?"

"Oh… nothing."

"Miss Jackson, I am calling to inform you that your son will be granted a short phone call. Please keep it short, and just to let you know, you will be on speakerphone."

"Lucky I am available to speak to him. Maybe next time you can give me more advance notice so that I can make sure I am not working?"

"Mama, it makes me so happy to hear your voice. I love it here. I am told to tell you that I am developing many skills, even the one nobody taught me, which you saw earlier."

In the background, Isabella could hear Delish say, "Aias, keep it short. There are many boys who wish to speak with their parents."

"Aias, you can visit me anytime."

Delish said in the background, "Aias, she knows you can't visit, right?"

"Ya, ya," he said as he nodded to Delish. Knowing his mother could hear everything and would catch on to his new secret of bilocation, he said to her, "Mama, make sure you don't tell anyone my secret. It's just for you and me. Okay?"

"Okay. I can keep a secret. I won't tell anyone that you are studying in India."

In the background, she heard, "You know she can tell people that you are here, right?"

"Ya, ya. Gotta go, mama, love you."

"Love you too."

Speaking to herself as she hung up, Isabella muttered, "So, Delish doesn't know that Aias can bilocate. Awesome. I will get to see my son more than I thought I would."

See, Isabella? God is looking after you and our son.

Isabella smiled. She loved it when Erland communicated with her.

Chapter 23

Lexi waited anxiously by the living-room window for Detective Redington's arrival. He had picked up Edward from the hospital and then drove to her mom's place to get her before heading back to his condo.

"Lexi, come away from the window. They will not get here any faster by you constantly looking for them," Olivia yelled from the kitchen.

"Mom, I can't help it. I am so nervous. I haven't seen Edward in three days, and I am praying that he recognizes me."

Olivia came up to her daughter and wrapped an arm around her shoulders, snuggling in. "Keep your faith, dear. Edward is in God's care and is being looked after. Trust that all will be well."

"I'm trying, but the mystery of not knowing is killing me."

Olivia squeezed Lexi's hand.

Just as Olivia was about to insist that they go sit down, Redington drove his car into her driveway.

"Oh my God, they're here."

Running over to the door, Lexi opened it as Redington came up the steps. "Where is Edward?"

"He is waiting in the car."

"Why?"

"Lexi, he still doesn't remember you. He is trying to be gracious but is annoyed with the doctor for insisting that you and I have to look after him."

"Are you saying that he doesn't want me to come to your place?"

"I am saying he knows he doesn't have a choice."

"Oh."

Redington picked up the two large suitcases and jokingly said, "How many months are you staying?"

A tear rolled down Lexi's cheek. "I didn't know what to bring."

Olivia hugged her daughter. "Chin up. Be strong, for Edward's sake. He needs you."

Lexi kissed her mom and said, "I'll call you in a few days."

Olivia whispered in her ear, "I'll pray for the two of you."

Getting into the backseat of the car, Lexi said, "How are you feeling, Edward?"

Turning his head slightly backward, he said, "Silly, actually."

"I don't understand."

"I feel fine. I don't understand why the doctor needs me to have babysitters."

Trying to take the focus off of Lexi, Red said, "I am sure it is only for a few days. Don't you have a doctor's appointment early next week?"

"I would have to see a calendar. I don't know what day it is."

"Let's see your appointment card," Redington commanded.

Edward took the card out of his jacket pocket and passed it to Redington.

"Yep, next Tuesday. That is only four days away."

"Well, at least now I know it is Friday." Changing the subject, Edward said, "So, what club are you guys taking me to this weekend?"

"Club?" Redington repeated.

"Oh… Don't tell me you don't like to party. Man, just my luck. I wake up months later to no memory of my past, and now I am stuck with two nursemaids that don't want to enjoy life."

"Edward, the doctor told you that you are a reverend, right?" Redington asked.

"He mentioned that, but I don't believe him. I am sure I would know if I was a man of God, and I am sure I am not. Those nurses in the hospital were sweet, and all I could think about was getting into their panties.”

Lexi gasped.

Edward turned his head slightly backward and said, “Oh right. I am supposedly engaged to you. Sorry, ma'am, but you are not my type. I don't think you would hang out with the likes of me.”

Lexi was glad that they had arrived at Redington's so that Edward didn't say anything else that she could hate him for.

As she walked around to get her luggage, Redington said, “Don't take anything personally. The doctor said that this is common and that he could get his memory back tomorrow.”

“I sure hope so because I don't know who this man is.”

Walking into the condo, Redington said hello to the doorman and introduced Lexi and Edward.

Redington lived on the second story of the building, and his condo looked out onto the Atlantic Ocean.

As he nudged Redington with his elbow, Edward said, “Now this is what I am talking about. Babes in skimpy bikinis lying on the white sandy beach, enjoying the ocean breeze. Detective, your digs are dope. I bet there is an excellent seafood restaurant nearby that also has lively parties around here.”

Lexi couldn't believe her ears. *Who are you, and where did you hide my Edward? At least Redington is behaving himself.*

Redington chuckled. "Edward, you surprise me."

"Come on, Tec. This place is rad. I bet you have a swarm of ladies swooning at your feet." Edward opened the balcony doors to get a better look. "Woo, baby, look at that one."

Redington came out onto the deck to see what Edward was getting excited about. There were some young things with their bathing suit tops undone to get an even tan on their back.

Nudging Redington again, Edward said, "Nice, right?"

He had to admit they looked pretty sexy from here.

"Red! Don't encourage him," Lexi said, waiting for him to tell her where she could put her things.

Turning to face her, Redington said, "I haven't had time to look out onto the beach for months. Let me enjoy the view."

Not used to either of the men's current behavior, Lexi threw her hands up in the air, walked over to the balcony, and said, "Listen, you two hooligans, while I am staying here, you will act like grown-ups." Then, Lexi shut the balcony doors and locked them out.

Redington knocked on the door. "Let me in. Don't be silly."

"Not until you promise to act like an adult."

"Lexi, let me in. It's my place."

"Tec, come on, they are calling us over."

Redington looked over just as Edward grabbed the railing and swung himself over. He hung from the deck for only a moment before lowering himself down, then landed safely on the sand.

Lexi quickly unlocked the door and ran to the railing to see if Edward was okay.

He was already headed in the direction of the girls.

"Red! You have to go after him."

Looking down, he said, "I'm not jumping."

"I don't care how you get down there. Just go and bring him back here."

Redington brushed past Lexi and went out the entrance door.

Moments later, Lexi watched as Redington walked over to the girls that Edward was now rubbing baby oil on.

"Great! What in the world are they even out there for? It's October," Lexi said, even though she already knew the answer was because of the Indian summer they were having.

Chapter 24

Furious that Redington sat down on the sand beside the girls, Lexi went back inside, slamming the glass door, almost shattering it.

Snooping through Redington's condo, Lexi chose the guest bedroom that didn't have a computer desk in it.

While sitting on the bed, Lexi was deciding whether to unpack her belongings when Susannah said, *Hey, baby sister, how are you doing?*

Tears started to trail down Lexi's cheeks. *Susannah, I don't think I can do this.*

Sure, you can.

No, really. I don't think I am strong enough for this. It is bad enough that Edward doesn't even know who I am, but now he is acting like a love-starved teenager.

It will pass.

It doesn't help that Redington is humored by it.

Ah, Edward has gotten under his skin for a long time now. He is just enjoying Edward's new persona.

New persona? Well, I hate it.

You don't mean that.

Right now, I do.

Lexi's cell phone rang. "Hello?"

"Hi, Lexi. It's Isabella. How are you and Edward doing?"

"Funny you ask. Susannah and I were just talking about that."

"She's with you now?"

"She was. She left when you called."

"Sorry, I can call back."

"No, no. It's okay. Susannah won't go far. How are you doing?" Lexi asked.

"Good," Isabella answered.

"I miss Aias. How big is he now?" Lexi was curious how fast he was growing.

"Lexi, you wouldn't believe it. To the world, he is a twelve-year-old boy."

"Holy cow, and he isn't even two, insane."

"I know, right?"

"So, where are you guys? Are you still in Switzerland?"

"No, actually, I am here in New York, making another movie."

"Oh, that makes me so happy to hear. I need a friend right now," Lexi said, wiping away her tears.

"Is everything okay, Lexi? You sound depressed. Is Edward okay?"

"Yes, in fact, he came out of the hospital today."

"Oh, I am so happy to hear that. Then why are you upset?"

"It's a long story, and it would be easier to show you. Can you and Aias come over for dinner tonight?"

"Sure, but Aias is not with me."

"Where is he?"

"He is at boarding school while I work on this film."

"Really? You left him?"

"It's a long story that I can tell you all about tonight."

"I can't wait to hear the details."

"What should I bring?"

"Nothing, just your pretty little self."

"I'll bring some wine."

"Maybe make that two, and bring an overnight bag."

"I'm not that far away. I can get a taxi to take me home if I drink too much."

"Not from here. You won't want to."

"Why, where are you?"

"Redington's."

"Why?"

"Another long story. Just get over here, and I can fill you in on what has been happening. I'll text you Redington's address."

About an hour later, the doorman rang up and announced that a Miss Jackson had arrived.

"Please, let her up," Lexi replied as she let go of the button on the wall.

Redington and Edward had not come back yet from the beach. Looking out toward where they had been sitting, she could not see them. Even the girls were gone.

A knock on the door brought her back inside.

Opening it, she gave Isabella a big hug. "I am so glad to see you."

"You too."

Coming in, she passed the wine to Lexi and said, "Nice place."

As she walked into the condo, a large antique mirror, framed in brushed gold, was on her right, with a small half-circle marble table under it. On top of the table was a cast bronze statue of a fierce-looking Poseidon, standing on a rock, holding a trident, ready to attack, and swimming around his feet was a sexy mermaid.

A closet was on the other side of the marble floor entrance.

The ten-foot-high ceiling gave the living room an even grander feeling with a clear view of the ocean through glass doors and wall-to-wall windows. The floor was made of dark mahogany, and the walls were painted taupe. The fireplace was an incredible mix of small and large strategically placed brown fieldstone rocks, and the mantel was darker mahogany than the floor. On top of a red area rug were two comfy brown leather couches on either side of a live edge wood and resin coffee table. The artwork in the room was a very large modern abstract that accented the colors perfectly.

As Isabella moved through the living room to the kitchen, she noticed a large sit-down bar off to the side with three comfortable light tan leather chairs that faced out onto the balcony that revealed the shoreline through the glass railing. Isabella had to take one step down into the U-shaped cabinetry from the one end of the bar. It was fully equipped with a small sink and stocked with every type of liquor she could think of. The lower cupboards and countertop of the far side had windows above that opened like an accordion to reveal a pass-through to the balcony. She could see that there were three more chairs on the outside of the bar, this time made out of rattan.

Next to the bar was a round distressed wood dining room table with six Santa Fe-styled designed chairs.

The large kitchen had black shaker cabinets and wild horse granite counters with matching tile—named like this because they resembled an appaloosa but contained hematite and white magnesite with brown mottling, just like the painted horse. The island was so large that it fit four chairs and had drawers on three sides. It also had a vegetable sink. Inserted into one of the wall cabinets were two ovens and a warming drawer, and over the gas-burning stove—attached to the wall—was a pot-filler water tap.

Continuing through the condo, she walked around the corner and found a wine vault with the same rock on its walls as the fireplace. Five open floor-to-ceiling wooden racks held many bottles of fine wine from around the world.

Walking further down the hallway was a reading nook—it had two leather chairs in front of a wall-to-wall bookcase—and the laundry room was as big as most people's kitchens.

There were four bathrooms in the condo, one closer to the living room and one in each of the three bedrooms.

The master bedroom also looked out to the ocean, but it had a floor-to-ceiling glass accordion door that opened the entire length of the wall onto the balcony. The room held an oversized king bed that faced a fireplace—with a large screen TV above and two leather chairs at the end. Redington's walk-in closet had a sit-down cosmetic desk with cabinets on both sides. It had rows of custom shelving units attached to three walls, with a matching dresser island in the center. It even had a stacking washer and dryer. His bathroom had a six-foot double-ended soaker tub that shared the same fireplace as the bedroom, a glass-enclosed shower that had three heads—one on two sides and one from the ceiling, and the "his and her" sinks were gorgeous.

"Lexi, why didn't you tell me he owned this place? It's incredible," Isabella said, coming back to the living room.

"I didn't know until today. Well, I knew he lived here a few weeks ago, but I had never been invited in."

As Redington and Edward walked in with three pretty girls, Isabella said, "Redington, you little devil."

"Isabella, nice to see you again. How is Aias?"

"Good. Aias is good."

One of the girls pulled Redington onto the couch in the living room as the other two made themselves comfortable at the bar with Edward.

Seeing the look on Lexi's face, Isabella said as she walked into the kitchen, "Red, can you barbeque these steaks? Lexi has made us dinner."

"Sure," he said as he pulled three more steaks out of the freezer. Then, coming back from turning on the barbeque, he said, "They'll be ready in about twenty minutes." He then opened the window above the bar to enjoy everyone's company while he was out on the deck.

Lexi watched in horror as Edward flirted with two of the girls. *They look like they are still in college.* Lexi whispered, "Isabella, I think I am in hell. I must be being punished for something I did."

Coming over and patting her shoulder, Isabella said, "It must have been something pretty bad to have Edward act like this."

"Thanks… You were supposed to be comforting me, not agreeing with me."

"Ah-huh. How long did you say you have to stay here?" Isabella asked as she stared at the shenanigans going on by the bar.

"Hopefully not long. I will end up hating Edward if he acts like this. Thank God his doctor's appointment is on Tuesday."

Chapter 25

Four days seemed like an eternity. Edward's doctor appointment didn't come soon enough for Lexi's sake. She had picked up her car the next day since Red worked such long hours, and Edward had insisted that Lexi take him to bars, nightclubs, and pubs every night since he got out of the hospital. Lexi decided she had to submit to his request, for he would have gone out by himself, and she couldn't have that. Unfortunately, she had to endure all of his flirtatious ways with other women.

Sitting in the waiting area of Doctor Singh's office while Edward was in a room being examined, Lexi was relieved to see him before he went in to talk to Edward. "Doctor Singh?"

Hearing his name, he turned and instantly recognized Lexi. "Miss Constantine, nice to see you."

Hurrying over to him, she pulled him aside and said, "Doctor, I can't do this. I can't watch over Edward. Please, let me go home."

"What happened?" he asked, knowing that it had to be severe for her to say something like that. Neo knew how much she loved Edward.

"He is not Edward. The man in that body is not the man I would marry. Not only does he not know who I am, but he also makes me take him out to meet other women. I can't do it anymore."

"I am so sorry, Miss Constantine. This usually never happens."

"So, you are implying that it can happen, though?"

"Yes."

"How long will he be like this?"

Neo paused and then decided to tell her the truth, "Miss Constantine, he may never remember who he was and may stay like this forever."

"Oh my God. I can't… I can't go on like this. You have to do something."

"Let me go and check on him. I will talk to you again after I see him."

About twenty minutes later, Doctor Singh came out of the room and walked over to Lexi. "He cleared all his tests. He seems to be healthy and back to normal. I would have never guessed if you weren't telling me that his personality wasn't like this. You can drive him to his place and drop him off. He can be on his own now."

"Are you sure there is nothing you can do to get his memory back?"

"I am sorry, Miss Constantine, I have done everything in my power."

"What do I do now?"

"Be his friend."

Lexi looked at the doctor as tears formed in her eyes. "A friend? I am not sure I can do that. I would never go out with a guy who has a personality like the one he has now."

"I am sorry, Miss Constantine. I wish I could tell you something more, but I can't."

Edward came out of the room buttoning up his shirt and smiled at Lexi. "Hey, babe, the Doc here says that I can go home. Isn't that great?"

Lexi looked with pleading eyes at the doctor, with no response, then looked at Edward and said, "Let's go get your things."

An hour later, she was driving Edward through the big gates at the entrance of his funeral home. Lexi prayed that it would jog his memory and he would return to normal. As she looked over, his head was leaned back, and his eyes were closed. Clearing her throat, she said, "We're here."

Edward didn't open his eyes until the car stopped.

Lexi watched as he looked at the building. "Do you recognize it?"

Edward stared. "No."

Lexi got out of the car and opened the trunk for Edward to get his bag.

Waiting for him to get out, she said, "Are you okay?"

He opened the door and slowly got out, all the time staring at the entrance. "Are you sure this is my place? It's kind of creepy."

"I'm sure. It has been in your family for generations. Here," she said as she passed him his bag, "I'll walk you in."

As Lexi opened one of the big wooden doors that led to the funeral home entrance, she had a flashback to the day that she had come knocking on this very door to beg him not to do Susannah's funeral. It seemed like yesterday, even though it had been two years ago. So much had happened to her, to them since that day, so many adventures. It was hard to believe that he didn't remember any of it.

Casandra greeted them just inside the door. "Oh, Edward, it is so nice to have you back. Reverend Bernardo has been great, but nothing like you."

Edward stared at the lady talking to him.

Lexi asked, "Do you recognize her, Edward?"

He shook his head.

"Maybe you will remember your office," Lexi said as she motioned for him to follow her.

"Oh my," Casandra said as she followed Lexi and Edward.

Once in the room, Lexi asked, "Anything?"

He shook his head but looked at the picture frames on the desk. Picking one up, he said, "Is this my dad?"

Lexi squealed. "You remembered!"

"No, but he looks like me." He then looked at a picture of himself smiling as he held onto a woman. At a closer viewing, he could tell that it was Lexi. "So, it is true that we were a thing."

"Yes…" Lexi said, disheartened.

"Hard to imagine. You're not my type."

Lexi could see the look on Casandra's face and gave her a slight smile, trying to make it better than it was.

"Let's see the rest of the place," Edward said as he set the picture down and walked out of the room.

Casandra led the way to the chapel.

Edward glanced from the door, then turned and went back into the main building.

Discouraged, Lexi slowly shook her head from side to side as she looked at Casandra.

Lexi saw that Edward had gone down the stairs. She quickened her step to catch up. As she descended the last step, she heard him groan.

Both ladies walked into the theater room just as he came out of a side room and threw up.

"What the hell? There are dead bodies in there."

"It's the morgue. It is where the bodies are placed before burial."

"I live in a morgue?"

"Technically, you live upstairs," Lexi said.

"Let's see that."

Casandra and Lexi followed Edward back up to the main level.

"Edward, I am going to let Lexi show you. I have to meet with a client."

Edward nodded.

"This way, Edward," Lexi said as she opened the door to the upstairs suite.

"Well, at least this isn't disturbing," Edward said as he walked up the marble steps.

"You did an amazing job with this place, Edward."

"I guess… If you like this kind of look."

"You don't like it?"

"It is a little old-fashioned for my taste. It reminds me of a place that a married couple would live and bring up children."

Trying to hold back a tear that was about to roll down her cheek, Lexi said, "You rebuilt it for us."

Looking at Lexi in disbelief, Edward said, "Hmm, well, this is not going to work for me."

"What do you mean?"

"I mean, that there is no way that I am going to live with dead people."

"But you own the place. It has been your home ever since you were born. It is your life."

"Correction. It was my life."

Lexi stood there dumbfounded as he walked away from her. *What does that mean?*

Chapter 26

Aias, who now had the maturity and looks of a fourteen-year-old, was learning the real reason behind the act of *padasparshan*—the act of touching feet. Acharya Shri Sharma was there visiting the students to witness their spiritual growth.

The guru speaking today was the same one that Aias had as a teacher the first day he arrived.

In Hindi, the guru said, "Showing respect for an elder by touching their feet is more beneficial than you may think."

Aias sat cross-legged as he listened under the giant Banyan tree.

"As you have learned in biology, the nerves in the human body start from our brain and end at our fingertips and toes."

Aias touched the tips of his toes.

"While doing *padasparshan*, your fingertips immediately create a closed circuit like a battery when you touch an elder's feet."

Aias boldly reached over and touched the foot of the boy sitting beside him, expecting a shock of energy like you would feel when you touch a battery, but nothing.

"Your fingers and hands become the receptors of that energy, while the feet of the elderly person become the transmitters."

Whispering, he said, "Maybe it only works when you touch an elder."

"When the elder accepts your respect, their heart becomes filled with good thoughts. This positive energy is sent to you via their feet."

Whispering again, Aias said, "Oh, you didn't send me positive energy."

The boy responded, "You tickled me."

"Only the feet of elders and such respectable people as your parents, grandparents, teachers, spiritual gurus, and other senior citizens are touched. Their acquired knowledge, experience, and virtues prove to be extremely powerful and benefit those who show them respect and seek their blessings." The guru noticed the boys talking and said, "Aias, please come up here."

Knowing that he was in trouble, Aias got up and walked over to the guru, and using the prayer hand mudra, he said, "Namaste." Which spiritually means *the light in me honors the light in you.* It is honoring the soul and the light within each and every being.

"Aias, please touch Acharya Shri Sharma's feet."

Aias went to do what was asked of him.

"Wait, you must bend your upper body in front of him, and without bending your knees, stretch your arms forward. Your arms should remain parallel and should be stretched in such a way that your right hand touches his right foot, and your left hand touches his left foot."

Aias took a breath, brought his arms forward, and crossed them as he bent at the waist to touch his grace's feet.

Acharya Shri Sharma felt a surge of energy come from Aias's hands. Moving to adjust his seated position, Acharya Shri Sharma realized that the chronic pain in his lower back was now gone. Placing his right hand on Aias's head, he said, "I bless you."

Aias stood upright and smiled and waited to be allowed to go back to his seat.

Acharya Shri Sharma asked, "What else can you do?"

Sensing that his grace felt the healing effect of his hands, Aias said, "So far, I know that I can also bilocate."

"Can you materialize anything?"

"I haven't tried."

"Try something easy like a pencil, eraser, or something sweet, like a candy."

Aias asked, "What color of pencil would you like?"

Smiling, his grace said, "Surprise me."

Turning around, Aias looked at his classmates. Taking a breath, he walked over to a boy sitting in the back and then opened his hand, palm up.

"What?"

"I need to borrow your pencil."

"Why me?"

"Because you are the only one here with a pencil."

"How do you know I have a pencil?"

"I just do."

The boy removed a rainbow lead pencil from inside his uniform and gave it to Aias. "But I want it back. My sister gave it to me."

Aias bowed his head and then returned to his grace and presented the pencil.

"This time, I want you to create a pencil from thin air."

Aias closed his eyes and thought about it. As he opened the hand holding the rainbow pencil, there were now two.

"Now, create a pencil for all the students."

Aias closed his hand, walked to each student, and passed them a rainbow pencil, lastly, giving the boy back his original.

"Now, create a pen."

Aias closed his eyes, but nothing appeared in his hand. Looking up, he said, "I can't."

"You will be able to soon. Keep practicing."

Aias nodded and sat back down in his spot.

As the guru started talking again, Aias quickly closed his eyes and bilocated to his mother, who was just in the middle of a scene for her new movie.

"Cut! How did he get in here?" the director yelled.

Isabella quickly said, "I need five," and walked over to Aias, saying, "Follow me."

Once out of the way of the crew, Isabella said, "Is everything alright?"

"Yes, I was just so excited to tell you that I learned how to do *padasparshan* today."

"What is that?"

"It is touching the feet of an old person to get their blessing."

"You mean of an elder?"

"Same thing. Can I touch your feet, mama, and show you?"

Teenagers. Looking around, Isabella said, "Can you make it quick? I have to get back. The director is moody today."

Aias took a breath, brought his arms forward, and crossed them as he bent at the waist to touch his mother's feet. "Oh, right. Your feet need to be bare. Can you remove your shoes, mama?"

"Aias, we will have to do this some other time. I have to get back to work. Hey, wait. You were going to touch me."

"Ya."

"You can become solid now when you bilocate?"

Quickly kissing his mother on the cheek, he said, "Oops, his grace knows I am gone. Gotta go. See you soon."

Opening his eyes, he noticed all the other boys had left. Only his grace was still sitting there.

"Where did you go?"

"To see my mom and tell her about what I learned today."

"Do you think it wise to tell her that you can materialize items?"

"Oh, no. My mom is not ready for that. I was going to practice *padasparshan* on her, but she had her shoes on."

"I see."

Chapter 27

Sitting in the waiting area of Doctor Singh's office, Lexi nervously twitched her foot. Across from her was a young mother holding a small child on her knee.

Smiling, Lexi asked, "What are you here for?"

The young lady said, a bit rudely, "If it were any of your business, I would tell you."

A moment later, the young lady and her son were escorted by the receptionist into an examining room.

A nurse passing by said to Lexi, "Don't take it personally. Her son has a brain tumor that is growing at a rapid speed."

"Oh, my. How stupid of me."

"You didn't know, but to be on the safe side, I wouldn't ask that question in here. All the patients have serious conditions, many that are incurable."

"Good point." Lexi sat up straighter in her chair and grabbed a magazine.

Fifteen minutes later, the receptionist showed Lexi into an examining room.

Doctor Singh knocked before he came in. "Miss Constantine, what brings you here today?"

It had been a month since she had brought Edward to see Doctor Singh. "I didn't know who else to talk to. I am concerned, Edward is not himself, and I think he is about to do something that will change his life forever."

Writing down something on a card, he passed it to Lexi.

"What's this? Is this someone Edward is supposed to go and see?"

"No, Miss Constantine, it is for you. It is time to let go of Edward. He is not your responsibility anymore. What decisions he makes now are all his choice. He is a healthy grown-up and has the right to choose his life's journey."

"But he is going to sell the funeral home!"

"He told me at our last meeting."

"You knew?"

"Yes."

"But it has been in his family for generations."

"It is his choice."

"But…"

"Miss Constantine, there is no but. He has made a decision that he believes is the right one."

"But…"

"As I said, the name on the card is for you. If there is nothing wrong with his health, we are done here. And, Miss Constantine, you cannot make an appointment again unless you are here because of a serious health issue. Do you understand?"

Lexi nodded and stood up, saying, "Thank you," and left the room.

Without starting the car and holding tightly onto the steering wheel, Lexi brought her head forward as she began to cry uncontrollably.

Why me? Why did you let this happen? First my dad, then my sister, and now my fiancé. Why do I lose the people I love?

Lexi, you haven't lost me. I am still here with you.

Susannah, it is not fair. I loved him.

I know.

I don't know how to go on. I left my job for him.

He didn't ask you to.

How could you say that? Of course, I had to. I loved him.

It was his destiny.

Destiny! It is all a bunch of crap!

Lexi, you know that a person's fate is unavoidable. The soul chooses before it is even born to live the life set before them.

But Tamara got to change her destiny. She changed her future.

Are you sure about that?

Yes. I was with Tamara in Alfheim.

No, Lexi, all of that was part of her path.

So, you are saying that I chose for Edward to get hurt and abandon me?

No, you chose to have the experience of being abandoned.

That is absurd. Why would I do that?

For the same reason everyone else does.

What reason is that?

Lexi, each soul, is a divine incarnation, an Avatar.

What is an Avatar?

An incarnation in human form.

What does incarnation mean?

The embodiment of a deity or spirit in some earthly form. You already know this stuff. You have been taking Tamara's classes, talking to me, talking to angels, having incredible adventures. Lexi, all that is happening now is that you are trying to find out the actual reason why you are here.

Susannah, I am not following you.

You are "feeling" the reason.

Plain English, please.

The reason every soul comes to Earth as a human.

Susannah! Just tell me.

To feel… to feel all the experiences… to experience all the emotions needed to complete the soul's journey.

A tap at Lexi's window snapped her out of her conversation with Susannah.

Looking out the window, she saw Redington. Opening the window a bit, she heard him say, "Are you okay? You have been sitting here a long time."

Shutting her eyes, she said, "He is selling the funeral home."

"Alexandra, open the other door."

Pushing the button to unlock the other door, Lexi just put her head back against the headrest and closed her eyes.

But instead of Redington going around and hopping into the passenger's seat, he opened her door and said, "Alexandra, move over. I think you need a drink."

Chapter 28

Redington drove in silence as Lexi cried the whole way from the hospital to his place. Knowing there was no use in stopping her, he just let her cry.

Walking around the car and opening her door, he helped her out.

"Why are we here?"

"I told you that you need a drink."

"I thought you meant at a pub or something."

"In your condition, I don't think the owners would like a woman sobbing uncontrollably. It's bad for business."

"Don't you have to work or something? How about your car?"

"As luck would have it, I was at the hospital with another officer who drove. See? My car is right there."

Lexi looked over and saw his beige 1967 Chevy Impala SS. "Why do you drive such a big car in New York? You do know that most people don't even own a car here."

"I guess it's sentimental. I loved watching one of my favorite actors drive his Metallicar."

"Is that so? You have a car because of a show?"

"It was an awesome show."

"So, why do you really have the car?"

"I guess I just like it."

"Fine, if you don't want to tell me. I get it."

"Why do you own your car?"

"Truthfully, because it is good on gas and will get me out of the city safely."

"Where are you planning on going?"

Lexi relaxed back into the passenger seat. "What?"

"You said it would get you out of the city safely."

"Ah. I don't know where. I just said the first thing that came to my mind."

"As a detective, usually, those are truthful answers."

Lexi sat there looking at him. "I don't know. I hadn't thought about where I would go."

Redington passed her the keys and said, "Come on, you still need a drink."

It had been a couple of weeks since she had stayed at his place, but walking into his condo this time seemed different. It didn't seem like a prison.

Redington walked in with his shoes on and threw his coat onto a chair at the bar.

"You know, my cousin in Canada would be horrified that you didn't take your shoes off at the door."

"Well, have you been to Canada? I would also take off my outside shoes if I had to truck through the slushy, salty, and dirty snow in the winter. Muddy, wet dirt in the spring. Stones, dog poop, grass, dried dirt, and other things in the summer."

Lexi laughed for the first time in a while. "Thank God our roads are relatively neat and clean, and we don't have to remove our shoes because they rarely get dirty when we are outside of the house. And by the way, she says it is the law now to clean up the dog poop during a walk."

"About time."

Redington passed Lexi a cocktail.

"What's this?"

"A Brown Cow."

"What's in it?"

"Kahlua, cream, and a maraschino cherry."

"Tasty. It tastes like chocolate milk," Lexi said as she drank it down in one gulp. "Can I have another?"

"Sure, but be careful. The cocktail catches up with you."

Lexi took her second drink and went and sat in the living room.

Redington turned on the fireplace.

Slipping out of her shoes, she put her feet up on the couch and said, "This is nice. Thank you." Then she drew the blanket tossed over the back of the leather couch over herself.

Redington sat at the other end of the couch and placed her feet onto his lap. Then, after putting his drink on the coffee table, he started to massage her feet.

She was emotionally exhausted, and this felt nice.

"Alexandra?"

With her eyes closed and her head leaning on the soft cushion, she said, "Yes."

"Have you ever thought about going to Cuba?"

"Not recently. Why?"

"It is somewhere that I have always wanted to visit."

"Then you should go one day."

"Ya, I might just do that."

"I imagine myself revisiting Paris. I love that city," Lexi said, with her eyes still closed.

"You've been?"

"Yes. Not only would I have to attend all the shows here in New York, but I would also have to attend the semi-annual events there. I loved seeing the famous brands like Dior, Chanel, Louis Vuitton, Givenchy, and Céline. The designers would host their shows in historical places like the Carrousel du Louvre or the Grand Palais. It was magical seeing the models all dressed up, walking down the runway. Some years, I used to travel to Milan and London."

"Do you miss your job?"

"Sometimes."

"Do you think you are going to go back to work now that Edward is out of the picture?"

Lexi pulled her feet out of Redington's hands and sat up. "Now that he is out of the picture?"

"Edward told me the other day that he was seeing one of those girls that he met on the beach. He even said that they are thinking of moving in together."

"Man, what I wouldn't give right now to have lost my memory."

"Don't say that."

Lexi started to cry again. "Why? Why does it have to hurt so much?"

Redington moved closer and pulled her in tight, rubbing her back. "I don't know."

Chapter 29

"How much did you let me drink last night?"

"Let you? Like I had a choice. Alexandra, you helped yourself after I went to bed."

Holding her temple, she said, "I think I took advantage of you."

"Hey, wait right there. Nothing happened between us."

Lexi looked up from squinted eyes. "I meant your hospitality."

Feeling awkward now, he said, "I knew that."

"I am going to take a shower," Lexi said as she got up and walked past him, almost bumping into him from the effects of being drunk last night.

As she stepped into the oasis of the guest bedroom, she slipped out of her clothes. The shower reminded her of going to the spa and entering a steam room. The water automatically turned on as she placed her foot down on the warmed tiled floor. The water cascaded down from the ceiling as if it were raining, and three jets sprayed out of the wall, hitting her back, buttocks, and legs. She tilted her head back to let the warmth of the water run down her long dark hair, washing away her woes. Relishing in the heat of the water, Lexi didn't hear the door open.

"Alexandra, you need to take this call."

"Get out!" she yelled, covering herself.

Quickly grabbing a towel and wrapping herself with it, she came out into the bedroom, but Redington wasn't there. Opening the door, she peeked into the hallway, but he wasn't there either. "Red!" Furious that he was playing games with her, she stormed into the kitchen, but he wasn't there. "Where are you?"

No answer.

"Red, this isn't funny."

She searched his condo, but he wasn't there. Then, as she turned to go back into the guest bedroom, she noticed a note.

Hey, Alexandra,

Help yourself to whatever you need.

I made coffee.

Talk to you later. I got called into work.

Red.

Picking up her phone, she called him.

He answered by saying, "Redington."

"Of all the nerve. How dare you come into the bathroom when I am having a shower!"

"Alexandra, what are you talking about?"

"Just a few moments ago, you came in and said there was an important call that I needed to take."

"Alexandra, I don't know what you are talking about. Sawyer picked me up about half an hour ago."

"Ha, ha. Funny. It wasn't even ten minutes ago."

"Alexandra, maybe you should go lie down."

"Don't patronize me."

"Alexandra, I have to go. We'll talk about this later."

"Well, of all the nerve." Looking around the condo, she reread the note. It had a coffee stain on it that had dried.

"Great, I am losing my mind."

"Alexandra."

Freaking out, Lexi screamed as she turned in the direction of the voice. "Who's there? Show yourself."

"Alexandra, you need to take this call."

"Red, stop it. This isn't funny!"

Lexi ran through each room, but no one was there.

Kneeling, she started to pray, "Oh, God almighty, please tell me what is going on. I am losing my mind."

"Alexandra, you need to take this call."

"Susannah! HELP ME!"

"Alexandra."

"Oh, my God, Susannah! PLEASE HELP ME!"

Running back into the guest bedroom, she shut and locked the door. Then after getting dressed in last night's clothes, she grabbed her purse and shoes and ran out of Red's condo to her car.

Fumbling with her keys as she tried to get them out of her purse, she dropped them.

As she bent down to pick them up, a stranger asked, "Ma'am, are you alright?"

Looking at the man, she went white as a ghost, terrified for her life. She pushed the button to unlock her car, getting in and instantly locking it, she started the engine. The tires squealed as she raced out of the parking lot.

"Alexandra…" was the last thing she heard.

#

"Red." Looking around, Lexi added, "Where am I? What happened?"

Caressing her finger gingerly, he said, "I got here as soon as I heard. Alexandra, you hit a telephone pole. You are lucky to be alive. They had to use the 'jaws of life' to get you out."

Just then, Olivia rushed into Lexi's hospital room. "What in Heaven's name were you doing, Alexandra Elizabeth Constantine?"

Barely able to keep focused, Lexi said, trying to smirk, "Ah-oh, I'm in big trouble now. She used my full name."

Redington chuckled. "I think I will go. It looks like your mom wants a heart-to-heart." Then, as he walked by her, he said, "Mrs. Constantine, she's all yours."

"What is he doing here? Doesn't he know you have a fiancé?"

"Had, mom. Had a fiancé."

"He'll be back. Edward can't stay away for long."

"Mom, he doesn't even know who I am. Besides, he is dating someone else."

"I can't believe that our Reverend is dating someone else."

"Not only is he moving in with this girl, but he also sold his funeral home."

"Blasphemy!"

Lexi tried to shake her head to insinuate she knew, but the pain stopped her.

"Lexi, my poor baby, does it hurt that much?"

"Only when I move."

"Should I go and tell the nurse to get you something for the pain?"

"No, they set me up with a morphine drip that I can control. I just have to push this little button, and then I am off to la-la land." Accidently, she pushed the button and drifted off to sleep.

Chapter 30

Before Doctor Singh came into the hospital room, he had pulled the chart from the nurse's station.

"How's your day going so far, Doctor?" a young nurse asked, flirting.

His head was down as he was going over the chart. "Fine, thank you." Then, not even looking at her, he turned and headed toward his next patient's room.

Entering, almost bumping into the man coming out, he said, "Detective Redington, what are you doing here?" Then, he looked down quickly at the chart again to reread the patient's information. That is when her name clicked. "Lexi?"

Redington followed him back into the room.

Hearing the doctor talk to Redington, Lexi groggily woke up. "Hi, Doc," she said through very swollen lips.

Olivia stuck out a hand and said, "I am Alexandra's mother."

Without shaking it, he said, "Nice to meet you. I am Neo Singh, the neurosurgeon checking in on her condition."

"Lexi? Is this the same doctor that you told me about? The one who helped Edward?" Olivia asked without taking her eyes away from the dreamy doctor.

"Yes."

"You didn't tell me how handsome he was and a surgeon like your father."

"I didn't know your father was a surgeon. Where does he practice?" Neo replied, still a bit shocked to see Lexi here in the first place.

Olivia answered for her, "Yes, he was a general surgeon at Brooklyn Hospital."

"So, he's retired then?"

Lexi answered since her mom still couldn't talk about him, "No, he passed away a few years ago."

"Oh, I am sorry."

There was an awkward silence in the room for a moment.

"Lexi, if you really needed to see me, I am sure I could have made an exception. Your accident is a bit radical. Don't you think?"

She laughed at his joke, knowing that the last time she saw the doctor was to complain about Edward selling his funeral home, which was yesterday. As she did, she started to cough up blood.

"NURSE!" Neo yelled as he pushed the emergency call button.

Being on the opposite side of the hospital bed, Neo and Redington couldn't catch Olivia as she fainted from seeing all the blood.

Being a doctor's wife, one would think you would be used to seeing blood, Neo thought to himself. *Luckily, she didn't hurt herself and only fell backward into the chair.* "We need to take Miss Constantine to the O.R. now!"

"But we don't have a doctor available," one of the nurses that had come rushing in called out.

"We don't have a choice. Miss Constantine is bleeding internally. I will have to do the surgery."

Redington spoke as Neo went by, "Doc, take good care of her, will ya?"

Neo nodded as he helped a nurse push the bed out into the hallway.

#

Three hours later, Doctor Singh came out of the operating room and delivered the news of Lexi's condition. "Mrs. Constantine, Lexi is doing fine. She has just been wheeled into a recovery room, and after she wakes up, we will be continuing to monitor her vitals."

"Thank God, my prayers have been answered," Olivia said, bringing her hands together in prayer formation.

Neo had heard it a thousand times, family and friends thanking God and not him for saving their loved ones.

"Doc? What was the problem?" Redington asked.

This is the part that I hate—giving people bad news. "I haven't told Lexi yet. So, you will have to wait until she tells you or permits me to."

Chapter 31

Lexi woke up from the anesthesia. Feeling a bit uncomfortable, she asked the nurse what had happened. "All I remember is laughing and then blood coming out of my mouth. What was wrong?"

"I am sorry, you will have to wait for Doctor Singh. He will explain all that he had to do."

"All that he had to do?" Lexi touched her head to see if there were any bandages. She knew he was a neurosurgeon, so she must have had some nerve damage somewhere if he operated.

The nurse noticed her panic and said, "He didn't operate on your head."

"So, what did he operate on?"

Just in the nick of time, Doctor Singh came in saying, "How is my patient?"

"Your patient? Am I going to walk? Am I going to go into a coma, like Edward? Oh, my God, do I have a tumor?"

"Miss Constantine, calm down. It was nothing like that. I had to do minor emergency surgery on your lungs and more on your uterus. The impact of the seatbelt damaged your body."

Taking a deep breath, she said, "Well, I seem to be breathing okay."

"Yes, it was a rib that was pushing on the lung and bruised it. Then, when you laughed, it caused pressure and started to bleed."

"Whew, that is good news." But the look on his face said something else was wrong. "What? What is it?"

"I had no choice but to remove your uterus. It was very badly damaged. I could do a partial, though, so you still have your ovaries."

It took a moment for Lexi to understand what he had just said. Then, tears started to run down her cheeks. "Are you telling me that I will never be able to have children?"

"I am so sorry, but yes, I had to remove your uterus."

Sorrow instantly transferred to anger. "Get out! Get out of here. You ruined my life!" Tears streamed down from Lexi's eyes.

"Nurse, she is going into emergence delirium. Give her a sedative."

Within moments, Lexi was in a dream state from the drugs the nurse had administered… She had married Edward and was upstairs in the suite at the funeral home. She was in the kitchen making supper when she heard a baby cry. Turning down the heat on the stove, she ran up the few stairs toward the sound. She stopped and turned into the nursery. Expecting to see Aias in the crib, she was surprised that it was a baby girl. Lexi recognized the baby instantly. It was her baby, hers and Edward's. Picking the little darling up, and as she rocked her in her arms, she started to sing, "Hush, little baby, don't you cry." The love she felt was beyond words. She started to cry as the dream faded and reality set in.

After the drugs had worn off, Lexi woke from her dream and instantly went into a depressed state. The hospital staff must have moved her because she was in a shared room on the maternity ward with three other ladies. Two of the other ladies were dying of uterine cancer and crying. The third had a hysterectomy after Lexi and was already up walking around.

Lexi had stopped talking and hardly reacted when a nurse came in and checked in on her. As her evening meal came around, she pushed the table away, not wanting to eat.

The pain Lexi was feeling wasn't only from her surgery. It was emotional pain from knowing what she had lost, the ability to have a baby. *What do I have to live for now? I am worthless as a woman. Who will want to marry me when I can't give them a child? Nor do I have a job.*

How did I get from traveling the world, having great friends, being a top fashion designer about to marry the man I love, to being a spinster and living with my mother, and not wanting to live?

All she wanted to do now was escape the pain.

Chapter 32

A little out of breath from running up the stairs to Luna's bedroom, Kesia shouted anxiously, "I just found out. Lexi is in the hospital. She was in a car accident."

"Is she okay?" Luna asked as she put down her athame.

"I think so. Redington says that her body has taken a beating, but her mind seems okay."

"Well, that's good at least."

Looking at the little sword on the floor that Luna had been holding, Kesia asked, "What are you doing?"

"Cleaning the tools I use in various Wiccan rituals."

Kesia sat down and waited for Luna to tell her about them, but she didn't, so she asked, "What do you do with them?"

Luna looked at Kesia and said, "If I tell you about them, then you will have to join my coven."

"Oh."

"Do you want to join my coven?"

"Ah, I never thought about it. What does it entail?"

"You will be initiated and bound by an oath of secrecy. We also meet in a secret location and practice rituals and magical workings during a full moon or to celebrate the wheel of the year."

"What are the rules?"

"There is only one 'rule' in Wicca: *Harm none, do what you will.*"

"I like that rule. How many people are in your coven?"

"You would make number thirteen. It is also the maximum number of people allowed in any coven."

"Oh, I would have thought there would be hundreds."

"Kesia, we are a priesthood, but Wicca is not like going to church. It is very intimate. You will be divulging your soul's deepest secrets, no matter how dark or light."

"Do you practice black magic?"

"Never, and we also don't cast harmful spells on people. We only cast spells for protection, prosperity, attracting love, and things like that. A spell must always have good intentions."

"What will be expected of me?"

"A Wiccan is a type of witch. And as a witch, we follow the moon cycles and the seasons of nature. We mostly work on shaping and empowering our spirit."

"Sounds intriguing. Yes, I would like to join your coven."

"Great, then we will start today."

"Cool, what do you want me to do first?"

"First, you must promise to take the oath of secrecy."

"Okay, how do I do that?"

Luna got up and took a bottle off a shelf, then opened the lid like it was a perfume bottle. Dabbing a little on Kesia's wrists, Luna said, "Kesia Bango, I bind you to the secrecy of our coven. What happens in our coven stays in our coven. What is said in our coven stays in our coven."

'That's all? Am I a Wiccan now?"

"No."

"But I thought you said I could join."

"You can, and if you still wish to become a witch, in one year and one day, we will have a ceremony, and we'll celebrate with our coven. Until then, you learn."

"Not what I expected, but I can live with that."

"Good."

"So, what do I get to learn first?"

"You might as well learn about our tools."

"Lit!"

Luna smiled. "I might as well teach you what these tools are." *It will be fun to have someone my age in our coven.*

Kesia leaned in to get a better look.

"This athame is a ritual knife, but one could also use a dagger or sword. Most covens consider the blade a fire element, and it is always charged with the owner's energy. It is used as a pointer to define space—such as casting a sacred circle—and as a conductor of the owner's willpower. I usually use it to direct energy when casting my magical spells, but it can also control spirits."

"It looks sharp."

Luna nodded and then moved on to the next item. "Next is a wand. Mine is made of wood but can be made from metal, gemstones, or crystals. It is considered an air element."

Kesia picked it up and said, "I see many tarot card readers with crystal wands on their table."

"Yes, a wand is an awesome tool to direct energy into something or out of something." Then, Luna pointed to an old-fashioned metal wine glass with engravings on it. "The chalice or goblet is considered a water element. Its symbolism is like the sacred Holy Grail, but rather than holding the blood of Christ, it represents the goddess's womb. The chalice is traditionally used to hold ceremonial wine."

Kesia nodded to confirm that she understood.

"This magical symbol." Luna pointed to the object, then continued, "The paten or pentagram, or you may know it as a pentacle, is considered an altar consecration tool. The five-pointed star is usually drawn, engraved, or inscribed upon a plate or disk of some kind. Although, many witches use chalk or salt to draw a version of the paten within the ceremonial circle. It is considered an Earth element."

"I have seen this symbol associated with Satan."

"No. Don't make that mistake. Many people confuse the paten with the satanic symbol of an upside-down, five-pointed star. Our symbol is an upright, five-pointed star, and the point at the top means triumphing over the world.

"So, we will never be praying to Satan?"

"No, absolutely not. In fact, most witches do not even believe that such a character exists."

"Good to know. Hey, I have seen you use other tools. Do I get to learn about those today?"

"There are many other tools, some you know already like incense, and some you probably don't know like the scourge."

"Nope, I don't know that one. So, what is a scourge?"

"A religious whip."

"A whip. Really?"

"Yes, it is used during an initiation and stands for the sacrifice and suffering that one is willing to endure to learn."

"They strike you with it?"

"You'll have to wait and see. It's a secret, remember?"

"Is there anything we can do for Lexi today? But not like with Edward. We don't want a walk-in to take over her body."

"You think that is what happened to Edward? He became a walk-in?" Luna asked Kesia.

"It is the only explanation I can think of. I believe Edward died the day of the beating, and on the hospital table as the doctor shocked the life back into him, another soul took his place."

"Interesting theory," Luna said as she looked for a healing spell in her witch's book of magic for Lexi.

Chapter 33

Early the next morning, a nurse came in and said to Lexi, "We need you to get up. You can't go home until you can walk to the bathroom and have a bowel movement. Here, let me help you."

Lexi didn't move. Mentally, the effort seemed too exhausting. She had spent the night listening to the two women dying of uterine cancer cry. To make it even worse, she could also hear the babies crying from down the hall, which reinforced the pain of knowing that she would never have one of her own.

"Miss Constantine, that is an order. You have to get up," the nurse said as she tried to move Lexi into a sitting position. Giving up, the nurse said, "Fine, we will try again in an hour," and left the room, never intending to come back.

Lexi just lay there, motionless, dosing in and out of consciousness.

An hour later, a different nurse came into the room to check the morphine drip. As she tapped the unit, she woke Lexi up. After checking Lexi's chart, the nurse asked, "Have you used the drip?"

Lexi looked over and said, "The doctor told me to use it if I am in pain. If I don't move, I feel no pain, so no, I haven't pushed the button for more morphine."

With an irritated tone, the nurse said, "You haven't used it since yesterday," and hastily left the room.

Within a few moments, she was back. As she pointed to Lexi to turn away from her, she said, "Turn onto your side."

Lexi winced as she turned.

Seconds later, the nurse stuck something up Lexi's butt.

"What was that?" Lexi asked, feeling invaded.

"I don't have time to deal with you today. You needed something for the pain!" the nurse said rudely and walked out of the room.

You never asked me if I was in pain. I wasn't until you had me move.

Lexi instantly fell asleep, knowing that the nurse must have given her a drug of some type.

When she woke, Lexi had enough of this gloomy place. So, when a different nurse than the tyrant who came in earlier and mistreated her came in, Lexi asked, "What do I have to do to get out of here?"

"You have to eat something, have a bowel movement, and be able to walk."

"Okay, and if I can do that, I can leave?"

"With the doctor's permission and sign-off, yes."

Lexi was determined to get out of the hospital that same day. She struggled to sit up due to the pain when breakfast came but forced a few bites down. *One goal accomplished.*

When lunch came, the same ordeal.

Finally having the urge to go to the restroom, Lexi lay there a moment, then using her arms, she shimmied her legs to hang over the edge of the bed. A sharp pain shot up her back. Lexi almost passed out but was determined to walk to the bathroom.

Once the pain subsided a bit, she used her arms again to sit up. Again, a sharp pain shot up her back. A few tears formed and ran down her cheeks. Biting her tongue, not to make a sound, Lexi tried to stand up by grabbing the edge of the bed. Just as she did, someone caught her as she screamed from the unbearable pain and collapsed into their arms.

Lexi looked up to see who had caught her. As she looked into her rescuer's eyes, a spark flickered. She couldn't describe it exactly, but she just knew it was some kind of cosmic connection—an invisible bond that occurs when you meet your soul mate. She wasn't sure if she had imagined it, but she thought for a second that he felt it, too.

At the same moment, Redington dropped the flowers, a beautiful bouquet of pink carnations and roses—Lexi's favorites—and saw the look on both their faces. Not caring about the flowers, Redington instantly went to help.

"I've got her," Dr. Singh said as he placed her back into her bed. "Where does it hurt?"

Lexi closed her eyes. The pain was like lightning bolts surging through her body. "Everywhere."

"Lexi, be specific. Where does it hurt?" Neo asked again.

With her eyes closed, she said, "My lower back."

"I'll return," Doctor Singh said as he left her room.

Redington sat down on the chair beside Lexi's bed and said as he picked them up, "I brought you flowers."

Lexi could hardly open her eyes because the pain was excruciating. "Thank you." With her eyes still closed, she said, "How did you get in to see me? I didn't think they were allowing visitors."

"Why did you think that?"

"My mom hasn't been in to see me."

As a cop would, Redington asked, "Did you call her?"

"No, my phone is dead, and I don't have my charger."

"Here, I'll call her for you." He pulled out his phone and dialed her mom's number.

"You have my mom's number on speed dial?"

Redington went a bit red. Ignoring her question, he said, "She's not picking up. Maybe she is on her way over."

Lexi got a sick feeling. "Red! Pass me that paper bowl." It was a false alarm, so she continued, "Can you do me a favor and drive over and check on her, please?"

"Well, since you said please."

Lexi winced as she attempted to laugh. "Red, are you trying to burst my stitches?"

As he was about to answer, Doctor Singh came back into the room. "Sorry to break you two love birds up, but Lexi, I have to do more tests."

Before Lexi or Red could say anything else, the awful nurse from earlier that morning came in, and as she butted in between Lexi and Redington, she said, "Sir, you are going to have to leave."

Not wanting to deal with a witch from hell, Redington got up and left. "I'll check in on your mom for you, Alexandra."

The nurse had just stuffed a thermometer into Lexi's mouth, so she couldn't even say thank you.

Chapter 34

$\mathscr{A}$ couple of weeks after being accepted into the coven, Kesia was sitting in Luna's room, looking at one of her Wicca books.

"Hey, you only talked about four elements when you explained the tools, and this picture shows five."

Luna went over and looked at the picture in the book. "The Wiccan Classic Element theory shows the four main elements: Earth, Air, Fire, and Water. I mentioned those while explaining the tools. The fifth element is known by a few names, Spirit, Aether, Sky, Wind, or the Void, and it is technically not considered an element."

"Why is that?"

"Because elements are believed to be the basic components of creation that come together to build all things, and spirit or the soul is not a constituent. In Wicca, we believe that it is the divine force of the fifth element that created the other elements."

"Okay, but why are these elements different from the ones that the Chinese talk about? Where are the elements of metal and wood?"

"I don't know much about the Chinese Five Element theory, but I do know that tarot cards use the same four Classic Elements as Wiccans, and so do the Native Indians with their Medicine Wheel."

"That's weird, don't you think?"

"Actually, now that I am thinking about it, the Japanese, Greeks, Tibetans, Hindus, and even the Babylonians didn't call any elements metal or wood."

Kesia's curiosity got the best of her, and she had to know more, so, of course, she consulted with her almighty oracle, the internet. "This website says that the Chinese Five Element Theory is also called Wu Xing. Everything between heaven and earth is influenced and categorized within the five basic elements of Fire, Earth, Metal, Water, and Wood. It says that these five elements are so powerful that they have the power to create and destroy."

"It doesn't sound the same as our Classic Elements," Luna said. "Does it say how the elements work?"

Kesia shrugged. "I think each element works with a meridian. It says that the five elements are continually evolving and changing within our bodies. By using the Chinese Five Element Theory, one can figure out what body system is unbalanced and how to use that knowledge to heal a sick person." Looking at Luna, she asked, "How do Wiccans use the elements?"

Smiling, Luna pointed at the arrows on the picture and said, "Not only do we use the appropriate tool while performing witchcraft, but we also pay attention to the direction of the arrows. Moving the tool in the direction to either *invoke* or *banish*, whatever it is that we are working on."

"Oh, that is cool, but not at all what I was expecting."

"Each element in Wicca, similar to the Chinese Five Element theory, also has specific healing traits and powers. Wiccans call upon these powers before casting circles, spells, cleanses, or during sacred rituals." Luna read from the book. "Here is what each of the four elements symbolizes:

Earth's colors are brown, green, and yellow.
   Cardinal direction is North.
   Zodiac signs are Taurus, Virgo, and Capricorn.
   Tarot card suit is pentacles.
   The Wiccan tools associated are salt and the pentacle.
Fire's colors are red, orange, and gold.
   Cardinal direction is South.
   Zodiac signs are Aries, Leo, and Sagittarius.
   Tarot card suit is wands.
   The Wiccan tools associated are candles and the wand.
Air's colors are white, silver, and yellow.
   Cardinal direction is East.
   Zodiac signs are Gemini, Libra, and Aquarius.
   Tarot card suit is swords.
   The Wiccan tools associated are bells, incense, and the athame.

Water's colors are blue and indigo.
  Cardinal direction is West.
  Zodiac signs are Cancer, Scorpio, and
  Pisces.
  Tarot card suit is cups.
  The Wiccan tools associated are the chalice
  and the cauldron."

"What about the Spirit element?" Kesia asked.

"As I said earlier, it is the substance that unifies the four material elements. Many Wiccans believe that Spirit is our higher self."

"Do the elements mean anything else?"

Luna turned to a page in the book, showed Kesia, and said, "Here, read this."

Earth

Matter, foundation, manifestation, money, incorporating, employment, touch, empathy, understanding, fertility, security, safety, home, prosperity, and business. Represents stability and physical endurance.

Fire

Energy, spirituality, passions, light, vitality, health, goals, desires, destiny, sexuality, purification, and sight. Represents courage and daring.

Air

Thought, creativity, knowledge, mental activity, study, speech, intellect, ideas, communication, hearing, travel, messages, eloquence, freedom, discovery, revealing hidden things, and secrets. Represents intelligence and the arts.

Water

Feelings, happiness, pleasure, love, children, friendship, marriage, family, ancestors, veils, home, taste, dreams, sleep, divination, purification, cleansings, healing, psychic, intuition, and the subconscious. Represents emotions and intuition.

Spirit

Spiritual energy, magic, empowerment, community, purpose, divine connections, interconnections, power. Represents the All, Deity, and the blending of the Elements.

"Oh, I like this book. May I borrow it?"

"No, but you can buy it off the internet or through a bookstore."

Looking at Luna's shelf, Kesia saw many books on Wicca. "Which one should I start with?"

"It doesn't matter. Just start to learn all that you can."

Chapter 35

Coincidentally, Aias, who now looked sixteen, also had to learn about the elements, but in much more detail.

Teaching today was Delish. "Pancha Bhoota, Air, Water, Fire, Earth, and Sky are Hindu and Buddhist elements. These five elements are the basics of all cosmic creation. The first is *Vayu,* the Vedic Sanskrit term for *wind or air*." Delish held up a toy wind spinner and blew on it.

Aias had never seen one before and excitedly hooted as the plastic tips started to spin, creating a flowery rainbow of colors. Aias put up his hand. "How does that work?"

Delish asked one of the boys up front to stand up. "Aias, a wind spinner, or some people call it a pinwheel, is a stick with twisted paper or plastic pieces that turn as they catch the wind. Here. Take the stick," he said, giving the stick to the boy. "You can blow on it to make it turn, move it through the air, or you can run with it."

The boy ran with it. The colors became a blur as the toy's petals turned so fast against the pressure of the air.

Aias watched as the boy ran back, holding the toy just right so that the friction of the air would quickly turn the colorful petals again.

Delish took the handheld wind spinner from the boy and then showed a beautifully designed mandala wind spinner. "This one you hang up outside, and when the wind hits the twirling metal pieces, it pops out in layers to reveal a vibrant three-dimensional design. Watching it in motion gives the viewer an inner calmness."

Aias liked that one, too.

"Air is considered the most spiritual element, for it corresponds to the breath and soul of our spirit. We need air to breathe. Without it, we would not exist. As you all should know by now, we teach you a breathing technique. What do we call it?"

Every boy in the group put up their hand.

Delish pointed to a boy and asked, "What do we call it?"

"Yogic breathing technique."

"Correct. Apart from sustaining life, what else is air good for?"

Many hands went up. Delish picked another older boy. "Our breath, mind, and body are so intimately connected. All three can deeply influence each other. If you are stressed, it can cause one or more to become dis-eased."

Delish nodded, then said, "The way we breathe is influenced by our…?"

"State of mind," one of the boys in the back called out.

"Yes, and our thoughts and physiology can be influenced by our breathing."

Aias put his hand up.

"Yes, Aias."

"How?"

Delish smiled. "Aias, have you ever been scared?"

"I guess."

"What happened to your breath?"

"I sucked it in."

"Okay, what about swimming? Have you ever swallowed water, and it went down your windpipe?"

"Oh, ya. I coughed for a long time to get it out."

"How about when you run around and play? What happens?"

"I have to stop sometimes and catch my breath."

"Right, your body needs air. Each breath you take goes into your lungs, sends oxygen through your blood system, and then comes back out your lungs as you exhale, releasing carbon dioxide. Without air, you could not live. So, this element is the most vital of all the elements.

Okay, everyone, hold your breath and see how long you can go without breathing."

Aias tested Delish's theory, took a big breath, and closed his lips tight. Then, a few seconds later, he plugged his nose not to cheat and started to count. Then, he let out a big breath of air. *Dang, I didn't even get to sixty.*

"Most people can only hold their breath for thirty seconds to one minute, but with training, you can hold it longer. But after six minutes, you start to deprive your brain of oxygen. If you go much longer, you could cause brain damage. So, your body has a fail-safe system, and it will make you faint and go unconscious so that you will breathe again."

Good to know, Aias thought.

"The second element is *Apas* or *Jala,* the Vedic Sanskrit term for *water.* How important is water for the body?"

Delish picked a different boy to answer.

"I read that we can only survive a few days without water."

"True. Dehydration happens quickly, causing extreme thirst, fatigue, organ failure, and death. A person may go from feeling thirsty and slightly sluggish on the first day with no water to having organ failure by the third."

"What about breatharians?" one boy called out.

Delish had to be careful about how he answered this question. "To live the rest of your life on the nourishment of light or air alone is dangerous. Without food, the body must find another way to maintain glucose levels. At first, it breaks down glycogen. Then, it turns to proteins and fats. Next, the liver turns fatty acids into by-products called ketone bodies until too many of them are processed. Then, the body goes into a life-threatening chemical imbalance called ketoacidosis. Then you die."

One of the boys rubbed his tummy as it grumbled. "I think I am dying of starvation right now."

All the boys laughed.

Delish laughed and said, "Keung, you just ate an hour ago."

As his stomach growled again, he said, "Tell that to my tummy."

"Students, there is a difference between fasting to cleanse your body, mind, and soul and not ever eating or drinking anything. Other than for medical tests ordered by a doctor, you should always drink water. Your body will become dehydrated without water, and that can cause many fatal health conditions. So, here, let's do a test."

"Aww, a test," one boy said and then quickly covered his mouth, remembering he was not allowed to complain.

Delish demonstrated what he wanted the boys to do. "Lightly pinch and pull up the skin on top of your hand. If the skin stays up and doesn't instantly go down to normal when you let go, you are dehydrated."

Aias tested his skin. It instantly went back down to its starting position.

"Your body is made up of almost seventy percent water, and depending on your weight, your body needs a certain amount of water to maintain optimum health. To determine how much water to drink daily, multiply your weight by two-thirds. For example, if you weigh one hundred and fifty pounds, multiply that by two and divide the answer by three, which would be about one hundred ounces of water per day. Now, if you divided that by eight, you would know that you need twelve and a half cups a day, but most people on average only drink four to eight cups."

Aias did the math in his head. *I am ninety-one pounds, so that would be… seven and a half cups of water per day. I'll have to make a mental note to drink more water.*

Delish continued with his lesson. "The third element is *Agni* or *Tejas,* the Vedic Sanskrit term for *fire.* In the old scriptures, Agni was a god and existed at three levels, on earth as fire, in the atmosphere as lightning, and in the sky as the sun. The Vedic believe that this triple presence connects Agni as the messenger between gods and human beings. Why is fire important?"

A smaller boy answered, "My mom says, for dust thou art, and unto dust thou shalt return. She says that fire is what turns people to dust."

"True, fire burns and turns everything to ash, or dust as you called it. During all Vedic rituals or fire ceremonies, such as celebrating a birth or wedding, and even at death, we use fire."

Aias put his hand up.

"Yes, Aias."

"What would happen if we didn't have fire?"

"Over the years, fire has provided cooked food, warmth, weapons, technology, medical solutions, jobs, and protection from wild animals. I guess we would go back before the caveman days or count on air and water to produce enough electricity."

"I am sure glad that we can create fire."

"Me too." Continuing the lesson, Delish said, "The fourth element is *Prithvi,* the Vedic Sanskrit term for the *earth*, also known as Mother Earth. This element is possibly the easiest to understand—it's what you can touch, taste, hear, see, and smell. Earth governs your bones and teeth, muscle tissue, and fat deposits. It's what gives you form and weight and what grounds you in the tactile environment."

Aias put his hand up.

"Yes, Aias."

"When you say earth, do you mean the planet or the dirt?"

"In science, it means heaviness, matter, and the terrestrial world. In Hinduism, it means mother goddess or mother nature. Some say that it is a personification of nature, motherhood, fertility, creation, a protective figure against destruction, or a deity that embodies the bounty of the Earth."

"Thank you."

"Now lastly, we have the fifth element, *Akasha,* the Vedic Sanskrit term for the *sky, Void,* or *aether.* The ethereal divinity of the elements. In Vedantic Hinduism, Akasha means the basis and essence of all things in the material world and was the first element created. I am going to state what Vedas say about creation."

Aias put his hand up.

"Yes, Aias."

"Explain what Vedas are."

"Vedas are the sacred text of Hinduism, just like the Bible is for Christianity."

"Oh."

"Creation, the world as we know it took place in the following order: ether (or sky), gas (air), fire, liquid (water), and solid (earth)."

Aias put his hand up.

"Yes, Aias."

"Why that order?"

"Without the ether, we cannot have air, without oxygen we cannot have a fire, without fire creating steam, we could not have clouds which make water, and without water to nourish the earth, we would soon be a moon."

"Okay, that makes sense."

"In Ayurveda and Indian philosophy, not only is the human body considered to be made of these five elements, but also all these elements are needed for healing. I will teach you which finger and thumb go with each element in our next class. Actually, I am going to teach you finger yoga."

Chapter 36

Doctor Singh had given Lexi a sedative to relieve some of her pain. He wasn't scheduled to be in today, but he felt obligated to check in on her since Lexi's hysterectomy.

As he helped the nurse wheel Lexi's bed through the halls, he couldn't help but look at Lexi. Her eyes were closed.

She looks like an angel.

Neo's heart skipped a beat. Flustered at his feelings, he quickly looked away as Lexi opened her eyes.

"Hey, Doc. What do you think is wrong with me?" Lexi asked.

The rude nurse answered for him, "If he knew that, he wouldn't be taking you for tests."

Neo replied, "Whatever it is, we'll figure something out."

Once in the MRI examining room, Neo helped the nurse transfer Lexi to the machine's bed. "You will have to lie very still."

Before he went to the monitoring area, he told the nurse, "She'll need gadolinium." Then said to Lexi, "There is going to be a loud clicking and beeping noise."

He watched through the window as the nurse administered the contrast agent through Lexi's intravenous drip.

"How does this machine work?" Lexi called out.

Neo spoke into a microphone from the monitoring station. "Don't move." Then, as the bed moved Lexi into the big machine, he answered her question, "The machine you are in uses a combination of a large magnet, radio frequencies, and a computer to produce detailed images of your organs and other structures within your body. The powerful magnets produce a strong magnetic field around you that forces protons in your body to align with that field."

He continued to talk to keep her calm. "A radiofrequency current is pulsed through you, and the protons are stimulated, and because of the pull from the magnetic field, it causes them to spin erratically. Then when we turn the radiofrequency field off, the protons will realign, and as they do, they send out a radio signal that the MRI sensors can detect. The computer receives the MRI's information and will then analyze and convert the signals into a two-dimensional image that we can see on our monitor."

Looking at Lexi's images on the monitor with concern, Neo said to her, "The MRI scanner is particularly well suited to examine bones, joints, and soft tissues, such as cartilage, muscles, and tendons for injuries or the presence of structural abnormalities or certain other conditions, such as tumors, inflammatory disease, congenital abnormalities, osteonecrosis, bone marrow disease, and herniation or degeneration of discs of the spinal cord."

Neo told the nurse to print the images, then turned off the MRI to get Lexi back into the room.

He could easily transfer Lexi to the movable bed himself since she weighed maybe a hundred and ten pounds.

"So, what's the verdict, Doc?" Lexi asked.

"It looks like traumatic spondylolisthesis," Neo answered.

"Oh my God! That sounds serious," Lexi gasped.

"It's not as bad as it sounds. It means that one of your vertebrae has slipped out of place."

"Am I going to need surgery?"

"I doubt it. Lexi, do you have any numbness, weakness, or tingling in your feet?"

Lexi moved her feet and winced. "A little bit."

As the nurse helped Neo push Lexi back to her room, Neo said, "Well, you won't be going home as soon as you would have liked."

Lexi let out a breath and rolled her eyes. "Can I at least be moved into a private room?"

Once they were back in her old room, he noticed her crying roommates and said, "I'll see what I can do. But, for now, bed rest is what the doctor orders. And the nurse will give you some ibuprofen to help bring down the swelling."

"Hopefully, it won't be up the butt again," Lexi said, worried, looking at the mean nurse.

"What?" Neo asked, surprised.

Before Lexi could say anything, the nurse said, "Doctor Singh, if that is the only way she will take her pain meds, then up the butt, I will do."

Lexi rolled her eyes again and replied, "I was only following orders to push the button if I was in pain. I wasn't, so I didn't."

Furious with Lexi, the nurse walked out of the room saying, "Fine, she can be in pain for all I care."

"What was all that about?" Neo asked Lexi.

"Ah? I am sure it was probably just a misunderstanding. I will take my pain meds. I promise."

"Good. I will be back later to check in on you."

As he was leaving, Lexi called out and said, "You'll remember to check on moving me, right?"

As he left the room, he said, "I'll do my best."

Chapter 37

Redington drove over to check on Lexi's mom. As he went up the steps to her front door, he picked up a newspaper.

He rang the doorbell and tapped a couple of times. "Mrs. Constantine, it's me, Detective Redington."

"She's not home," he heard from the bushes at the side of the house.

Looking over, he said, "How long has she been out?"

"A couple of days. Olivia usually pops over for a nightcap, but I guess she forgot to tell me she was going away. I haven't seen Lexi either." As a gray-haired older man with a goatee came through the bushes, he said, "I'm Frank, her neighbor."

"Alexandra is in the hospital. She had an accident," Redington informed the man.

"Oh! Is Lexi going to be alright?"

"I think so."

"That's good to know," Frank said.

"Though, it is strange that Mrs. Constantine would go away when her daughter is in the hospital," Redington said, getting tingles. He knew by now to trust his Spidey senses when something wasn't quite right.

Frank was now on the front step beside Redington. "Wow, how tall are you?"

"Six-foot-four."

Frank knocked on the door. Trying the knob, he said, "Olivia, it's me, Frank." The door was unlocked. "That's strange."

Both men went in.

"Olivia, you home?" Frank said.

No answer.

Looking at Redington, he said, "She is usually in the kitchen," and led the way.

Red noticed Lexi's and Susannah's baby books and an open bottle of Pinot Noir on the kitchen island. As he came around the island, broken glass and red wine were lying on the floor. Red's detective instinct set in.

Heading down the hallway and running up the stairs, he looked into the bedrooms until he came to the master suite. There she was, sleeping in her bed.

Frank was right behind Redington, a little out of breath from running up the stairs. "Olivia." Running over to her, he said, "Olivia! Wake up." He shook her.

She didn't move.

Redington saw the sleeping pills on the bedside table and instantly checked her neck for a pulse.

There wasn't one.

Taking her hand, Red knew she had been dead for at least four hours and less than forty-eight because rigor mortis had already started.

"Frank, call 911!" Then, running his fingers through his hair, he said, "Damn it, now her mom. Alexandra can't handle all this."

#

Redington and Frank were outside when the ambulance arrived.

"Detective Redington! Was it a homicide?" one of the EMS personnel said, recognizing him.

"No, a friend's mom."

"I'm sorry."

"Me too."

A few moments later, a police car pulled up.

"Fletcher," Red said as the officer got out of his vehicle.

"Red, what happened?"

"It looks like an overdose of sleeping pills, but we'll know more once there is an autopsy," Red said, knowing the drill.

As the ambulance took Mrs. Constantine's body away, Fletcher asked Redington, "Why are you here?"

"I was checking in on her for a friend of mine who is in the hospital. She was worried about her mom."

Looking at the report, Fletcher said, "Constantine? Isn't that the girl that you got caught up with a while back?"

"It is. It's Alexandra's mom."

"Damn, what luck you have," Fletcher said, shaking his head. Then, pointing to the old man, he continued, "What is the story with this guy? He looks pretty shaken up."

"From what I can gather, he was the boyfriend. He lives next door. He thought Mrs. Constantine was away," Redington said as he looked at Frank sitting on the bottom step.

As Redington started down the steps, Fletcher called out, "Don't worry, Red. I can take it from here."

"Thanks, Arrow," Redington said using his nickname. Touching Frank's shoulder as he came down the last step, he said to Frank, "Let me walk you to your place."

Frank got up but didn't say anything.

Redington led the way down Olivia's driveway and around the bushes to Frank's place.

Frank opened the door and asked, "Do you want a beer?"

"Sure. I wasn't on duty today. I was just helping Alexandra out."

Frank popped the lid on a couple of chilled beers and passed one to Redington. "I was going to propose."

Red knew that Frank wanted to talk a bit longer, so he said, "Man, I am so sorry. Can I see the ring?"

Frank went to a drawer and pulled out a blue and gold velvet box. Opening it, he showed it to Redington.

"Nice. Olivia would have loved it."

Tears started to roll down Frank's cheeks. Brushing them away, he said, "Now what do I do?"

Redington took hold of Frank's arm and said, "Is there someone I can call to come over?"

Frank shook his head. "I'll be fine. I'll call my daughter later."

Finishing his beer in silence, Redington said, "I'll make sure the arrangements for the funeral are taken care of. I will let you know when and where, when I figure it all out."

Frank nodded.

"I'll let myself out," Redington said and then left.

Red sat there a moment after getting back into his car... *How the hell am I supposed to tell Alexandra?*

Chapter 38

"Hey, Doc. Just the man I need to see. I was hoping to run into you," Redington said to Neo. "I have a problem, and I am hoping you will have a good answer."

Recognizing the man's voice talking in the waiting area by his office, Neo turned to look at Redington. Knowing that he didn't have an appointment, he said, "Detective Redington, to what do I owe the pleasure?"

Coming closer, Redington said in a quiet voice so waiting patients in the room wouldn't hear, "Can we speak in private? It's about Alexandra's mom."

"Don't tell me she needs a doctor," Neo said as a joke.

"She is dead."

Neo pulled Redington by the arm into his office. "How did it happen?"

"I am not positive, but it looks like an overdose of sleeping pills."

"Does Lexi know yet?"

Redington hated that Neo was so informal with Alexandra's name. "No. I wasn't sure if I should tell her or not. Do you think she can handle it? Were her tests okay? Man, what am I saying? I am a cop, for goodness' sake. I know I am supposed to tell her right away, but this is Alexandra, and she has been through so much lately. It will break her heart."

Neo looked at Red and said, "You are just going to have to rip the band-aid off. She is tough. She'll be able to handle it."

Redington stared at Doctor Singh for a moment, then opened his office door and left.

"Hope I was of some help," Neo called after him.

Redington didn't turn around but gave him the finger. *I think I hate that guy.*

Redington's phone rang. Listening to his captain, Redington said, "Sure thing Cap, I'll get right on it."

#

Not long after, he was at Mrs. Constantine's place. Her silent alarm had warned the police that there was an intruder.

Pulling out his gun, Red went in through the open door of her house. "Frank, what are you doing?" Redington said, putting his gun away.

"I am looking for her Christmas ornaments. She always put her decorations up after the Thanksgiving long weekend."

"Frank, how did you get in here?"

"She hid a key in one of the planters. I would use it late at night when she didn't want to come downstairs to open the door for me."

"Frank. I need you to put the box down," Redington said calmly, knowing that Frank wasn't quite himself. "How much have you had to drink tonight?"

"Just a couple."

Walking over to Frank, Redington took the heavy box from him and set it down. "Come on. I'll walk you home."

Frank blankly followed Redington's order and followed him out.

Redington turned off the lights, set the alarm, and locked the door as he left.

"Do you want to come in for a cold one?" Frank asked.

"Not tonight. I'm on duty. Hey, what is your daughter's phone number?" Redington said, knowing that Frank wasn't okay to be by himself.

"Let me get it for you." Fumbling around in a drawer in the hallway, he pulled out an address book. "It is… I can't read the numbers. Here, you look."

Redington took the little book, typed the phone number into his phone, and then asked as he dialed, "What is her name?"

"Linda. She's married, though, so don't think about asking her out on a date now, young fella," Frank said a bit slurred.

Redington saluted Frank as he said, "Hi Linda? I'm Detective Redington… No, he is okay, but I do need you to come over. Can you do that right now? I see… How soon can you be here? Mrs. Constantine died, and your dad needs someone for a few days to help him through this tough time… Great, I'll wait."

Hanging up the phone, he said to Frank, "She'll be over in about an hour."

"Oh, that is nice of her. I would love to see her. I wish she came over more often, but with her schedule, you know, she is swamped."

Redington sat down on Frank's couch and said, "Can you make me a coffee, Frank?"

"Ya, sure. I can do that," Frank said, walking toward his kitchen.

Hearing a lot of banging in the kitchen, Redington went to look. "What are you doing, Frank?"

"Ah, I can't find the beans."

"You mean you don't have any ground coffee beans?" Redington asked, now wishing he hadn't said anything.

"Olivia used to make the best coffee, so I stopped buying any." Then, pausing, he said, "Hey, I can go over and get hers."

"No, that won't be necessary. I'll just have a glass of water while I wait."

Redington didn't have to wait long for Linda and her husband, Bob, to show up.

"Frank, your daughter has agreed to take you to her place for a couple of days. I'll make sure Olivia's place is okay."

"You sure? I don't mind. I can still smell her perfume when I am over there." A tear dropped to Frank's lip.

"I'm sure," Redington said, as he took a deep breath so that he wouldn't get caught up in Frank's emotions.

Chapter 39

$\mathcal{N}$eo had been away for a couple of weeks due to a conference in Geneva, Switzerland. He decided he had better go check in on Lexi.

Walking into her hospital room, he said, "So, they were able to find you a private room."

Lexi gave a slight smile. "No thanks to you, I hear. Your replacement found it for me. He is a nice guy, by the way, and a good doctor, too."

Neo smiled. "How are you doing? Is the physiotherapy working?"

"I am trying to do what they tell me, but it still hurts terribly."

Neo went over and checked Lexi's vitals, then her feet. Touching them, he asked, "Any numbness, weakness, or tingling?"

"Not really, just mostly pain when I try to stand or sit up."

"I'll have some more tests ordered."

"Great, just what I want, more tests," Lexi said with sarcasm.

"Hey, I am sorry about your mom. How are you doing?"

"What are you talking about?"

Neo stared at Lexi, not sure what to say. "Ah… Redington was in, right?"

"Yeah, a couple of times. He's been really busy, though, with a case. Why?"

"What did he tell you about your mom?"

Lexi looked at Doctor Singh with concern. "That Frank surprised her with a trip to Barbados. Why, is everything okay?"

Stalling, Neo said, "Lexi, there is no easy way of telling you this. Your mom is dead."

"She's what?"

Neo watched Lexi's eyes change in an instant. "I'm so sorry."

"Is Frank alright? How did it happen?"

"Lexi, Redington lied to you. They never went on a trip. She died a couple of weeks ago."

"Why would Redington lie to me?" Lexi said, just before she screamed.

"Lexi! Lexi, you need to calm down," Neo said, as he now knew why Redington didn't tell her. Then, panicking for the first time since he was in med school, Neo pushed the button to get help. "Lexi, stop! You can't pull out your intravenous."

"Just watch me."

"She needs a sedative," Doctor Singh said to the nurse as she came quickly into the room.

"No! I am signing myself out of here. You said if I can eat, walk, and go on the toilet, that I can leave."

"Can you walk?" Neo said, not sure what to do.

Lexi said, determined, "I'll manage." Then, as her adrenaline pumped through her veins, she tried to stand up but screamed from the pain.

Doctor Singh had to hold Lexi down. Then as he nodded to the nurse to administer the drug, he said, "I am sorry, Lexi, this is for your own safety."

A moment later, Neo watched as Lexi went limp and fell asleep. "Make sure she doesn't wake up for a couple of hours. I have to go and check on a few things before letting her out of here.

Walking out of Lexi's room, Neo phoned Redington's precinct. "This is Doctor Singh. I need to speak with Detective Redington. It's an emergency."

After leaving a message with the police station, Neo locked himself in his office. He had ordered the nurse at the front desk to take all his calls and only disturb him if it was Detective Redington.

He didn't have to wait long.

"Detective, what the hell were you thinking?"

"I am guessing that we are talking about Alexandra."

"Yes, who else would I be talking to you about?"

"I contemplated my decision and decided that she wasn't healed enough to know that her mom had died."

"You could have warned me," Neo said.

"Aww, the way I see it, you deserved this since you were an ass the other day when I asked for your help."

Neo hung up the phone. *What do I do now? She can't walk. She is still in pain, and she has no one to look after her.*

The nurse called over on the office phone's intercom. "Doctor Singh, it is your mother. What should I tell her?"

Shaking his head to clear his thoughts, he said, "I'll take it."

Picking up the phone, he said, "Hi mom, what's up?"

"Dear, I am just reminding you that tonight is the start of the 'Family Festival of Giving.' You'll be able to make it, right?"

Neo forgot about going to his parents' place, though it gave him a good idea. "Yes, I'll be there, but mom… I'll be bringing a guest."

"Oh, how very nice, dear. We look forward to meeting her."

"I didn't say it was a 'her,' mom."

"You didn't have to. See you around seven."

The Christmas season for the Singhs began on December twenty-first to December twenty-fifth, celebrating his dad's Hindu beliefs, and then right after that, his mother's Greek Orthodox side kicked in. Celebrating the twelve days of Christmas, starting December twenty-fifth, and finishing January sixth, when his family celebrated Epiphany—The Feast of the Holy Theophany.

Against hospital protocol, Neo signed Lexi out and brought her with him to his parents. He was almost at their house when Lexi woke up.

"Doctor Singh? Where are we?" Lexi asked groggily as she looked at him and then out the window.

Pulling into his parent's home, Neo answered, "At my parents' home in Newark, New Jersey."

"Why?" Lexi was so confused.

"That is an excellent question," Neo said as he parked the car, got out, and popped the trunk to get the portable wheelchair he borrowed from the hospital. Then, after opening Lexi's side door, he said, "You need a change of scenery and someone to look after you."

"I could have gone home."

As he gently lifted Lexi into the wheelchair, he said, "As I said, you need someone to look after you."

"Do you live here?" Lexi asked as she smelled the aroma of his cologne.

"When I am not at the hospital, which isn't very often." *What was I thinking to bring her here?*

As they came through the front door, the color yellow was to be seen everywhere. Knowing Lexi probably didn't know about this Hindu tradition, Neo said, "Pancha Ganapati marks the worship of five different forms of Lord Ganesha, to mend the past mistakes and start a new beginning. For the next five days, my mom will change the color in the house to match the specific day's celebration. Today we celebrate yellow. This color stands for love and harmony among *all members*."

"What are the other four colors?" Lexi asked, mesmerized by all the yellow.

"Tomorrow, she'll decorate the place in blue. Blue represents creating or restoring a vibration of love and harmony among *neighbors, relatives, and close friends*. It includes a ritual of presenting heartfelt gifts and offerings to people outside the home."

"And the next day?"

"Red. Great color to establish love and harmony among *business associates* and the public. It is the day to present gifts to fellow workers and customers and honor employers and employees with gifts and appreciation. It is also the best day considered to clear all debts and disputes."

"Interesting. What color is on the fourth day?"

"Green stands for joy. We can do anything that involves music, art, drama, and dance."

"Red and green are taken, so what color is displayed on Christmas Day?" Lexi asked.

"Orange, which stands for *charity and spiritualism.* But don't worry, this day is the most exciting, especially for children. We also get to open gifts and eat lavish treats."

Wheeling Lexi into the living room, Neo introduced her to his family.

After meeting everyone, she asked Dr. Singh, "What is the meaning of the boat that is lit up?" Lexi pointed to the one in front of the living room window.

Neo looked over to the carved wooden boat with a six-foot sail draped in Christmas lights, standing in place of a Christmas tree. "Ah, that is a Greek tradition. Usually, the boat wouldn't be decorated until January sixth, but mom gets excited and decorates it early. Notice that the bow is pointing inwards?"

Lexi looked again and nodded.

"Greece is known for their men going out to sea. During the dark winter months of ferocious, stormy, and dangerous seas, the women spend their days fretting over fathers, husbands, and sons battling with the waves, praying for their safe return. It is a celebration that symbolizes their successful homeward journey."

"Ah, that is so sweet," Lexi said, enjoying the cultural differences.

Moving a chair aside for Lexi's wheelchair, he pushed her up to the dining room table.

Neo's mom, Naida, had made dinner with foods close to the color yellow. It consisted of baked potatoes, roasted chicken, cheese bread, and buttery corn on the cob.

Neo leaned over and whispered to Lexi, "For dessert, she will have made BBQed caramelized bananas."

"Yum," Lexi said, not sure if she was hungry enough to eat anything.

Neo's pager vibrated. Looking down, he knew he had to go back to the hospital. Getting up, he said, "Mom, can I speak with you, please?"

Once in the privacy of the kitchen, Neo said, "I need a big favor."

"Don't worry. I can look after Lexi for you."

"How do you do that?" Neo asked his mom, hugging her.

"It used to be stray dogs that you brought home. Do you know how long it has been since you brought home a girl?"

Ignoring her question, Neo kissed her and walked back into the dining room. "Sorry, Lexi, I have to go back to the hospital."

Putting down her fork, Lexi said, "It was nice while it lasted."

"No, Lexi, you are going to stay here. My mom will look after you while I am gone. You'll sleep in the den. She used to be a nurse and knows what to do. I'll be back as soon as I can."

Chapter 40

Lexi woke up to the smell of bacon.

"Good morning, sleepyhead," Neo said as he came in to check on her.

"What time is it?" Lexi asked, stretching due to having the first good night's sleep in a while.

"Six-thirty."

"In the morning?"

"Yes. My mom doesn't make bacon at night."

"Wow. I slept all night."

"You did," Neo said happily.

Wincing from Neo placing her into the wheelchair, Lexi said, "Am I ever going to feel better?"

"We'll know more in a week or so. Your body needs to mend those stitches. My sister, Evangeline, and her son, Todd, will be over tonight. She is hoping that you will allow her to work on you."

"Oh, I don't know. What does Evangeline do?" Lexi asked, now nervous.

"She is a massage therapist. I think it would be good if you let her do some lymph drainage."

"What is that?" Lexi said, making a weird face by scrunching up her nose.

"The lymphatic system in your body works with your immune system to clean up any toxins, inflammation, and dead cells."

"Doesn't my body know how to do that without a massage therapist?"

"If you are active, yes. But right now, you are barely moving. Lymph is not like blood. This system needs movement in the body to have it work."

"Oh. I guess your sister can work on me. Will it hurt?"

"No. The pressure she uses is approximately the weight of a nickel."

"My, that is light. Are you sure it will work?"

"Lymph moves in the direction of the heart. She will use her thumbs to do the light feather strokes. The liquid in your lymph will move to your digestive system to be eliminated."

"How long does it take?"

"It will depend on what she can do on you. If you move into a position that hurts, she might not be able to do everything today, but normally it would take about an hour."

Coming into the kitchen as they were finishing their conversation, Naida said, "My daughter is very skilled at her job. She has the hands of an angel. You'll love whatever she does on you."

"Okay, my mom might be a bit biased, but she is good."

Lexi saw what Naida had made for breakfast and asked, "Is an army coming to eat all this?"

Naida laughed and said something in Greek.

"My mom said, 'Breakfast is the most important meal of the day.' Plus, today is the blue day, which means she is feeding our neighbors, relatives, and close friends," Neo explained.

"Oh my." Panicking, Lexi said, "I need a bath and to get cleaned up if people are coming over. Neo, I have nothing to wear."

"Calm down. I am sure we can find you something. Do you want me to go to your place and grab some clothes for you?"

"Yes, please. Can I come? It would be easier," Lexi said, then thought twice about it. "Maybe not. I don't think I am ready to go home yet."

"There is plenty of time before you need to go home. Just make a list of what you want, and I can go get everything on my way back from the hospital."

After Neo gave Lexi some paper and a pen, she made a list of things she would like and gave the list to him. "Oh, ya, make sure to get my phone charger, please."

"Noted. Now let's eat."

Lexi was hungrier than she had been in weeks. Being at Neo's seemed almost normal.

After Neo headed out to work, Lexi noticed Naida moving from room to room, holding a bowl and a cross. "What are you doing?"

"It is an ancient tradition. This shallow wooden bowl has been in my family for generations."

Lexi saw a wire suspended across the bowl with a sprig of basil wrapped around a wooden cross hanging from the wire.

"See?" Naida said as she took the cross out. "Inside the bowl is some water to keep the basil alive and fresh. Once a day, I dip the cross and basil into the holy water and use it to sprinkle in each room of the house."

"Why?"

"It is believed to keep the *kallikantzaroi*—evil spirits—away."

Lexi looked around the room she was in. *I don't sense any evil spirits. However, I don't sense any good ones either. Actually, I don't sense Susannah, for that matter.* "Naida, can you please help me back into the bed I am using?"

"Sure, dear."

Naida stopped what she was doing and came over to wheel Lexi back into the den.

"Thank you. I think I will take a nap for a bit," Lexi said, hoping that Naida would leave quickly.

"Call out if you need anything. I won't be far."

"Thanks, I should be good for a while."

Closing her eyes, Lexi thought, *Susannah. Are you there, Susannah?*

Hi, little sis. It's been a while.

Where have you been, Susannah?

Right beside you.

I couldn't hear you.

Energy is weird like that. When a person is sick or has had trauma, they can't seem to hear the celestial world.

I needed you. Mom died. Did you know?

Yes, I knew. Mom is here with dad and me.

What happened to her? Why did she have to die?

Lexi, sometimes a soul just can't heal from this lifetime's experiences. Mom had just found out that you couldn't have any children, and she had a bit too much to drink. Her sadness led her to have insomnia, so she took some sleeping pills, forgetting how much wine she had consumed. The next thing she knew, she was on the train toward the pearly gates. By the way, she passed the test with flying colors.

Of course, she did. She was a good person.

Hey, Lexi?

Ya.

Redington found mom's will and cremated her. You will need to get her ashes from him and set a date for her funeral.

I don't think I can talk to him right now.

That's too bad.

Do you know why Susannah?

Lexi, I know everything you are thinking. So yes, I understand why you haven't forgiven him yet.

That is true. But that's not the only reason.

Yes, I know the other reason, too. You're…

Naida came into the den and asked, "Lexi can I get you anything?"

"Oh my, she's gone."

"Who dear?" Naida asked, confused.

Lexi took a breath and said, "I must have been dreaming." *Come back, Susannah.*

Chapter 41

$\mathscr{A}$ couple of days later, Lexi woke up to music playing.

Neo came into the den and said, "Mom's started day four, green day."

"Right. What does that color stand for?"

"Joy."

"Oh, right."

Lifting her into the wheelchair, Neo said, "Hope you like green eggs and ham."

"Isn't that the name of a kid's book?"

Neo laughed. "I never connected that before."

"Neo, I think I need to go home."

"Lexi, tomorrow is Christmas. There is no way I am letting you be alone on Christmas."

"I have overstayed my welcome. I can't keep imposing like this."

"My mom will forbid me to take you out of this house." Changing the subject, he asked,

"How are you and Evangeline doing on the treatments?"

"She is excellent, but she thinks I need a chiropractor."

"Hmm, medical doctors disagree on the subject of manipulating bones. We think a physiotherapist is needed instead."

"Your sister said that she can always tell when it is a bone out of place."

"Really? How does Evangeline know that?"

"She says that if she can't get the pain to go away, it is one of three things."

"Which are?"

"An internal organ issue, a torn ligament or tendon, or it is a bone pinching a nerve. Now before you say anything, you have done tests and told me the first two aren't the issue, so I am guessing that Evangeline is right, and it is a bone issue."

"I'll talk with her tonight, after dinner," Neo said, not happy with Evangeline's suggestion.

"Hey, you never gave me my charger cord. Didn't you find it?"

Neo couldn't lie. "Yes, I found it."

"Well, can I have it, please?"

"After Christmas. I promise."

"Why?"

"You need to be stress-free, and that won't happen if you are talking to people about your mom and her funeral arrangements."

"That reminds me. I need to get her ashes from Redington. Hey, has he tried calling?"

Again, Neo couldn't lie. "Yes."

"Yes, and you haven't told me?" Lexi said, perturbed.

"He is not good for you, Lexi."

Taken aback, she said, "And how would you know that?"

"You need someone in your life that loves you more than they love themselves."

"Does that person even exist? Besides, he is more like a brother to me," she lied.

"I don't think he knows how you feel," Neo said, remembering Redington giving him the finger.

As Neo pushed Lexi out of the den, Naida said, "Neo, can you please put Lexi in the bathtub? I will be right there."

Horrified, Lexi said, "Is she crazy? You're not going to see me naked."

Neo laughed.

"What's so funny?"

"Lexi, I have seen you naked a few times."

"What? When?"

"I operated on you, remember? I am a doctor. I think I can put you in a tub."

Lexi went red.

Lexi watched as Neo swirled the water with his hand as it filled the tub. The shirt he was wearing was a bit tight and showed the outline of his muscles. She bit her bottom lip.

He picked her up like she weighed nothing and put her in the tub, nightgown and all.

"Hey, what the?"

As he sat down on the lid of the toilet, he said, "Well, this way, you aren't naked. Mom will be here in a moment."

"You're impossible. Just when I think I know you, you do something like this," Lexi said as she struggled to get out of the wet nightie.

Neo helped her, even though he couldn't stop staring at her beauty. "How are the scars coming?"

Looking down, she said, "They will always remind me of what I've lost."

Neo caught the tear that ran down Lexi's cheek with his fingertip. "I haven't told too many people, but I can't have children either."

Lexi looked at him. "Really?"

"Really."

"What happened?"

"I had a bad groin accident when I was five, and it damaged my testicles. The doctor who operated said that he wasn't able to repair them."

"I am so sorry," Lexi said, looking down at her scars.

"That is why I don't date much. Most women want children, and I can't, so I break it off before it can get serious."

Neo poured some water over Lexi's shoulder. It dripped over her breast.

Without warning, he bent over and kissed her.

His lips were so tender and warm. Lexi could have melted right there and then.

Chapter 42

$\mathcal{L}$exi had never seen so much orange in her life. Christmas morning had always been about red and green and the smell of cinnamon and a roasted turkey. This seemed so wrong; even the Singhs' clothing was orange. *At least the tradition of opening presents is still the same… Oh my God, the presents! I didn't get anyone a gift.*

Evangeline came over to Lexi and asked, "Are you in pain, Lexi?"

"Ah, I forgot to buy everyone a gift."

Neo, hearing Lexi, said, "Don't worry, I wrote your name on my gifts to everyone."

Dumbfounded, Lexi just smiled. *He hasn't said a word since the other day about the kiss. He must not have liked it as much as I had.*

Naida said, to the group, "Okay, let's go, or we will be late."

Lexi looked over to Evangeline and said, "Where are you guys going?"

"We all, including you, are going to the mandir."

"The what?"

As his mom dressed Lexi in a warm orange coat and orange blanket, Neo came closer and said, "You get to come with us to the mandir, the largest Hindu temple in the USA."

Lexi was in some pain during the car ride to the temple but was happy that she was outside for the first time in what seemed like forever.

The temple was impressive, as it was made entirely of hand-carved marble.

Lexi listened to Neo say, "Thirteen thousand, four hundred, and ninety-nine pieces of Italian marble and stone, quarried in Italy and carved in India, were imported through the New Jersey Marine Terminals. The temple you are looking at, Lexi, is one hundred and thirty-three feet long, eighty-seven feet wide, and forty-two feet tall."

Not really caring about that much detail, Lexi was most impressed by the intricate carvings.

Neo continued, "Ninety-eight carved pillars, sixty-six peacock style arches, one hundred and forty-four sacred figures, ninety-one elephants with various musical instruments and flowers, fifty-eight decorative ceiling designs, and all this on a stunning one hundred and sixty-two acres."

Being polite, Lexi said, "Wow! You sure know a lot about this place."

As they entered the main worship room, which looked like an amphitheater, Lexi watched as a man dressed in gold and sitting on a throne of flowers greeted his disciples in Hindi.

"That is His Holiness Mahant Swami Maharaj," Neo whispered to Lexi.

Neo stayed in the back with Lexi as the others went down the stairs and kneeled on mats closer to the altar. Leaning over, Neo whispered this time, "We believe that he is in constant communion with Bhagwan Swaminarayan—the manifestation of Akshar—the perfect devotee of God. His Holiness was presented with the mayors' key to various cities in Georgia, Texas, and Illinois. He was also presented with a key to the city of Toronto in Canada."

The altar, to Lexi's astonishment, wasn't anything that she had expected. On top of a couple of small, crisscrossed rugs was a fancy square box holding a lit fire. Lexi could smell the intoxicating fragrance of incense burning from where she was sitting. She could hear someone playing a type of piano and many people chanting and clapping to the music.

Neo whispered, "This is the elaborate pūjā. Today, the deity—in this case, the statue of Lord Ganesha—is invited to the ceremony. As you can see, they are washing his feet, as well as his head and body. After which, he will be adorned in beautiful cloth, and perfumes will be applied.

He will be offered water to drink, flowers as gifts, and incense will burn in his honor."

Next, Lexi watched as a burning lamp was waved in front of his statue, and then he was offered foods, such as cooked rice, fruit, clarified butter, sugar, and betel leaf.

Lastly, the devotees bowed and circled his statue before they took their leave to meditate further.

Lexi bowed her head and prayed. *God, I give you thanks for allowing me to witness this celebration. I pray that you will bless me no matter what temple I am in. I believe these people believe in their gods as much as I do in you. I believe that the energy of prayer, no matter what language, is for the good of humanity and that your grace is gifted to all.*

Lexi opened her eyes as Neo's fingers intertwined with hers. Looking into his eyes, she saw love.

Chapter 43

The following week went by in a flash, and Lexi was the happiest she had been in months. Neo was so loving when he was around, which wasn't as much as she would have liked. But, growing up with a surgeon for a father, she knew the drill. Neo was dedicated to the hospital.

As promised, Neo had given back her phone charger. Looking at it, she finally decided to read and listen to all the messages.

Redington had called a couple of dozen times. Even Isabella had left a few messages.

Lexi called Isabella first.

"Lexi! Where in God's name are you?" Isabella said, almost yelling. "I have been worried sick ever since Redington started leaving me messages."

"I am at Naida and Paal's house."

"Who are they?"

"Neo's parents."

"Neo? Who's Neo?"

"You remember Edward's doctor?"

"Edward's doctor. The cute neurosurgeon?"

"Yep, that's the one," Lexi said, now a bit embarrassed.

"How did that happen?" Isabella said as she sat down on the couch in her hotel room.

"It's a long story. How are you and Aias doing? Did you get to see him for the holidays?"

"Uhmm, kind of."

Puzzled, Lexi asked, "What does that mean?"

"Well, let's just say he pops in now and again."

"He pops in?"

"Yep, as in bilocation."

"He can be in two places at once?" Lexi almost screamed.

"I know, right? It freaked me out the first time. Aias is growing so fast. You're not going to believe what he looks like."

"He would be how old now?" Lexi asked, not sure what age a half-elf would be by now.

"In elf years, he is now eighteen. He looks identical to his dad."

"How is Erland taking all this?"

"I think he is okay. I never asked him that question. I will next time I speak with him. Hey, back on the subject of you. How are you doing?"

"I think I am in love."

"Wow, Lexi, that is amazing. Congrats."

"I know, right? Who would have believed that I could find happiness again? Now, if I could just get out of this wheelchair."

"You're still in a wheelchair? Lexi, I am so sorry. What does the doctor say?"

"Neo is still trying to figure it out. His sister has been an angel and has been giving me massages. She wants me to go to a chiropractor. What do you think? Should I go?"

"I have been a few times. I swear by them."

"I have never been. It seems a little scary," Lexi confessed.

"No. The secret is to relax. The tighter your muscles, the harder it is for the chiropractic doctor to manipulate your bones. I researched it before I went, and coincidently, it is your tight muscles that can pop your bones out of place."

"You're kidding?"

"No. Really. You've had a spasm, right?"

"Ya. Hurt like crazy."

"Well, muscles are attached to bones by tendons, and when contracted, they are strong enough to pop a bone out of place. Though, in your case, I am sure it was the car accident that dislodged your bones."

"That makes sense," Lexi agreed. "I'll make an appointment for next week."

"Hey, Lexi, what did you tell Redington?"

"What do you mean? I didn't tell him anything."

"You know he is in love with you, right?"

"No, he isn't. What gives you that idea?'

"Lexi, be real. Think about it. He was with you every step of the way with Edward."

"Well, he has a funny way of showing it. He disappeared after my mom died. And I haven't seen him in weeks."

"Lexi, from what he tells me, Neo kidnapped you."

"Neo did what? He didn't kidnap me."

"Redington said he took you from the hospital and wouldn't tell him where you were. Neo pulled the doctor's power over Redington. Redington had no way of figuring out where you went or if you were okay. He called me every day to find out if you had talked to me yet. I'm telling you, Lexi, Redington is in love with you."

"Iss, as crazy as that may sound, I am sure he would do the same if it were you in my place."

"Ya, no. Have you called Redington yet?"

"No, not yet. Redington still has my mom's ashes. And I haven't wanted to deal with the funeral and all the people."

"So, what I'm hearing is that you are hiding out at Neo's parents' place."

"You make it sound like I am doing it on purpose."

"Well, are you?"

Lexi had to think a second. *Maybe she is right. Maybe I am hiding out.*

"Give him a call, Lexi. He at least deserves that much."

"Ya, I will."

"Today, Lexi. Call him today."

"You sound like my big sister, ordering me around."

"Some days, I feel like I am your sister. I love you enough to be one."

"Ahh, Isabella, that is the sweetest thing anyone has ever said to me. I love you too."

Neo came into the den and said, "Who do you love?"

"Ah, Isabella, I have to go. But I promise I will call. Luv ya. Talk to you soon." Lexi hung up her cell phone. "That was Isabella. You met her in the hospital when she visited Edward."

"Aww, the one with the son."

Lexi laughed.

"What is so funny? Doesn't she have a son?"

"Yes, but most people would have said, the famous actress."

Lexi loved Neo's smile. It made her heart sing.

Chapter 44

Kesia was dreaming that she was astral traveling through the Milky Way galaxy with Galileo di Vincenzo Bonaiuti de' Galilei, the Italian astronomer.

As they traveled through space, the stars appeared to Kesia as mere blazes of light, and the planets resembled colorful balls.

"I spent the last ten years of my life under house arrest," Galileo told Kesia.

"Why?"

"For stating that the earth rotated around the sun."

"But everyone knows that it does," Kesia said, remembering the astronomy lesson in science class.

"Back in my time, the Catholic Church disagreed, and the Roman Inquisition investigated my theory. And since it contradicted the Holy Scripture, it was

concluded that heliocentrism—in which
the Earth and planets revolve around the Sun—
was foolish, absurd, and heretical."

Kesia looked at him briefly and said, "I find it crazy how people are treated when they have opposing beliefs. The funniest one I ever heard was that you would fall off the edge of the Earth if you traveled too far. A flat Earth, how crazy is that?"

Galileo smiled at her.

"I've noticed that a belief, until proven true, seems to be ridiculed until the majority of people believe the same thing. Take the cell phone, for instance. If you go back far enough in time, even a landline seemed impossible. And don't even get me started on airplanes," Kesia said, thinking about how if people can't touch it, see it, feel it, they can't conceive it.

"What is a cell phone and airplane?" Galileo asked as they flew past a constellation.

Kesia forgot that he had died years before they were invented, so she just ignored his question.

Forgetting that he had asked a question, he said, "This pattern of stars is associated with the figure of Asclepius, the Greek god."

"Who is that?"

"He was the son of the god Apollo and a famous healer in Greek mythology. Mythology says that he was able to bring people back from the dead with his healing powers."

"Was he born with his healing powers?" Kesia asked, curious if he had attained them another way.

"Legend has it that Asclepius witnessed a snake slithering toward a dead snake and placed an herb on it, which miraculously brought the dead snake back to life. Soon after Asclepius witnessed this, the king's son, Glaucus, fell into a jar of honey and drowned. Asclepius, remembering the miraculous resurrection, took the same herb and placed it on the body of the king's dead son. Within minutes of placing the herb, the king's son was resurrected to full health."

"So, you're saying that he learned the skill of healing?"

"Yes. Asclepius was raised by Chiron, the wise centaur, who taught him the art of healing."

"What else can you tell me about Asclepius?"

Galileo thought for a moment. "Another myth speaks about how Asclepius was given the blood of the Gorgon Medusa by the goddess Athena. Mythology says that the Gorgon's blood from the veins on her left side was poisonous, but the blood from the veins on her right side was able to bring people back to life."

"So, Asclepius could use blood and herbs to heal?"

"It was said that Asclepius grew so skilled in the craft of bringing people back from the dead that Hades, the god of the underworld, was concerned that the flow of dead souls into his domain would dry up as a result of Asclepius's healing ability, and complained about this to his brother Zeus. Zeus looked into the matter and became worried that the human race would become immortal with Asclepius around to heal them all, so he killed Asclepius."

"How do you kill a god?"

"Zeus destroyed him with a thunderbolt."

"What happens to gods after they die?"

"Zeus placed Asclepius's image in the sky to honor his gift and good deeds. The healer became the constellation Ophiuchus, the Serpent Bearer."

"Are all these constellations gods?"

"Most of the constellation names we know came from the ancient Middle East, Greek, and Roman cultures, and yes, they did identify the clusters of stars as gods and goddesses, but other cultures identified the clusters as objects and animals, such as the zodiac signs."

"Why do we still believe in the constellations?"

"To tell time. The Native American, Asian, and African people used constellations to create and track the calendar in ancient times. It was very handy for the farmers to know when to plant or harvest."

"Oh right, I forgot that part of science," Kesia said as she thought back to her classes.

"And in some cases, the constellations have had ceremonial, ritual, and religious significance."

Kesia's dream of astral traveling through space with Galileo came to an end. Her next dream wasn't really a dream but a memory of the other night with Luna.

Kesia was celebrating with the other Wiccans, one of the eight Sabbats—Yule, Yuletide, or better known as Winter Solstice. This Sabbat starts on the longest day of the year—December 20th or 21st—and depending on the coven, the celebration lasts anywhere from one to twelve days.

Wearing long red hooded capes, Kesia and the other twelve witches stood in the woods, in a circle formation, around a blazing fire created from sacred Yule logs.

Kesia listened as the high priestess said, "Some say that the origin of the name 'Yule' comes courtesy of the Norse god Odin. Odin was chief among the Norse pagan deities. He was spiritual, wise, and unpredictable. In centuries past, the Norse legends say that when the midwinter Yule celebration was in full swing, Odin, other gods, ghosts, lost souls, and his sword-maiden Valkyries went soaring above the rooftops on one of their midwinter 'Wild Rides.' The hunting party would fly over the villages and countryside, terrifying anyone who happened to be out and about at night. But… as many don't know, it is said that children would fill their boots with straw for Odin's flying eight-legged white horse, Sleipnir, to eat while Odin would slip down the chimney or fire hole to leave gifts and candy behind."

Kesia remembered whispering to Luna, "Is that a true story?"

To which she answered, "Legend has it that honoring Odin became forbidden, and the chief god was replaced by the godly Christian Saint Nicholas, a fourth-century Greek bishop, who was always portrayed wearing a red cloak. Saint Nicholas, or better known as Santa Claus, became the patron saint of giving, and Odin was forgotten."

Kesia remembered how Luna had grabbed her hand as the high priestess said, "With the Winter Solstice constellation of Capricorn, the yule logs, which represent the old year, are tossed into the fire so that the embodiment of cold and death of winter can be replaced by heat and light."

Kesia remembered feeling Luna squeezing her hand as they listened.

"Yule is to honor the sun king and the return of the sun. The Christmas star on top of the tree represents the Star of Bethlehem, which symbolizes the sun king. All because way back, some two thousand years ago, due to some bright planets aligning—Saturn and Jupiter being two of them—in the rising sun's glare, the illusion of one massive star was created. This anomaly was believed to be a miracle throughout the world, and so the star now represents the birth of Christ and a new day. Thus, Yule is a celebration of rebirth, the coming of a new year, quiet introspection, hope, setting intentions, and the celebration of light and the days becoming longer."

Kesia was drawn to these words that the high priestess said next, "Just as we can draw down the energy of the moon, so too can we tap into the celestial magic of the universe. Wiccans call it *star magic*. Truly, as above so below."

After the celebration, Kesia had gone to Lunas's and remembered that she could smell cinnamon sticks, citrus fruits, star anise, and cloves before entering her bedroom. The altar Luna had created for the Yule celebration was decorated with evergreen branches of cedar, pine, hemlock, and spruce, as well as sprigs of holly, pinecones, and other festive winter flora. Once entering the room, Luna had lit four candles, a red, green, white, and gold one.

Kesia remembered Lunas's comment about how the Yule log, a Christmas tree, wreaths, and even caroling, are actually rooted in pre-Christian pagan traditions. And how this is the time of year to let go of clutter in your life and clean out the old, literally by cleaning your house—cleaning the windows to see the new year better, sweeping the old energy out, and scrubbing down the bathrooms. Not only that, but if you hadn't worn it, used it, played with it, listened to it, or eaten it in the past year, you had to pitch it. It is a celebration to make room for the new year and all it brings.

Kesia then recalled the Yule smudging ritual Luna did. Luna moved the incense around each door and window using a smudge stick made of sage, sweetgrass, pine needles, and mistletoe. She went through each room of her house, following along the lines of the walls while saying, "Yule is here, and I smudge this place, fresh and clean, in time and space. Sage and sweetgrass, burning free, as the sun returns, so it shall be."

Then drifting from this memory, Kesia fell into a deep, peaceful sleep.

Chapter 45

Getting up the nerve, Lexi finally called Redington. "Hey, Red, it's me."

"Lexi, my god, where have you been? I left you like a million messages. So, why didn't you answer me?"

"I didn't have my phone."

"Well, couldn't you have used someone else's?"

"I didn't have your number. It's on my phone."

"I am sure you could have looked up my precinct's number."

"Actually, what is the number of your precinct?" Lexi asked.

"You mean the phone number?" Redington asked.

"No, your precinct number?"

"There isn't a number. It's called the Midtown South Precinct."

"Oh. See, I wouldn't have figured that out."

"Lexi, I am sure if you said my name, someone at any of the precincts could have gotten a hold of me."

"I guess. Sorry, Red."

"Lexi, I don't think you know how worried you had me."

"Isabella told me that you called her every day."

"She told you that?"

"Yes."

"Did she say anything else?"

Crossing her fingers, Lexi said, "Not really."

"I see," Redington said as he kicked a pebble on the sidewalk where he was standing.

"Red?"

"Ya."

"What should I do about my mom's ashes?"

"I don't know, but she did have in her will that she wanted to be buried with your dad."

"I forgot about that. That's right. But ugh, that means I have to go to Edward's funeral home."

"Yes, but it isn't Edward's anymore. I can go with you if it helps."

"Yes, I would like that. Can we go tomorrow?"

"I'm working tomorrow. I can come and pick you up right now. What's the address?"

"Sure, that will work." Lexi gave him the address, and he was at the front door within an hour.

Naida came to the door and let Redington in. "She will need help, you know?"

"Yes, Ma'am. I can see that she is in a wheelchair. I will take good care of her."

"You better, or I'll have your hide."

Lexi saw Redington smirk before he said, "Yes, Ma'am."

As soon as Redington had Lexi in his car and was in the driver's seat, he squeezed her hand. "I missed you."

Maybe Isabella wasn't joking. Lexi looked over at him and said, "Redington, I have to tell you something."

"It can wait. Let's get this thing with your mom over with first, okay?"

Lexi looked at him for a moment, then responded, "Sure. It can wait."

As they drove through the big metal gate at the funeral home entrance, Lexi's stomach somersaulted. "Red, stop the car. I think I am going to be sick."

Red stopped the car, ran to the passenger's door, and opened it. "Here, let me help you." But it was too late. She threw up all over his shoes.

"I'm sorry, Red. I don't think I can do this."

"Lexi, you have no choice. It has to be done."

"Can you do it for me? Please, Red. Can you give her ashes to the minister to bury her with my dad?"

"What about a funeral? She needs a funeral."

"For whom? I am her only family left. I don't need a funeral. I know where she is."

"Lexi, you don't mean that. Of course, you want a funeral," Red said, not knowing what to do, drive her to the front door or head back out. He chose to head back out and drove around for an hour. Finally, he stopped the car.

Preoccupied in her thoughts, while they had been driving, Lexi said, "Where are we?" Then she saw the blue awning and knew exactly where she was and allowed Redington to lift her into the wheelchair and take her up to his place.

Once inside his condo, he said, "Lexi, I have something for you. Wait here a second."

Calling after him, she said, "Where am I going to go?"

He had the fireplace going, and she thought she heard the wood crackle. Hearing him come back into the room without looking, she said, "Nice effects."

He didn't answer.

Turning her head to where she heard him, she said, "Red. Are you there?"

He didn't answer.

Louder, she called out, "Red!"

"What?"

"Don't do that?"

"Do what?"

"Hide on me."

"Lexi, are you losing it? I was in my bedroom getting you this."

Lexi took the small gift bag. "I didn't get you anything for Christmas. I can't take this from you."

"Just open it."

"But—"

He cut her off and said, "Listen, just open the damn gift, will ya?"

Lexi slowly opened the gift. Inside the box was a Swarovski crystal angel. "Red, it's beautiful. You shouldn't have."

"When I saw it, it reminded me of how we met. If it weren't for your sister, we wouldn't have ever met."

"Red, I have to tell you something."

"Fine, go ahead. Tell me."

As she was about to speak, Lexi's phone rang. Picking it up, she said, "Hello?"

There was static on the line. Lexi couldn't make out any words. "Hello," she said again.

The phone went dead.

"That's weird," she said to Redington as she looked to see the number that had called.

"Everything okay, Lexi? You seem a little freaked out," Redington asked, concerned for her.

The memory of the last time she was here came full force. Lexi's face went white as a ghost.

"Red! Get me out of here! Now!"

Chapter 46

Kesia was invited to join Luna at the high priest's home. It was just before midnight during the first full moon after Yule, the "wolf moon."

Not knowing what to expect, Kesia was mesmerized by the looks of his home. It looked like a mix between a hobbit house and a witch's house. It was made of wood shingles, and the roofline had multiple pitches that were slightly curved like haystacks. There were various-shaped dormers, turrets, and even a steeple. The outside walls were built with rocks, and around each window, the wooden arches were outlined with curved stones like a wood fire oven, and the decks were made with thick wooden beams.

As she walked inside, it was a magnificent log cabin. To the right of the entrance was a stairway that led upstairs. The handrail was made of many intertwining branches. Even the table legs in the living room were made of branches. There was an upside-down broom hanging on a wall.

"Why is that broom upside-down?" Kesia asked Luna as she took a seat beside her on one of the chairs set out for the coven.

"It means good luck."

"Oh."

As the high priest walked into the living room, he was dressed in a tux that one wore when going to a formal black and white dinner party. Upon his head, he wore horns to honor the Horned God, who Luna previously mentioned had other names: Cernunnos, Herne, Dionysus, and Osiris—the Egyptian Horned God. In Wiccan belief, the Horned God is Lord Pan, the god of the wild earth. He is associated with nature, wilderness, sexuality, hunting, and the life cycle.

Pan is best known for being the Greek Horned God, who has the body of a man and the head of a goat. The Horned God symbolizes the personification of the life-force energy in animals and the wild.

Luna had also told Kesia that the church so hated Pan's worship that his image became known as the Lord of all Evil, the Devil.

Like yin and yang, the two horns upon Pan's head represent his dual nature—bright and dark, night and day, summer and winter.

"Tonight, we practice magic," the high priest said to the gathered Wiccans.

Kesia felt her arm being squeezed as Luna grabbed it and said, "I love learning magic from this guy. He is so dramatic."

As the high priest walked around the group, he poured salt to encircle them, saying, "We cast a circle of salt to keep all the good within and all the bad without."

Coming back to where he originally was standing, he continued, "We acknowledge all the elements." He poured some dirt onto his hands from a wooden cup while he said, "Earth." Then saying, "Air," he whooshed his hands around, making a wind sound. "Fire," and threw something that sparked flames in the fireplace, creating an instant fire. Lastly, he said, "Water," and snapped his fingers. From the edge of the second-floor platform that looked upon the living room, a waterfall started to come out, landing on the rocks embedded in the floor just below, collecting the water. "We now call the element's earthbound symbols, gnomes for the earth, fairies for air, dragons for fire, and mermaids for water."

Kesia looked around anxiously, waiting to see what would happen next. She jumped as she thought she felt something brush up against her leg, but as she turned to see what it was, nothing was there.

The high priestess joined the high priest as he said, "We call up the Triple Goddess, the Maiden, the Mother, and the Crone."

The high priestess's body started to shake as if something was in her trying to get out. Then, her voice changed to sound like an old crone as she said, "The new moon is a time for renewal spells, starting new projects, planting seeds, and starting over. As the moon gets closer to full, it is considered 'waxing.' This is a good time to build momentum, gather information, or work spells to increase love, wealth, and good luck. The energy is strong and intense during the full moon, so you should be cautious, meditate, focus on good health, and have fun! As the moon goes from full to crescent, it's called a 'waning' moon. This is a good time to finish existing projects, tie up loose ends, and take time to relax. The moon can also be useful to 'recharge' oneself, especially during a full moon."

Kesia was fascinated as the high priestess had changed her persona and became an old lady.

"Each phase of the moon correlates with a phase of a woman's life. The *Maiden*, represented by the new moon, embodies purity, youth, creation, pleasure, naivety, and new beginnings. The Maiden invites you to explore your spirituality, sensuality, and creativity."

Kesia looked over at Luna, who was chanting something under her breath.

"The *Mother*, represented by the full moon, embodies love, fertility, nourishment, responsibility, patience, gratitude, power, and self-care. The Mother invites you to master giving and receiving love."

Kesia watched Luna's eyes close, and her body started to sway.

"The *Crone*, represented by the fading waning moon, embodies endings, wisdom, death, acceptance, and culmination. The crone invites you to accept that without death, there is no birth."

Surprising Kesia, Luna's head moved backward, and her hands turned toward the ceiling just as the moonlight shone through the windows into the living room as the high priestess said, "I stand in the moon's glow, arms outstretched with palms upwards, and imagine my palms absorbing the moon's rays. I call upon the Greek goddess Hecate, who is associated with crossroads, entrance-ways, night, light, magic, witchcraft, knowledge of herbs and poisonous plants, ghosts, necromancy, and sorcery." A window blew open, and a gush of wind made the flames burn higher.

Without even flinching, the high priestess continued, "Normally, we would honor you, Hecate, on November thirtieth, but tonight is necessary. We need your expertise in witchcraft."

Luna leaned over and said, "What she just did is called 'drawing down the moon.'"

Kesia nodded to affirm that she understood, but in reality, she was a little freaked out.

The high priest came around and passed everyone a piece of paper and a pen.

The high priestess continued, "Write down your wishes, wants, dreams, and desires for this coming year. When you are done, go to the fireplace and throw what you have written into the flames, allowing the words to travel throughout Earth, Heaven, and even the underworld."

At first, Keisha didn't know what to write down but decided to make something up fast. Getting up, right after Luna did, she followed her toward the fireplace. When it was Kesia's turn, she tossed the piece of paper into the fire and watched it catch flame and turn to ash just as fast.

As a food table was brought into the circle, the high priest and priestess came over to stand behind it.

Holding his hands above the food, the high priest said, "We thank the elements, the triple goddesses, and the goddess Hecate for blessing us tonight."

"What happens now?" Kesia whispered to Luna just as the high priest said, "The circle has been opened, and this space is no longer consecrated. So now we eat and be merry."

Luna repeated, "We eat and be merry."

There was a simple feast of crescent-shaped cookies and cakes and white liquid on the table.

As Kesia tasted each, she was pleasantly surprised that the drink was milk.

A moment later, the deep sound of a drum being played could be heard, and the vibration echoed throughout Kesia's body. Looking in the direction of the music, she noticed the drum was a djembe—a sizable goblet-shaped, rope-tuned, skin-covered drum originally from West Africa—being played with bare hands.

To Kesia's delight, some coven members started to chant, while others started to dance to the beat of the music.

Luna grabbed Kesia's hand and pulled her to join her in the celebration.

Smiling as she danced with Luna, Kesia immensely enjoyed her first Esbats.

Chapter 47

As Redington drove Lexi back to Neo's parents' place, Lexi said, "Red, I have to tell you something." She remembered the voice in Redington's condo.

"I know. You are seeing the Doc."

"Well, yes, but that wasn't what I was going to say."

Redington looked at her for a second, then back at the road. "Lexi, you're making me nervous. Crap, you have cancer, right?"

"No. Not that I know of."

"Then, what is it?"

"I heard a voice in your condo."

"Tonight?"

"No," Lexi said, having a hard time getting comfortable while in the car. The pain was back full force.

"Are you okay? You look like you are in a lot of pain," he said as he tried to keep his eyes on the road.

"It's my back. The pain shoots down my legs."

"The Doc hasn't figured out what is going on?" he said with real concern.

"His sister thinks it may be a pinched nerve."

"His sister is a doctor?"

"No, a massage therapist," Lexi answered through gritted teeth and pushed down on the seat of the car, lifting herself to take the pressure off her lower back.

"What are you going to do about the pain, Alexandra? You can't go on like this."

"I have a chiropractor's appointment this afternoon, actually."

"I've been to one. The guy fixed me in one session," Redington said, thinking back to his treatment.

"What was your problem?"

"A pinched nerve. I was playing baseball with the guys from work and slid home. Guess I twisted funny, but I got a home run."

Shaking her head, Lexi said, "Guys and their sports."

Pulling into the Singhs' driveway, Lexi noticed Neo waiting for her outside.

"Uh, oh, looks like you're in trouble. Hey, what about the voice you were telling me about?"

As her car door opened, she said, "I guess it will have to wait."

"Lexi, what were you thinking? Now look, you are in major pain again," Neo said, lifting her out of the car.

"Here is the wheelchair," Redington said as he quickly pushed it to Neo.

Barely looking at Redington, Neo said, "Just put it by the stairs," and carried Lexi into the house.

Redington gave a fake wave as he turned back to his car. Knowing she couldn't hear him, he said anyways, "Talk to you soon."

As Neo put her down on the couch, Lexi said, "That was rude. He was only trying to help me."

"He'll get over it."

"Neo, you can't be mad at him for caring about my welfare."

"Want to make a bet? Besides, he started it."

Lexi tried to laugh, but the pain was too much.

"What's so funny?"

"You two are acting like teenagers."

Neo ignored her and went to get her a glass of water.

Lexi's phone alarm went off.

"What was that set for?" Neo asked, bringing back her water.

Taking a sip, Lexi said, "I need you to drive me to the chiropractor. If not, I can get an Uber."

"No need, I can drive you, but I wish you weren't going."

"What is it with doctors and chiropractors?"

"If you have seen some of the cases I have from a person going, you would think twice about it. Plus, you still have numbness and tingling in your legs."

"Why don't you come in with me and see what he does?" Lexi said, trying to ease Neo's concern.

"I might just do that."

It didn't take long to get to the clinic. The chiropractor was a friend of Evangeline's and worked near Neo's parents.

Once in the waiting room, the receptionist at the front desk gave Lexi a couple of forms to fill out.

"Wow, he wants a lot of information," Lexi said to Neo as she was filling out the forms.

Neo looked over and read the questions. "Good, at least he isn't a quack."

"Shh, be nice. Someone might hear you," Lexi said quietly.

"Miss Constantine, Doctor Roy can see you now," the receptionist said. "Follow me, please."

Lexi let Neo push her wheelchair into the session room.

Before shutting the door, the receptionist said, "The doctor will be with you in a moment."

Lexi waited nervously. She looked at the human skeletal and nervous systems posters, then at the doctor's credentials. "At least he went to a good school," Lexi said, pointing to his diploma.

Neo just shrugged.

There was a tap at the door before Doctor Roy came in.

Lexi was surprised that he was so young.

Obviously, so was Neo. "How long have you been practicing chiropractic?"

Smiling, Doctor Roy said, "I get that a lot. I guess I come from good genes." Then, pointing to his diploma, he said, "Ten years." Then, looking at Lexi, he said, "Now, Miss Constantine, it says on the form you filled out that you were in a car accident."

"Yes, that is correct. I hit a telephone pole."

"I see. So, it was a head-on collision, then."

"Yes."

"I will need to see an X-ray of your spine. I'll need you to ask your doctor to send them over so I can view what is really going on."

Lexi looked at Neo as he was typing something into his phone.

Neo looked up and said, "The X-rays will be emailed to you within a few moments."

Looking at Neo, Doctor Roy said, "Who are you exactly?"

"I am her neurosurgeon."

Lexi patted Neo's leg and said to Doctor Roy, "He is also my boyfriend."

Doctor Roy's eyebrows lifted as he said, "I bet it took a lot for you to come in here?"

"More than you know," Neo said without smiling.

Looking back at Lexi, Doctor Roy said, "Lexi, I need you to stand. Can you do that?"

"Not without a lot of pain."

Looking at Neo, Doctor Roy said, "Can you help me get her onto the table?"

"Is it necessary?"

"If you want me to do my job correctly, it is."

"Fine." Neo lifted Lexi onto the automated chiropractic table—it resembled a skinnier version of a massage table.

"Lexi, I can't do any manipulations today. So today, I am just going to get an idea of what is going on," he said as he lifted the back of her shirt and applied a hand to her back. "Any pain here?"

"Not where you are touching, no."

"How about here?" He moved his thumb to her hip.

"No, mostly it is when I sit up or try to walk."

"Can you lie on your back?"

"Not without help."

"Okay, no need right now."

Doctor Roy bent down and touched the toes of Lexi's right foot. "Any numbness or tingling?"

"A little bit."

"Which one, numbness or tingling?"

"Numbness."

Turning to Neo, he asked, "Did she have a herniated disk?"

"No, we suspect it is a traumatic spondylolisthesis, but we won't know for a few more weeks if we will have to fuse the disks."

Lexi looked at Neo. "You didn't tell me that."

"I was waiting to make sure before I told you anything else. You have so much inflammation that it is hard to see what is going on," Neo said honestly to both of them.

"Lexi, I will need you to come back in about a week, so I can see if the swelling has gone down enough that I can help with the dislocation issue." Then, looking at Neo, he said, "I will need another set of X-rays, though. Do you want us to take them, or can you send me a copy?"

"I'll send you a copy. We were going to have Lexi get another exam next Tuesday."

"That will be perfect," Doctor Roy said to Neo. Then, turning to Lexi, he asked, "What meds are you taking right now?"

Turning to Neo, she said, "I think it is tylenol 3 with codeine."

Neo nodded.

Speaking to Neo, but looking at Lexi, Doctor Roy said, "The acetaminophen tylenol is okay, but I suggest that she add 500 mg of ibuprofen at least twice a day for the next three days."

"What do the drugs do?" Lexi asked.

Neo started to answer her question at the same time Doctor Roy did but shut up instantly, letting him answer.

"Acetaminophen helps relieve pain and fever. Ibuprofen is a nonsteroidal anti-inflammatory drug that can help reduce pain and inflammation. My clients swear that it helps even within a few hours of taking the two together. You should feel much better in no time."

Lexi looked over at Neo and said, "Whatever you think."

"It can't hurt to try."

Before opening the door to let Lexi and Neo out, Doctor Roy said, "Make sure to make an appointment with the receptionist on your way out." Then turning to Neo, he said, "Nice to see a surgeon with an open mind."

Lexi smiled as Neo pushed her wheelchair out of the building. "He seems like a nice guy."

"I'm sure he is," Neo said as he placed her into the car.

"Can we stop and get some? What did he call it? Oh ya, ibuprofen."

"I have some at my parents' that you can have. It's not a prescription. It's an over-the-counter drug, so anyone with pain can use it."

"Good to know."

Chapter 48

Kesia's Wicca homework assignment was to study dark entities. "Hey, Luna, why are we studying demons and such if Wiccans don't practice dark magic?"

Luna answered while lighting a candle, "If you want to embrace the light, you must understand the darkness."

To study demons, Kesia chose her favorite device, her almighty oracle, the internet, and started to do her research. "It says here that Lucifer is the father of all demons, husband to Lilith, and ruler of Hell. He has also been called Prince of Darkness, Moloch, Samael, Iblīs, and the Devil."

"True, but no matter what name you call him, he is considered the ultimate nemesis of good people everywhere," Luna added.

Reading on, Kesia said, "Hey, get this, it says that at one time, he was God's most beautiful angel, called the morning star and that he was an anointed guardian cherub, an angel of the royal guard with access to the holy mount of God, and could walk among the fiery stones."

"What are the fiery stones?"

Kesia read, "The cosmic mountain. The place where heaven and earth meet."

"Interesting. Do you know the most common folklore of how Lucifer became a fallen angel and why he was cast out of Heaven?"

"No," Kesia answered, now curious.

"It goes something like this… He became so impressed with his own beauty, intelligence, power, and position that he began to desire for himself the honor and glory that belonged to God alone. Which also became the first of the seven deadly sins, *pride.*"

"Actually, I kind of get that. Remember Amber in eighth grade?"

"Ya."

"She thought she was all that. Boy was her ego big," Kesia said, thinking back at how much Amber irked her.

Shaking her head and laughing, Luna said, "Ya, she thought she was something, alright. Sometimes I do wish I did dark magic."

"Luna!"

"Well, she would have deserved it," Luna said, then continued her story about Lucifer. "In rebellion against the Creator, more than one hundred 'Fallen Angels' followed Lucifer out of heaven and descended upon the earth—BUT… Get this. Some believe that the Devil was actually a type of angelic Santa Claus?"

"What?" Kesia said, shockingly.

"Ya, just as Saint Nick checked his list twice to see who's been naughty or nice, Lucifer's new job of reigning over Hell was to test people's virtues and to report their sins to God?"

"Wow, that puts a new twist on the devil." *What a theory.*

Luna nodded. "Pride and the other six deadly sins—greed, lust, envy, wrath, gluttony, and sloth all have demonic energy."

"What do you mean?"

"Each sin is controlled by a demon, and when a human acts upon a sin, it creates a vibrational disharmony that attracts the corresponding demon to that person. That is when the demon can create havoc and dis-ease in a person's body, mind, and soul."

"Wow!"

"Virtuous and sinful vibrations in the body are scientifically called frequency or hertz. And a healthy frequency from the neck up is 72-78 megahertz, and from the neck down is 60-68 megahertz. According to Tainio Technology, disease starts at 58 megahertz, cancer at 42 megahertz, and death begins at 25 megahertz."

"I wonder what Lexi is vibrating at?" Kesia said.

"That would be interesting to find out," Luna said. "There is also an odor—a chemical pheromone released—when a mammal, including a human, perceives it is in danger."

"I heard that animals could smell fear."

Nodding, Luna said, "The vibration of FEAR, any type of fear—fear of loss, fear of the unknown, fear of punishment, or fear of death is 19 megahertz. And a human's aura surrounding the soul creates a unique vibration that malevolent spiritual beings can detect when the person is in fear. This vibration is perfect for demons and dark entities to feed on a human's life-force energy. Fear is the superpower that feeds the devil's army."

Kesia started writing down these keynotes, knowing that this would come in handy one day.

"Only the mind can produce fear, not the soul, nor the core of a person. If one could shift their fear, one could heal. See, Kesia? This is awesome information that we can incorporate into our spells."

"How so?"

"Archangel Raphael was initially known as Labbiel and is the guardian of the tree of life, with its twelve healing branches, growing in the Garden of Eden. He represents the 'virtue' of humility and is the opposing force to Lucifer and the 'sin' of pride."

"Okay, but I am not getting it. How can we use this information?"

"We use the vibrational power of Raphael's ring."

"His what?"

"On Archangel Raphael's right hand is a ring called the pentalpha—a five-pointed star that has the power to command entities of the lower realms."

"Is that like a pentagram?"

"Yes.

"He is also known to be carrying a medical book, which contains the keys of life."

"So, Archangel Raphael is the healer angel?"

"Yes. Michael is the warrior of the four angels, Gabriel is the messenger, Uriel holds the wisdom, and Raphael is the healer. They are the four spiritual bodyguards to God's throne and are represented as the four cornerstone constellations—the lion, the eagle or serpent, the bull, and man."

Kesia got excited. "Hey, the tarot card 'Wheel of Fortune' has all four of these same creatures on it. It represents the Roman goddess Fortuna, associated with chance, luck, and good and bad fortune."

Luna added, "The four Royal Stars are also called the four cornerstone constellations. Back then, it was believed that the sky was divided into four districts, with each community being guarded by one of the four constellation creatures."

Kesia was impressed with Luna's knowledge.

As she went to get one of her spell books, Luna said, "Ophiuchus, one of the four cornerstone constellations, is tied to healing and

Archangel Raphael, and it's called the Serpent Bearer. The constellation has a serpent coiled around it, like the snake coiled around the staff of Asclepius."

"Wow. Lots to learn."

"Kesia, don't get overloaded. The secret to healing is maintaining a healthy and vibrant frequency in your energy field… your aura… your electromagnetic field."

"Easier said than done."

"Healing is all about virtue and sin, and the guardians of heaven—known as the sons of God, the watchers—especially the regulus, the watcher of the north."

"Who's that?" Kesia asked.

"Archangel Raphael. Kesia, don't you see that with his help, we can create vibration, quantum healing, and even green spells that can heal the body, mind, and soul?"

"So, what I am hearing is that when a person is in fear or is sick, demons can feed on their life-force energy, and Archangel Raphael's power can heal them?"

"Yes." Opening her spell book, Luna said, "Joy in all things is the path that leads to health and happiness."

Chapter 49

*I*t had been a while since their class on the five Vedic elements. "Who can tell me the names of the five Pancha Bhoota?" Delish asked the boys. Aias's hand went up.

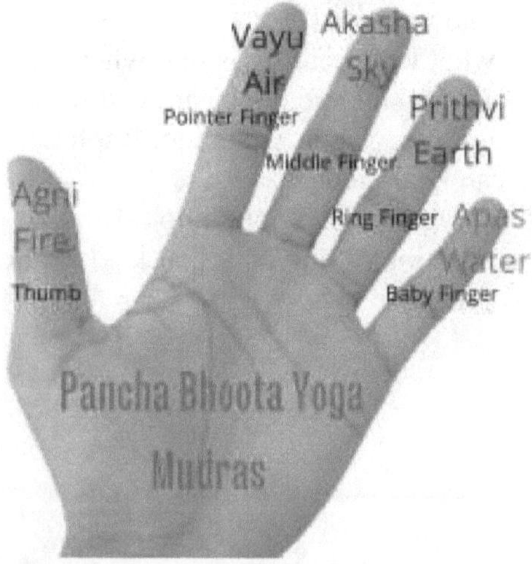

"Yes, Aias."

"Do you want to know them in English or Sanskrit?"

Clever kid. Delish answered, "Sanskrit."

"Agni, Vayu, Akasha, Prithvi, and Apas."

"Correct. Now in English."

"Fire, Air, Sky, Earth, and Water."

"Correct."

Aias smiled.

"Okay, everyone, to balance the elements in your body, we are going to learn Pancha Bhoota yoga mudras—finger yoga. To begin, start by sitting in a lotus position," Delish instructed.

Aias's hand went up again.

"Yes, Aias."

"What if my mom can't do the lotus position? Will this work if she is sitting in a chair?"

"Yes, but it is best if a person could cross their legs."

"Why?" Aias asked.

Delish smiled at Aias's curiosity, then said, "The lotus pose not only facilitates the deep breathing necessary to obtain a meditative state by maintaining proper posture and spinal alignment, but also various parts of the body press into the acupuncture points of the stomach, gallbladder, spleen, kidneys, and liver meridians. Thus, bringing about positive changes in the metabolic structure and brain patterns. Not only is this position good for your body, but it also holds the potential to awaken the dormant energy known as kundalini at the base of the spine, moving the kundalini energy up through the chakra system."

"Wow. So, you're saying that my mom won't be able to achieve all that by sitting in a chair?" Aias asked, concerned for her welfare.

"No, but don't worry, the mudras will still help her."

Aias looked very concerned.

"Let me explain. Mudras are linguistic, symbolic gestures practiced in Hinduism, Jainism, and Buddhism."

Aias's hand went up.

"Yes, Aias."

"Is a gesture like waving, the peace sign, or sign language?"

"Yes. Everyone knows at least one good or bad symbolic gesture."

Many boys laughed. Delish knew they were laughing about a bad finger gesture.

Trying not to smile, he continued his lesson by saying, "Each specific mudra gesture is considered kinetic because of the movement aspect. In sports, a coach has an athlete imagine the outcome of his action prior to the action. An example would be a golfer imagining the ball sailing through the air and landing within inches of the hole, even before he hits it. Mudras are like guided imagery, as they set the intention of what is desired. But instead of imagining the outcome in your mind, mudras use the kinetic action of the hand movements to achieve the desired outcome."

Aias put his hand up and said, "I don't understand."

"Each mudra has qualities and traits associated with it. As you move your hands into a mudra gesture, this action triggers the subconscious to remember what the specific mudra represents."

Aias put his hand up and said, "I still don't understand."

Delish took a breath and said, "Aias, if you put up your middle finger, what would happen?"

"I would get in trouble with my mom."

"So, the action of putting up the middle finger triggers a negative emotion in your body?"

"Yes. I wouldn't want to get grounded."

Another boy yelled out, "Or spanked."

"Lucky for all of you, mudras produce a positive emotion, and in turn, shift your vibration accordingly."

"So, are these hand movements subconsciously beneficial?" Aias asked for confirmation.

"Definitely. Let me show you the five main finger yoga mudras. First, take a breath and rest the back of your hands, palms up, one on each thigh. Take another breath. Mudras are usually practiced during a meditated state and can be practiced not only in the lotus position but while sitting on a chair or lying down in bed."

Delish watched to make sure the boys were following his instructions.

"Great. Now relax your fingers and shake them out. This time, show me your thumbs."

Delish watched as the boys held up their thumbs. "This digit represents the *Fire* element, and this mudra gesture we are about to perform is called Agni Mudra.

As he told them what to do, Delish demonstrated the next mudra for the boys to see. "Start again from the position of palms up on your thighs. Take a breath. Now, bring your hands together by interlacing your fingers with both hands, and comfortably place your wrists on your tummy. Make sure your thumbs are straight up and touching each other. This thumb action will activate the fire element. Take a breath, and if you like, close your eyes."

Delish scanned the boy's hand positions while he told them what the fire element represented. "When your body is out of balance, and the fire element is in excess, this element represents danger, anger, fury, and fear. We all need a balanced fire element within us to boost our immune system and keep our metabolism strong. To balance your fire element, hold this position. This mudra represents prana—your life-force energy, the sun, heat, vitality, masculinity, strength, enthusiasm, intellect, ambition, and power. Fire is also connected to transformation, change, and the ability to burn impurities in the body."

Aias's hand went up.

"Yes, Aias."

"How long do we hold this position for?"

"It is different for each person. Mudras are an easy form of meditation to practice directing a specific flow of energy within the body. Each day may be a different amount of time. Soon, you will trust your intuition's timeline."

"How long are we going to hold this position for right now?" Aias asked, making sure he was doing it perfectly.

Delish couldn't help it and said, "Until I tell you to stop." Then added, "Most people hold each mudra for a minimum of thirty seconds."

Delish watched as Aias nodded and shut his eyes.

"Now, relax your fingers by slightly flicking them. As I said earlier, each finger represents an element. This next mudra gesture connects us to our higher self. It is called Gyana Mudra or Chin Mudra and is one of the most famous mudras. Some people even chant the 'Om' sound while holding this position, with their hands open. While the fingertips are facing up toward the sky, bring a pointer finger to touch the tip of each thumb, forming a circle. Keep the other three fingers lightly stretched, and take a deep breath. This action balances the *Air* element's energy so that it can flow freely throughout the body. This element represents breath, freedom, lightness, movement, rhythm, and connection. You'll know when it is in excess because it causes instability, anxiety, weakness, disassociation, and disorientation. If you turn your fingertips to face downward, this mudra position is called Jnana Mudra and is the gesture to download intuitive wisdom and knowledge."

Delish listened to many of the boys start to chant the Om sound as they held the Chin Mudra. He smiled when he saw Aias shift his finger position to Jnana Mudra. "Relax your fingers. Now, bring your middle fingertip to your thumb's tip. Keep the other three lightly stretched and take a deep breath. The *Sky or Aether* element is known as the Akasha Mudra and represents openness, eternity, stillness, endless possibilities, clarity, light, our voice, and the ability to speak. When balanced, it creates space for the other elements to fill. In excess, we will feel empty, unsettled, insecure, and unconnected."

Delish closed his eyes for a moment and did this mudra to balance his soul.

"Relax your fingers. Now, bring your ring fingers to the tip of your thumbs. Keep the other three fingers together lightly stretched, and remember to breathe. This mudra gesture is called Prithvi Mudra and represents the *Earth* element. It is all about our connection with our physical bodies and our connection to the planet Earth. It is perfect for grounding and anchoring. This gesture makes us feel stable, secure, and well-rooted. It's about finding ourselves and connecting with our primal instincts, our basic needs and our desire for survival—food, shelter, and reproduction. Unfortunately, too much of this element can make us feel heavy, dull, lazy, or lacking in energy."

Aias's hand went up.

"Yes, Aias."

"If we hold this mudra too long, will it create too much of this element?"

"No. Your body will intuitively know when to release the position."

Delish waited a few moments before demonstrating the next mudra.

"Relax your fingers. Now, bring your little fingers to the tip of your thumbs. Remember to keep the other three lightly stretched and breathe."

Delish watched as the boys changed fingers. "This is the last of the main mudras that I am going to teach you today. It is called Jal Mudra or Apas Mudra. It is the *Water* element and represents mental clarity, openness, and fluid communication. In excess, it can cause obesity, as well as stomach and digestive issues."

Delish took a breath and enjoyed the moment of balance within his body, mind, and soul as the boys started to go into a deeper trance state. "There are at least 43 mudras that I will teach you eventually, but these are the main ones. Let's do a quick recap of each element's meaning. The thumb represents the fire element, the universal soul consciousness. The index finger represents the air element and the individual soul. The middle finger represents the sky element and the ego. The ring finger represents the earth element and illusion, and lastly, the little finger represents the water element and karma. By balancing all five elements, we keep the energy flowing freely throughout our body, mind, and soul."

Aias's hand went up.

"Yes, Aias."

"Does doing these mudras heal the organs in the body?"

"Yes, but that is for another class."

Aias's hand quickly went up again.

"Yes, Aias."

"Can you teach us one more, please?"

Delish thought about it, then said, "Okay, one more before we end. This mudra is called Surya mudra and also balances the fire element in your body. Fold your ring finger to the base of your thumb—the meaty part—on each hand. Next, place a thumb on top of each ring finger, giving both a light pressure. Keep your other fingers as straight as you can and hold that position. Take a deep breath. This hand gesture helps to calm a restless and anxious mind."

Aias said, "I like this one."

Delish smiled, knowing that he would.

After a few moments, Delish said, "To end this class, we will use the *heart* mudra, also known as *Namaste hands* or *Anjali Mudra*—the salutation mudra often accompanied by the expression Namaste. Bring your palms together in front of your heart. This action is to recognize the wisdom that lies within your heart."

After a moment, Aias's hand went up.

"Yes, Aias."

"So, by preprogramming each specific element's qualities and traits to a mudra, when I kinetically practice these finger positions, my body will eventually associate the feeling of the mudra with a vibrational response throughout my body to balance it, if needed?"

"Exactly."

Chapter 50

Aias was excited about today's class. Delish would teach them about healing the body, mind, and soul using the seven chakras.

"Good morning, everyone. Please, have a seat."

Aias sat up front so he could see the whiteboard that Delish had set up. It had a drawing of a person sitting in a lotus position.

Delish asked, "Does anyone know the names of the seven chakras?"

Aias didn't know, so he didn't put his hand up.

After a boy answered, Delish nodded, then wrote the chakra names beside each symbol on the whiteboard.

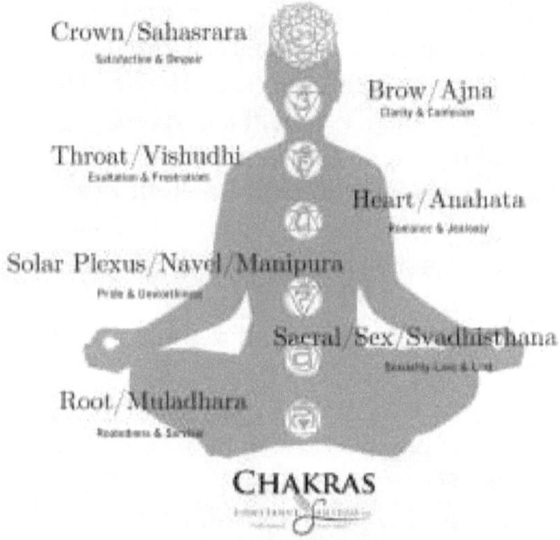

Passing out a piece of paper and seven crayons to each boy, Delish instructed, "Draw these seven circles a couple of inches above one another, creating a vertical line. The chakras are the color of the rainbow. Pointing at the bottom circle, he said, this red circle is called Muladhara and represents the root chakra. Color the bottom circle red."

The boys did as they were told.

"The next circle is orange, and it is called Svadhisthana and represents the sacral or sex chakra. Using the orange crayon, color in that circle."

Delish waited between each chakra for the boys to color. Then he said, "The yellow circle is called Manipura and represents the solar plexus or navel chakra. The green circle is called Anahata and represents the heart chakra. The blue circle is called Vishudhi and represents the throat chakra. The indigo circle is called the Ajna and represents the brow or Third Eye Chakra. Lastly, the violet circle on the head is called the Sahasrara and represents the crown chakra."

Looking at his paper, it did remind Aias of a rainbow.

"Today, we are going to learn about the emotional healing that can be performed using the chakra system."

Aias was a little disappointed. He really wanted to know the reason he could physically heal people when he touched them.

"The boys that are here from the West, you probably know of the solfege of 'Do, Re, Mi, Fa, So, La, Ti, and Do.' But today, we will be using the Indian Solfege of 'Sa, Re, Ga, Ma, Pa, Dha, Ni, and Sa.' When I tell you to, I want all of you to hum 'Sa.' Make the base of your body, your root chakra, vibrate." Delish waited for about thirty seconds. "How many of you could lower your voice enough to make your tailbone area vibrate?"

A few hands went up.

"Now hum 'Re' and this time make the area below your belly button vibrate." Again, he waited.

"How many of you could make this area vibrate?"

A couple more hands went up.

"Now hum 'Ga' and this time make the area above your belly button vibrate." Again, he waited.

"How many of you could make this area vibrate?"

A few more hands went up.

"Now hum 'Ma' and this time make the area above your heart vibrate." Again, he waited.

"How many of you could make this area vibrate?"

All hands went up.

"Now hum 'Pa' and this time make the area above your throat vibrate." Again, he waited.

"How many of you could make this area vibrate?"

All hands went up.

"Now hum 'Dha' and this time make the area between your eyebrows vibrate." Again, he waited.

Aias started laughing as all the boys began to make high-pitched girly noises.

Giving Aias a look that said, "behave," Delish continued, "How many of you could make this area vibrate?"

Through a lot of laughter, only a few hands went up.

"Now hum 'Ni' and this time make the top of your head vibrate." Again, he waited.

"How many of you could make this area vibrate?"

Hardly any hands went up, but even more laughter.

"In your own time, practice making these Solfege sounds until you can make each chakra area vibrate."

Aias put up his hand.

"Yes, Aias."

"Why do we have to learn the emotions with each chakra?"

"Good question. I am sure you are aware of the Western hospitals and medical practices back home."

"Yes, I have been to a hospital before," Aias confirmed.

"Ayer Vedic Medicine considers Western medicine *'Emergency Medicine'* because it deals with acute or chronic physical issues. This is because most people go to see their doctor or the hospital when they are sick, hurt themselves, need an operation, or are dying."

"Emergency Medicine doesn't consider a person's emotions?" Aias asked.

"Not unless the person is showing signs of psychosis or schizophrenia, and still, the doctors believe it is due to a chemical imbalance, not an emotional imbalance."

"What about the other kinds of healing?"

"You mean like Natural Medicine?"

"Ya."

"Natural Medicine deals with exercise and nutrition. Eastern Medicine, Complementary, or Alternative Medicine are modalities like Aromatherapy, Herbs, Hypnotherapy, Acupuncture, Shiatsu, or Nero Linguistic Programming. Integrated Medicine mixes quantum medicine, Western and Eastern Medicine. There are also modalities like Iridology—the study of your eyes that can tell your constitution from birth, and Reflexology—the study of your feet that can tell your health history."

"My mom gets massages. What are they considered?" Aias asked.

"Massage leans more toward Western Medicine because it is proven to help the circulatory, lymphatic, and digestion systems in the body."

"So why do we have to study emotions instead of physical healing?" Aias asked.

"Because stress is the number one issue behind most health conditions and dis-ease."

Aias said, "My mom was sad when her fiancé died, my dad. I remember her crying when she was talking on the phone to a friend about him."

"That sadness causes disharmony in the body and makes the chakra areas vibrate negatively, causing dis-ease in the body."

"The chakras are emotional?" Aias asked.

"Yes." Delish used this opportunity to continue his lesson. "The root chakra controls a person's *basic survival and rootedness needs* like breathing, food, water, sex, sleep, excretion, and homeostasis. Any physical, emotional, mental, or spiritual situation that causes a negative cellular shift in the body will cause this chakra to close up and not allow the energy to flow freely."

Aias put up his hand.

"Yes, Aias."

"What do you mean 'close up?'"

Delish had a small metal steamer on a table beside him. He picked it up and opened it all the way. "Too much energy is just as bad as not enough energy." He closed the sides again. "What we are always striving for is balance or

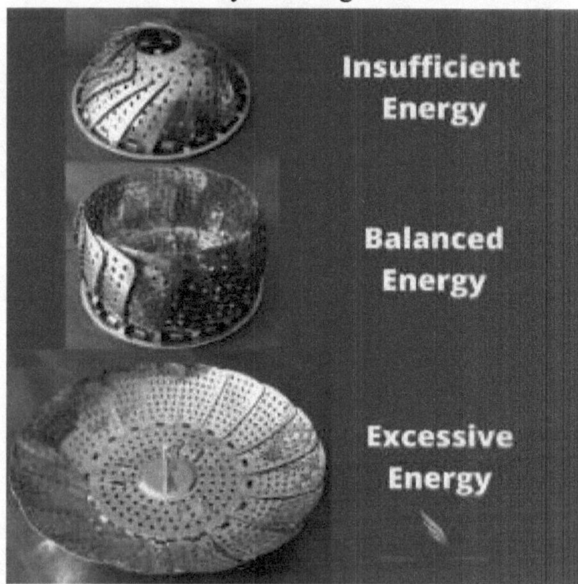

homeostasis." He held the metal steamer and opened it up halfway. "This is like what a chakra can do, be closed and have insufficient energy, be balanced, or overflow and have an excessive amount of energy."

Aias liked that analogy.

Delish continued to explain each chakra. "The Sacral chakra controls your sexuality—love and lust."

Aias wasn't quite interested in girls yet, so this chakra didn't matter to him.

"The Solar Plexus chakra controls your pride and unworthiness. The Heart chakra controls romance and jealousy. The Throat chakra controls happiness and frustration. The Brow chakra controls clarity and confusion, and the Crown chakra controls satisfaction and despair."

Aias put up his hand.

"Yes, Aias."

"I think I understand. Depending on our emotions, our chakras change with our moods."

"Yes, and if you stay in a negative mood for too long, the chakra will have insufficient energy and will cause dis-ease in the body. It would also not be good if you were over-excited for too long. That too would also cause issues."

"So, you're saying that we are always supposed to strive for balance?"

"Yes. Exactly!"

Chapter 51

The pain had subsided, but Lexi still couldn't walk, so Evangeline took Lexi to her next chiropractic session.

Once in the session room, Lexi said to Evangeline, "How do you know Doctor Roy?"

Evangeline smiled and said, "I dated him back in college. Then during pre-med, he decided that working in a hospital and all the bureaucratic stuff that comes with it wasn't for him, so he switched and became a chiropractor."

Just as Lexi was going to say something else, a tap at the door was heard before Doctor Roy came in.

"Well, isn't this a pleasant surprise?" he said as he saw Evangeline.

"Hi Jeff, how have you been?"

"Good, thanks, and you?"

"Good."

"Well, Miss Constantine, you are in good hands if you know Evangeline."

Lexi smiled. "I am lucky for sure. I have her as my massage therapist and her brother for my neurosurgeon."

"That was your brother that came in last time. I should have known."

"Known what?" Lexi asked, confused.

Jefferson shook his head and said, "And here I thought it was because he was a surgeon. But instead, he acted like that because I forgot who he was. Although, to be fair, I only met him once, and it was a short visit."

Evangeline laughed. "Oh right. He didn't like you back then either."

Lexi felt a little out of the loop. "What happened back then?"

Evangeline looked at Lexi and said, "Neo."

"That's right, that's his name. If he had said it last week, I would have recognized him."

Evangeline started again, "Neo didn't think that Jefferson was good enough for me. Actually, I think Neo thought that anybody that would give up being a doctor to become a chiropractor was crazy."

Lexi smiled, getting the picture.

"Miss Constantine."

"You can call me Lexi. Now that family connects us."

Evangeline stopped smiling and sat up straight.

Jeff caught Evangeline's change in attitude and started the session on Lexi.

"Lexi, I need you to sit on the table, please."

With Doctor Roy's help, Lexi shifted from the wheelchair onto the table.

"I am going to lay you backward. Just let me have all your weight."

Jeff applied a finger to Lexi's spine as he held her tightly and then let her down.

Lexi could feel a little pop in her back.

He then moved her in a few other positions, and again, Lexi felt her spine move. Finally, for the first time in weeks, she was able to lie with her legs outstretched.

He then sat on a short stool behind her head and cradled her skull with his hands. "I am going to need you to take a deep breath and wiggle your toes."

Lexi followed his instructions and wiggled her toes as he quickly adjusted her neck.

Finally, she felt like she could breathe without pain.

He made a few more adjustments and then said, "Good. That was good for your first session." After helping her sit up, he said, "Can you stand up?"

Lexi tried to stand up with his help and winced slightly as she did. The pain was still there, but not at the same intensity.

"No problem, it is still progress, Lexi. I will need to see you in about three days."

"I was praying that all the pain would be gone," Lexi uttered.

"Lexi, your muscles have had a very traumatic accident. It can take up to two years to heal. It may even take longer. The problem is that muscle has memory, and since yours have been contracted for weeks, your brain isn't ready to relax yet. It is trying to protect you, so you won't move and injure yourself even worse. It will take a few treatments to prove to your brain that this alignment is the proper one, not the one you have been in since the accident."

"Oh, that makes sense. I didn't know muscles have memory," Lexi said, learning something new.

"Yes, and for us chiropractors, it is what makes us look like we are after more money when really it is because your vertebra will slip out of place again. For some people, all they have to do is bend down and pick up a pencil, and bam, they are on the ground in excruciating pain."

"Lexi, when we get back home, I will teach you what I call the quick fix," Evangeline said as she smiled at Jeff. Then she said to him, "Thanks Doc, I will keep sending you referrals."

"Thanks, I appreciate it. And vice versa… Lexi, see you in three days, okay?"

"I'll make the appointment on my way out."

In the car, Lexi asked Evangeline, "Did I offend you in some way?"

"What makes you say that?"

"When I said he could call me Lexi. Your attitude changed."

Evangeline took a breath and said, "He doesn't know."

"Know what?"

"About Todd."

Clueing in, Lexi was dumbfounded. "Does Neo know?"

"I don't think so, but he is a genius, so maybe."

"Does Todd know?" Lexi asked.

"No. I told him that his dad died when he was young, and my family never corrected my story."

"There are tests you can get that would prove it," Lexi said, trying to be supportive.

"I don't need a test. I didn't sleep with anyone else. Jeff was my first and last."

"Your last?" Lexi said, shocked.

"I am still in love with him, but after he finished college, he left for a couple of years, and I didn't know how to get a hold of him. Then, when he came back, it seemed too late. So, I never told him."

"Evangeline, I don't know what to say."

"Just don't tell Neo, okay?"

"It is not my secret to tell. I promise I won't say a thing."

Chapter 52

Aias was sitting in the back of the group listening to Delish's words. It had been four months since he had arrived at the *gurukula*. He had aged eight years in that time and now looked and had the maturity of a twenty-year-old man.

Aias put his hand up.

"Yes, Aias."

"When are we going to learn about how to heal the body?"

"Everything I am teaching you is to heal the body, mind, or soul in some way or another," Delish answered. "Mantras are a great way to affect your overall well-being."

"How is saying a mantra going to help heal someone?" Aias asked.

"Simple words and phrases have the power to stop negativity and invite change into your life," Delish said to all the students, not just Aias.

"A mantra is an instrument of the mind—a powerful sound or vibration that you can use while in meditation. Stress can cause many people to repeatedly think the same negative thought and spiral into depression, which creates more negative thoughts. The vibration of negative thoughts can create your tears to change the pH in your body from alkaline to acidic, and once the body becomes acidic, it sends out a specific frequency. Pathogens—bacteria, parasites, viruses, and fungi—are attracted to this vibration. The only job of a pathogen is to decompose, to remove its prey from existence."

Aias put his hand up.

"Yes, Aias."

"A thought can kill us?" Aias said, having a hard time believing it.

"Over time, yes." Delish continued the lesson, "While chanting a mantra, you're doing a mini-meditation. The sound you make has a vibration that can be felt within your body. This vibrational sound can reduce stress and shift the body's pH, thus changing the brain's chemistry."

Aias said, "You mean change the hormones being produced like dopamine, serotonin, oxytocin, and endorphins?"

"Yes." Delish explained further, "A mantra is a sacred utterance, a mystical sound, a syllable, or word. The most basic mantra is *Om*." Delish wrote the symbol for *Om* on the whiteboard . "I would like you all to practice making the om sound. It sounds like this—a-ā-u-ū-m-(ng)."

Aias tried.

Delish corrected the students by saying, "Open your mouth wide as if you want to take in the fullness of the universe. Pursing your lips together helps stretch out the next two syllables. Place the tip of your tongue on the roof of your mouth to sound the last two syllables, 'm and ng,' which symbolize the close of the creation cycle. Let the silence drape over you before inhaling again."

Aias tried again. He could feel the vibration start from his throat, but from there, it expanded up to his head and down through his fingers and toes.

Delish said, "This particular vibration allows both sides of the brain to work together, as in hemispheric synchronization."

Aias could feel shivers on his skin as he adjusted the sound. The energy was moving from within outward. He could also feel the vibration of the person chanting beside him. *I understand how this would shift energy and thought patterns.*

Delish said, "In Hinduism, *Om* is called the first sound of the universe and is one of the most important spiritual symbols. According to the Hindu scriptures, om connects all living beings to nature and the universe. This mantra refers to Atman—soul, self within—and Brahman—ultimate reality, the entirety of the universe, truth, divine, supreme spirit, cosmic principles, and knowledge."

Aias put his hand up.

"Yes, Aias."

"How long do you practice a mantra for?"

"There are two simple ways to incorporate mantras into your daily life; on an *as-needed* basis, for five to twenty minutes. For example, you are having a super stressful day, and your mind is filled with drama and stories. Chant a mantra in your mind. Or the second way is a dedicated *40-day* practice. You would choose a mantra and repeat it every day for 40 days, chanting it 108 times per day. You can always do more than 108 times but never less than 108 times. Most people use a mala necklace—like a rosary or prayer beads—to help keep track of the counting."

"My mom would not be happy if I made this much noise," Aias said matter-of-factly.

"Then say it without noise. You can move your lips and tongue, or not, but you will not make a sound, only your mind."

"Will that still have the same effect?"

"Try it."

Aias tried it. He could still feel the vibration going through his body. "How is that possible?"

"Actually, silent mantras are more effective because they require a greater level of concentration, focus, and attention."

"Are there other ways that we can create this vibration in our body?" Aias asked.

"I'm glad you asked. Yes, Tibetan bowls, crystal bowls, tuning forks, gemstones, incense, food, water, negative ions, and music can all produce a vibration that brings about healing."

"What are negative ions? They sound bad," Aias asked.

"That is for another class, but for now, just know that they are good for you," Delish said before he had the students practice another mantra. "You can do mantras while meditating, working, or during a walk. And after a while, you will suddenly realize that the chanting has fallen away, the mind has become silent, and the healing has begun."

Chapter 53

"Alexandra, Frank keeps asking me when your mom's funeral will be. What should I tell him?" Redington asked when he called her.

"Red, I have already told you that I do not want a service," Lexi answered a bit on the defensive side.

"Hey, don't get mad at me. I am just delivering the message."

"You're right. I'm sorry. It is just a touchy subject."

"How have you been? Are you able to walk without pain yet?"

"No, and I am getting frustrated. It has been almost three months since the accident. You would think I'd be healed by now."

"I guess it takes as long as it takes. How have your chiropractic treatments been going?"

Lexi let out a sigh. "It helped a bit, but it doesn't seem to be doing anything lately."

Hating that Alexandra was in pain, Redington said, "How about acupuncture? Have you tried that?"

"No, but I am willing to try anything. Do you know of a good practitioner?"

"No, but I can ask around at the precinct and find out if any of the guys have a good Chinese Medicine Doctor."

"Hey, Redington, I have to go. Evangeline is here to give me a massage. I'll ask her if she knows anybody. Talk to you later. And Red, tell Frank I will drop by tomorrow and talk to him."

"Will do. Take care, Alexandra."

"Thanks, you too."

Lexi wheeled herself into the living room, and with Evangeline's help, got up onto the massage table.

"Was that the Detective, again?"

"Yes. Redington was telling me about my neighbor, Frank, wanting a funeral for my mom."

"Are you going to have one?"

Shaking her head slightly, Lexi said, "No, I don't think so."

After applying the oil onto Lexi's back, Evangeline said, "It might help, you know. It brings closure."

"What do you guys do in your culture?"

"Which one, Greek Orthodox or Hinduism?"

Lexi smiled, enjoying the massage. "Both."

"Well, my mom was brought up to believe that death separates the soul from the body and is the beginning of a new life in either Heaven or Hell. Whereas my dad's faith is centered around reincarnation—the belief that when someone dies, the soul is reborn as a different form."

"What do you believe, Evangeline?" Lexi asked curiously.

"That is a good question. I have contemplated the answer and have not come up with a definitive one. Do we come back down and live a new life as someone else, or do we just exist in the afterlife? Or is it just over? What do you believe, Lexi?"

Lexi had to take a breath. *Do I tell her the truth?* "I was brought up Catholic, so I was brought up to believe that a soul that led a good life gets to go to Heaven, and a soul that led a bad life goes to Hell."

"Okay, but is that what you really believe, Lexi?"

Thinking about Susannah, Lexi said, "I believe that there is a test you have to pass based on your own judgment of your virtues and sins. That it is you, and you alone that chooses if you were virtuous enough to get through the pearly gates."

"But do you believe in reincarnation, like my father?"

"I believe that whatever belief a person has about the afterlife is what happens to that person. If they believe, then so it will be."

Asking Lexi to turn over, Evangeline then said, "So, what you are saying is whatever I believe at the time of my death I will create in the afterlife?"

"Yes."

"Fascinating theory," Evangeline said, helping Lexi sit on the massage table. "Lexi, I told you the other day that I was going to teach you the 'Quick Fix.' I know we didn't get a chance, but I will teach it to you now. It helps with eliminating pain."

"Oh, that would be nice if it works," Lexi said as she adjusted the sheet to allow her legs to hang over the edge of the table.

Evangeline passed Lexi a piece of paper with a drawing on it.

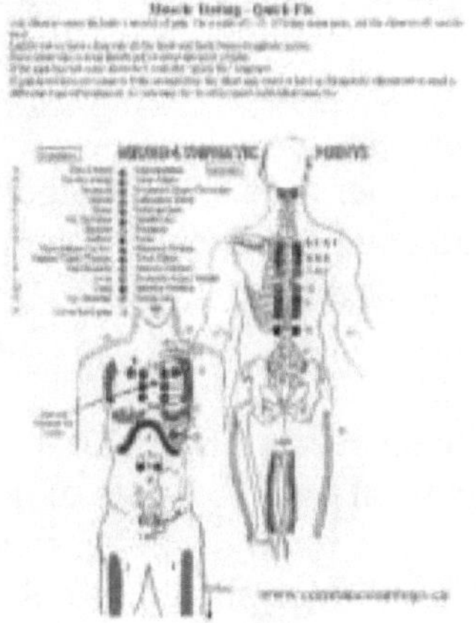

"What is this?" Lexi asked.

"It is a type of Kinesiology. This diagram shows the main points on the body that refer to specific muscles and meridians. When you lightly rub the area, it triggers a balancing reaction in your body, bringing it to homeostasis."

"I have never heard about this before," Lexi said. "Does it work? It seems too easy just to rub a few spots."

Evangeline smiled, knowing the amazing power of this technique. "Let's try. First, I want you to tell me where there is pain in your body and give it a number between zero—no pain, to ten—major pain."

Lexi thought about where the pain was in her body. Then, bringing her hand behind her back, she touched above her right hip. She said, "Here. It is about a five right now, but it can be an eleven if I try to walk."

"Anywhere else?"

Lexi moved her head and shrugged, trying to sense any other pain. "There is a pain level of one in my shoulder."

"Okay, now follow my actions. Do what I am doing."

Evangeline placed a finger and thumb under her collarbone on opposite sides of her sternum and started to rub lightly with her right hand. "Rub these spots. You should be able to feel a slight indent. Lightly, it doesn't have to hurt."

Then Evangeline rubbed up and down her sternum. "This motion activates six spots."

Lexi copied the same motion.

"Now, either side of the armpit."

Lexi copied her actions.

Evangeline said, "With both hands, rub under the breasts," and watched as Lexi rubbed the area. "Now, the edge of the ribcage."

Lexi moved her hands and, using her thumbs, rubbed her ribcage.

"Now, either side of your belly button. Use your pointer fingers and thumbs to activate all four spots."

Lexi alternated, pushing in with each hand.

"Good, now with the edge of one hand, rub across your groin."

Lexi did what Evangeline was doing.

"Then, with two hands, rub down on the outside of your thighs three times. Then on the inside of your thighs."

Lexi copied.

"Now, at the base of your skull with your pointer fingers, rub either side of your spine."

"Oh, that feels good," Lexi said.

"Next, if you can reach, rub down your spine on your back, starting about the bra strap line."

"Ah, it hurts to twist like that," Lexi said.

"No problem. I'll do it for you. If you could walk, you would find an open doorway and rub your back on the edge."

Lexi laughed.

"What's so funny?"

"That image reminds me of a bear rubbing its back on a tree."

"See? Even nature knows how to look after itself," Evangeline said, smiling. "Now, lightly pinch across the top of each shoulder. And then once you are done, repeat the steps three times."

Lexi looked at the diagram and rubbed all the spots. "Does it matter which order I do them in?"

"Nope."

Once Lexi was done, she asked, "What now?"

"Take a breath and recheck the original areas that you had pain. What number are they now?"

Lexi moved her head. "The pain in my neck and shoulders is gone. And my back is down to a two."

"Great. Now do this a couple of times a day. Personally, I do it while I am on the toilet. Might as well use that time efficiently."

Lexi liked that idea. "It did help, Evangeline. Thanks."

"Good. I am glad."

"Hey, you mentioned meridians. What are they?"

"Meridians are based on Chinese Medicine. There are fourteen channels in your body that Chi—life-force energy—runs through. Twelve of the meridians are connected to an organ. The other two are called Ren and Du. These last two connect a circuit that activates when you touch your tongue to the top of your mouth."

"Are these channels like arteries?" Lexi asked, trying to envision them.

"No. That is why Western medicine doesn't believe in them. Although, in Eastern medicine, acupressure and acupuncture use a combination of the three hundred and sixty-one tsubo—points—to balance your body."

"Oh, that reminds me. Redington suggested that I see an acupuncturist. Do you think I should?"

"You never know what treatment might fix your condition. No matter what, it can't hurt you."

"Do you know of a good therapist to go to?" Lexi asked, hopeful.

"Actually, I do. Let me get my phone and look up her number."

After giving the number to Lexi, Evangeline said, "I have to run, but I'll see you at dinner tonight."

"Oh. Is there something special happening? Neo didn't mention anything."

"It's a surprise. See you tonight."

Lexi wheeled herself into the kitchen to see if Naida was there, but all she found was a note.

> Lexi,
>
> I'll be back in about an hour.
>
> Mom

Lexi just stared at the note.

Chapter 54

Kesia woke up early. It was January 31st, and she knew that during today's Sabbat, the high priestess would teach them about Candlemas.

Later that day, entering the meeting room at the high priestess's home, Kesia sought out Luna, who was sitting by a newcomer named Vanessa.

Before she could ask Luna which member had left the coven for Vanessa to join, the high priestess started the meeting by saying, "Candlemas is traditionally a Christian celebration. This two-day holy day celebration starts on February 1st and continues through February 2nd. It is also referred to as the Feast of Pan, Feast of Torches, Feast of Waxing Lights, and Oimelc. No matter what name you call it, it celebrates the coming of spring and recovery of the Earth Goddess after giving birth to the Sun God at Yule."

Whispering to Luna, Kesia asked, "Is the Earth Goddess, Mother Earth?"

Luna shrugged.

Hearing the two of them whispering, Vanessa said quietly, "The Earth Goddess is Mother Mary."

Whispering to both of them, Kesia asked, "Does that make the Sun God, Jesus?"

Vanessa nodded.

Kesia tried to focus on what the high priestess was saying.

"For many traditions, it is a time for initiations, re-dedication, and pledges for the coming year."

Vanessa confessed to the girls, "I love Imbolc."

Never having heard the word before, Kesia whispered, "What is Imbolc?"

Before Vanessa could answer, the high priestess said, "We are here today to celebrate Brigid, the goddess of inspiration and healing."

Vanessa motioned to Kesia that what the high priestess just said was Imbolc.

The girls turned their heads from Vanessa back to the high priestess.

"The word Imbolc means in the belly of the mother. This is the time of year when the seeds of spring are beginning to stir in the belly of Mother Earth. We also celebrate Oimelc, which means lamb's milk. Spring is when many herd animals give birth to their first offspring of the year. As a result, they are producing milk. This creation of life's milk is a part of the symbolic hope for spring."

Kesia asked the girls, "Do Wiccans always celebrate the seasons?"

Luna said, "Always. We give thanks to the many blessing that the Horn god and Mother goddess provide for us."

As the high priestess held up a corn husk doll, Kesia's attention was brought back to the high priestess.

"It is time to honor Brigid. It is time to ask the goddess to help us. It is a time for spiritual cleansing and renewing our vows." The high priestess then placed some white flowers, a bowl of milk, and candles into the circle's center. "Before we initiate some of our new members, join me in chanting this prayer to receive a blessing from Brigid… *Mother of the earth, sister of the faeries, and keeper of the eternal flame. We thank you for stoking the fire in the hearth once more, bringing light and life. Bless us now as you do the soil so that our lives blossom abundance and richness.*"

Kesia felt a tingle ripple throughout her body that brought goose pimples to the surface of her skin.

"Years ago, people had to have faith that the sun would come again and bring with it new life. There is a Scottish tradition that seeing a serpent meant that spring is near," the high priestess told the group.

Kesia thought about the snake for a moment. *Who would have thought that a person would be happy to see a snake?* Then, turning to the girls, she whispered, "I always thought they looked for the groundhog."

The girls tried to hold back a giggle.

Kesia watched as the high priestess tore a large strip of her skirt into thirteen pieces and gave each member a portion of the cloth, saying, "I gift you this Brid Brat, for you to take home and leave out on the washing line, on a bush, windowsill, or tied to a door knocker. It is said that Bridget wanders the roads at night and blesses the Brat with healing powers. Tomorrow morning, retrieve it and rip it into many smaller pieces. Throughout the next few days or weeks, gift a piece of it to someone who needs healing, making sure to keep a piece for yourself. The Brat is now considered a healing object and will protect its keeper."

Kesia took the piece of fabric and looked at it. *I am starting to believe that whatever one wishes to believe in, be it Brat, placebo, talisman, or cross, it is the person's belief that holds power and that they possess the ability to heal, not the object.*

Chapter 55

$\mathcal{L}$exi took a nap while waiting for everyone to come back for supper. When she woke up, she could smell something sweet baking in the oven. She assumed she would find Naida cooking in the kitchen; instead, she found her praying.

Looking up, Naida said, "My dear, I was just giving thanks for the *Presentation of Our Lord and Savior in the Temple* Today, February 2nd, is the day that the Virgin Mary had finished her forty-day purification after the birth of her firstborn son. She had brought him to the temple in Jerusalem, where the sacrifice of a pair of turtle doves was required."

"Is that where the two turtle doves came from in the Christmas song? I always wondered about that," Lexi said, linking the connection.

"Even though it is after Christmas, there is no reason for you not to learn about this song. As you now know, the Greeks start to celebrate

Christmas on the twenty-fifth and celebrate for twelve days. The partridge in the pear tree represents Jesus Christ. The two turtle doves represent the old and new testaments. The three French hens represent faith, hope, and charity. The four calling birds represent the four gospels and or the four evangelists. The five golden rings represent the first five books of the Old Testament—the Pentateuch—which gives the history of man's fall from grace. The six geese a-laying represent the six days of creation. The seven swans a-swimming represent the seven gifts of the Holy Spirit—the seven sacraments. The eight maids a-milking represent the eight beatitudes. The nine ladies dancing represent the nine fruits of the Holy Spirit. The ten lords a-leaping represent the ten commandments. The eleven pipers piping represent the eleven faithful apostles, and the twelve drummers drumming represent the twelve points of doctrine in the apostle's creed."

Interested in what Naida had just told her, Lexi said, "Thanks for clarifying that."

"You're welcome," Naida beamed.

"So, what can I help with?" Lexi asked.

"Oh, you must be feeling better."

"I am, thank you. Whatever Evangeline did, it really has helped."

"What did she do?"

"I think she called it the quick fix."

"Ah, yes. That is a wonderful technique, and, as the title states, a quick fix."

"Ya, who knew that something so simple could have such a profound effect?"

"The Chinese are brilliant when it comes to healing," Naida said.

"I am going to try an acupuncturist. Have you ever been?"

Naida put down the spoon and said, "No, but Evangeline has."

"I wonder if it hurts?" Lexi said, hoping it didn't. And the thought of not just one needle but many scared her a bit.

"I don't believe Evangeline complained about it, so I would say no."

"Good to know." Lexi took a big whiff, saying, "Supper sure smells yummy."

"Mmm, I love turtle doves."

Lexi's eyes went big. "We're eating turtle doves?"

"Yes, pigeons are very tasty. You haven't tried it before?"

"No."

"I bet you haven't tried rabbit either?"

"No, I haven't."

"Well, I know you love chicken, so I know you will love turtle doves."

"It tastes like chicken?"

"Yes, God's favorite food," Naida smiled as she said it.

Lexi had to ask, "God's favorite food?"

"Why, of course, dear, chicken is God's favorite food."

"Why is that?"

"Because everything tastes like chicken."

Lexi laughed at Naida's joke.

"Hey, I hear laughter," Neo said as he came into the kitchen and kissed Lexi on top of her head.

"How was work today, dear?" Naida asked her son.

"Same old, same old. Just saved another life is all."

"Is all. My son is so humble," Naida said as she came around and kissed him on the cheek.

"Well, you taught us to be that way, mom. Humble." Then, looking at Lexi, he said. "*Pride* is Lucifer's sin, and *Humility* is Archangel Raphael's virtue."

Lexi got shivers as she heard Neo's words.

"Mom, do you have any idea what the surprise is tonight?"

"No, I was hoping that you were proposing to Lexi, but if you are asking, then that's not it."

Lexi almost spat out the water she was drinking.

Naida looked at her son and Lexi. "What? A mother can hope, you know."

Neo patted Lexi's shoulder. "That's my mom for you."

Lexi wasn't sure how to take Neo's reaction.

Just in the nick of time, Evangeline's son, Todd, came leaping into the room. "Boo."

Neo pretended to be scared.

Lexi laughed.

"Hey, everyone," Evangeline said as she came into the room. "You remember Jeff."

Popping his head into the room, he said, "Hi, Mrs. Singh. It's been a while."

"Jefferson, so nice to see you. Yes, it has been many years."

Todd squealed. "Guess what, Yia-Yia?

Lexi knew that is what he called his grandmother.

"What dear?"

"Jeff is my dad!"

The room went so silent that you could have heard a pin drop.

"What did I just hear?" Paal said as he came in from the garage.

Evangeline took hold of Jeff's arm. "It is true. Dad. Here, with Jeff's approval, I had a paternal test done to prove it." Evangeline gave the paper to her dad.

"Well, that is a surprise," Neo said.

Lexi wheeled over to Jeff, whom she had gotten to know over the past few weeks. "Congratulations."

"Thanks, Lexi. I am thrilled to have found out. I wish I had known sooner, but I guess I understand why she didn't tell me until now."

Todd grabbed onto his dad's arm and said, "Come on, let me show you how to win at Hearthstone."

"What is Hearthstone?" Jeff asked as Todd pulled him into the living room.

Lexi could hear Todd say, "It is a game I play on my phone."

"Evangeline, don't you think you could have warned us?" Neo said.

"Ah, Neo, let your sister be. She had her reasons," Naida said as she motioned to Paal to clean up before dinner.

"Forty-day purification, more like ten-year purification," Neo said as he pulled a couple of beers out of the fridge. "Great, sis, now I have to like him, chiropractor and all."

Lexi smiled at Evangeline. "Congrats. I like him."

"Thanks, Lexi. Actually, it is because of you that all this happened."

"Why is that?"

"If your back wasn't hurting, I wouldn't have had a reason to go and see him."

"Ah, so it was destiny?" Lexi said, smiling.

"Something like that," Evangeline said, smiling back.

Chapter 56

"Lexi, I have something special planned for Valentine's Day. I hope you don't mind that I made reservations without asking you," Neo said hesitantly.

Secretly thinking that he was going to propose, she said, "I am sure I will love whatever you have planned."

"Good. Make sure to dress warmly. We will be outside," Neo said with a grin.

"Okay, not what I had in mind. Are you talking hat, mitts, and scarf kind of warm?"

"Yes, that will do the job."

"Neo, are we celebrating Valentine's Day the Hindu way or the Greek Orthodox way?" Lexi asked, curious about both customs.

Neo looked at her and said, "Actually, in India, most Hindus find Valentine's Day an insult to their religion and beliefs. It is a Western thing."

"Oh. What about your mother's beliefs? Do the Greek Orthodox believe in Valentine's Day?"

"No, she doesn't either. I did a school report on Valentine's Day when I was in high school. I needed to prove to my mom and dad that it wasn't as bad as they thought."

"What did you find?"

"It came about because of two Italian priests. Bishop Valentine, renowned during his lifetime as a healer of the sick and blind, and Presbyter Valentine, a courageous steward of marriage."

"Which one became Saint Valentine?" Lexi asked, now interested in his report.

"Presbyter Valentine became known as Saint Valentine."

"Why?"

"Back in the day, Roman Emperor Claudius II banned marriage to Christians unless they fulfilled their military obligations to the Empire."

"So, you're telling me that Presbyter Valentine ignored the emperor's ruling?"

"Exactly. He married young couples anyways."

"I wonder why it mattered to Valentine so much?" Lexi queried.

"From what I gathered, Valentine was willing to sacrifice his life to sanctify and make whole the union of young couples through the blessing of God's love."

"Oh, how beautiful," Lexi said as she brought her hands up to her heart.

Kissing her on top of the head, Neo said, "I have a short day at the hospital today, so I'll come back to pick you up around seven tonight."

"Sounds great. I'll be waiting in warm clothes," Lexi said, smiling.

Neo smiled back and went out the door, blowing her a kiss.

The day seemed to move like a turtle, very slowly. Lexi was trying to decide what lipstick to wear when her phone rang. Not looking to who the caller was, she answered, "Hello."

"Happy Valentine's Day, Alexandra. I was hoping that you could tell me what you told Frank."

"Redington. I… I forgot to go and talk to him. I'm sorry. It totally slipped my mind."

"He is going crazy. He has called me three times today, asking if I have talked to you yet. Alexandra, you have to deal with this."

"I will, but not today."

"Great. Well, when Frank calls next time, I am giving him your phone number. Your mom's funeral is not my problem. Actually, your mom's house isn't my problem anymore. If you don't care enough to look after it, well, then I sure in hell don't have to."

Shocked, Lexi went to say something, but it was too late. Redington had hung up.

Sitting there wondering what she should do, she decided to call an Uber to come and pick her up.

A few moments later, Lexi was being driven to her mom's house in Brooklyn.

Lexi hadn't been there since her car accident.

The Uber driver helped her with getting the wheelchair out of his car, then after she paid, he said, "Sorry ma'am, I can't help you with those stairs, sore back and all."

Lexi looked at the stairs and said, "Oh, not a problem. Thanks for the ride."

Looking at the stairs again, Lexi wasn't sure how she would get into the house.

"Lexi, is that you?" Frank said from behind the bushes.

"Hi, Frank. Sorry I haven't called."

As he came through the bushes, he said, "I understand. I haven't been able to get over your mother's death either."

Lexi looked at him and gave him a slight smile.

"Can I help you up the stairs, Lexi?"

"I don't know if I can go in yet."

"Ah, well, let me take you over to my place for some tea while you decide."

"That would be nice, Frank. I would like that."

He had already made some peppermint tea and poured Lexi a cup. "Where have you been staying?" Frank asked, wondering about her whereabouts.

"At a friend's home."

"How have you been feeling? I see you are still in the wheelchair. Redington told me about your accident. I'm sorry. I have been looking after your mom's place the best that I can, but the police won't let me go inside."

"Thanks, Frank. That means a lot."

"Lexi, please have a funeral. Your mom would have wanted all her friends to have a chance to say goodbye."

"Frank, she was cremated. Her body won't be at the funeral. So, there will be nobody to say goodbye to."

"Please, Lexi. I will look after all the arrangements. I promise it won't be anything too extravagant. Just something intimate for her closest friends and, of course, you."

"Frank, why is a funeral so important to you?" Lexi asked.

"I have been mourning your mom for weeks now. I need closure. The funeral ritual is a way to express our deepest thoughts and feelings about life's most important events. It will give testimony to your mom's life, as well as encourage the expression of grief for the rest of us."

"Frank, if having a funeral will help you move on, then, by all means, you have my blessing to arrange whatever it is that you think she would have wanted."

Frank hugged Lexi. With a tear rolling down his cheek, he said, "Your mom loved you so much. She was so proud of you and Susannah."

Lexi teared up as he spoke.

"Lexi, I've lived next door to you guys all your life. I know all the good times, as well as the bad. Your mom and dad were so good to me after my wife died. I can never repay them for the friendship they gave me. Lexi, I loved your mom and was going to propose to her." Tears streamed down Frank's face.

Lexi was crying now, too. She knew why she hadn't wanted to come, and this was why. She didn't want to feel all this grief. Feeling uncomfortable, she finally said to Frank, "I should go and see how my mom's place is doing."

As she was wheeling herself over to the door, Frank asked, "Can I come with you?"

Looking at him, she couldn't say what she was thinking. So instead, she said, "Sure. That would be nice."

As it turned out, it was a good thing she did let him come over. As they got closer, they heard a crash. Hurrying up the driveway, they saw a couple of guys running out the front door with a duffel bag.

Pulling out her phone, she called the only cop she had on speed dial.

"Please leave a message after the beep, and I will get back to you as soon as I catch these bad guys. BEEP!"

"Redington, that's not funny. Two guys broke into my mom's house."

Serious now, Redington said, "What? I'll be right there. Don't go in. Promise you'll wait for the police to show up."

Lexi nodded.

"Alexandra. Promise me," Redington said, not hearing her answer.

'I … I promise."

Within minutes, Lexi and Frank could hear sirens.

The police arrived long before Redington.

Seeing Redington come into the house, Lexi said, "Don't get mad. The police needed me to come in and see what was stolen."

"Hi, Frank. So, I see she finally came by."

"Yes. I don't know how I missed them, the robbers. I notice everything."

"Don't worry, Frank. I am sure you were distracted. Alexandra has a way of doing that to people."

"This is not the time to be funny, Red," Lexi said to him.

After speaking with the other officers, Redington came back and said, "It looks like all your mom's jewelry, silver, and anything else worth something has been taken. I'm sorry, Alexandra."

Looking at her childhood home, she said, "It's time to sell."

Mortified, Frank cried, "What do you mean, sell?"

"It is time to let this old house go to a family who wants to live in it. I am barely able to sit in here, let alone ever live here again."

Turning to Redington, Lexi said, "I permitted Frank to make the arrangements for my mom's funeral. I will have a realtor come by in a few days and sign the papers to sell. Soon I won't be a bother to anyone. I am sorry that I put you all through this drama."

Pulling out her phone, Lexi called for a ride. "Can someone please help me out to the driveway?" she asked.

While waiting for her taxi, Lexi's phone rang. "Hello?"

No answer.

"Hello?"

No answer. Getting shivers, she hung up.

A moment later, Neo called. "Lexi, where are you? I've been waiting for an hour."

Confused, she said as she looked at the time, "Oh, my God, Neo. I lost track of time. I am so sorry. I am in Brooklyn. There was a break-in at my mom's house."

"Are you okay?"

"Yes, but they stole all my mom's valuables."

"Lexi, they are just things. As long as you are okay, that's all that matters."

Just things. How could Neo say that, just things? Those things are all the memories I have left. They are symbolic of my family's life. "I am just waiting for a ride. I should be home in about an hour."

"No rush, we missed our reservation anyways."

"Neo, I am so sorry."

"Me too."

Lexi's ride pulled up.

"My ride is here. I'll see you soon."

Taking out the velvet box in his pocket, Neo said, "Yep," as he hung up.

Chapter 57

"I love Valentine's Day," Kesia said to Luna just before getting onto the chartered bus. She had waited all day for this. "I am so excited to learn how Wiccans celebrate today." As Kesia sat down in the back of the bus, she asked Luna, "Hey, do you know where we are going?"

"It's a surprise. I don't even know. Every year, it's somewhere different."

As the bus started on the journey, the high priestess picked up a microphone and said to the coven, "Thank you for joining me on this enchanting day of love and celebrating those whom we love."

Kesia noticed that the bus was traveling north, in the direction of High Point State Park. As a kid, she used to love hiking through the Kittatinny Mountains with her family.

The priestess continued speaking, "We are headed to the highest peak in New Jersey to act out the ritual of the ancient Festival of the Arcadian Lykaia."

Turning to Luna, Kesia said, "I knew we were going there."

"Not only love but betrayal marks this day," the high priestess said dramatically. "As the legend goes, the Roman King Amulius ordered Romulus and Remus—his twin nephews—to be thrown into the Tiber River to drown in retribution for their mother's broken vow of celibacy to his brother. However, instead of just tossing them into the water to drown, a servant placed them inside a basket, which traveled downriver until it became caught in the branches of a wild fig tree. Amazingly, the young brothers were rescued by a she-wolf and kept alive in her den at the base of Palatine Hill in Rome."

The rest of the story was postponed because the bus had stopped. And with the high priestess leading the way, Kesia followed her and the coven out of the bus. Waiting for them in a clearing was a couple of Wiccan members who had set up the sacred space for tonight's celebration by lighting many lanterns.

The high priestess raised her arms and said to the group, "Not only are we here to honor these brothers that became shepherds, but we are here to celebrate Lupercalia, also known as Februa or Februatio. Lupercus is the god of shepherds and the Roman equivalent of the Greek god Pan."

The sound of beautiful flute music started to play from behind the high priestess. Kesia loved the ambiance that her coven always seemed to create.

"We are here today to honor the god Pan. The god who looks after the wild, shepherds, their flocks, and rustic music. On this day, legend has it from the slopes of Mount Lykaion, 'Wolf Mountain,' the highest mountain in Arcadia, that Pan—half-man and half-goat—cleansed the city of all evil spirits, and people's souls were purified, bringing health and fertility to Rome."

Kesia watched as two men were marked with fake blood—representing the goat sacrifice of the day of old—and holding onto what looked like leather straps, these two men started to walk around the group.

Kesia's mouth dropped open as the high priestess untied her strap at her shoulder and let her garment fall to the ground. Then, naked as the day she was born, the high priestess started to prance through the field.

Tonight's celebration stunned Kesia. She wasn't sure what to take from it. *These witches take their rituals seriously.* Kesia continued to watch as the two men, laughing, chased the high priestess, and as one of the men struck her lightly with the leather, Kesia asked Luna, "I don't get it, what is happening?"

"As the ancient ritual goes, Februa is a purification ritual performed to drive away evil spirits in the community and ensure fertility for the spring or planting season. Any lady who wishes to become pregnant participates in this ritual. It is considered to bring fertility and good luck if hit by the leather strap."

After the high priestess was dressed again, she took hold of a stick and drew a large heart in the dirt, saying, "I call down the goddess Juno, the goddess of love, marriage, and women. Juno, who is usually pictured wearing a goatskin cloak and in the company of a peacock, I call down thee. The one whose sacred plant is the wild fig tree."

Kesia waited anxiously for what was going to happen next.

"Valentine's Day wouldn't be complete without love magic," the high priestess said. "This spell is to attract love and will ensure the intended success in love and romance."

Kesia watched as a folding table was assembled in front of the high priestess. A small jar, some honey, a bottle of vodka, a rose quartz crystal, a piece of paper and pen, a pink birthday candle, and a lighter, some herbs—cinnamon, patchouli, and oregano—and flowers—rose petals, blue lotus, and lavender were placed on top of it.

As the high priestess placed the items into the jar, she said, "I add a bit of honey and alcohol to sweeten the love. Rose petals and their thorns to represent love with healthy boundaries. Blue lotus for an aphrodisiac, lavender for healing, cinnamon for lust and sex, patchouli for passion, and oregano for good luck."

Kesia wondered how many witches used love spells.

As if reading her mind, Luna said, "I have created a few love spells for kids at school."

As Kesia watched the high priestess add the crystal to the jar, she said to Luna, "Really?"

"Ya, you wouldn't believe what some people will do to get the person of their dreams."

"Crazy." Next, Kesia watched as the high priestess gave some paper to one of the witches and said, "Write your intention in the past or present tense only, never future tense. You can write something like: 'I found my perfect lover.'"

Once the girl placed the paper in the jar, the high priestess closed the lid and shook it up, saying to the girl, "Visualize your intention."

Kesia watched as the high priestess passed the pink candle and lighter to the girl, then said, "As you light this candle saying your intention out loud to the universe, visualize what it would be like to attain it."

As the girl chanted, "I now have my true love," the coven joined her in her chant while they danced around her in rhythm to the beat of the drum.

The group continued to chant and dance until the candle had burned down to nothing.

At that point, the high priestess ended the ceremony by saying to the girl, "Take a moment to thank the universe, Pan, and the goddess Juno for working with you."

Kesia was impressed. Before getting ready for the drive back home, the group helped clean the area. The coven cleaned up so well that no one would have ever known that they were there in the first place.

On the drive back, the bus stopped at an intersection, and Kesia watched as the girl quickly got out and tossed the items in the jar into a garbage can. "What did she do that for?" Kesia asked Luna.

"It represents the modern-day crossroad. Years ago, people used to bury their wishes at a crossroads. It represents knowing that your spell is complete."

"What is a crossroad?"

Luna looked at Kesia. "There is so much to teach you. A crossroad represents a location 'between the worlds' and, as such, a site where supernatural spirits can be contacted, and paranormal events can take place."

Grabbing onto Luna's arm, Kesia said, "Hold on. I remember hearing something about a crossroad."

As she removed Kesia's hand from her now hurting arm, Luna said, "Well, don't leave me in suspense."

"Something about the blues and a guitar player. Oh ya, the guitar player made a deal and sold his soul to the Devil."

Giving Kesia a funny look, Luna said, "You're making this up. How bizarre. Kesia, I have told you before, we don't do dark magic."

"It is believed that this guy went there on purpose with the intent of furthering his career. That he waited at a crossroad reciting an ancient incantation until the Devil showed up. The myth says that the Devil tuned his guitar, and after that, the bluesman's fingers danced over the strings from then on, and he could play with a supernatural flair. But, while he sang, his voice moaned and wailed, expressing the deepest sorrows of a condemned sinner." Whispering closer to Luna's ear, Kesia said, "I don't know, Luna. Don't you think tonight was pretty bizarre?"

"Okay, I admit that there were a couple of similarities to what the high priestess had the girl do and your story of this guitar player."

"See? I told you," Kesia said.

"No. The only similarity in both cases was that a crossroad was used—a place known to contact the spirit world. Both people had a motive, but the big difference was that Old Scratch was not summoned in the love spell that the girl did."

"First off, who is Old Scratch?" Kesia asked, never having heard the name before. "And secondly, how do you know?"

"Old Scratch is a nickname for the Devil. And we never summon the Devil in Wicca. But, as you will recall, the high priestess called down Juno, the goddess of love. Kesia, I know this is all new to you, but as I said, we don't do dark magic."

Kesia sat back in her seat. *I don't know. Using a crossroad seems a little dark to me.*

Chapter 58

The spring funeral Frank planned was more than Lexi would have done. Her mom used to love it when the crocuses were out. She would have loved this funeral even though she would have never wanted anyone to bother over her death.

Hey, little sister, are you okay?

Hi Susannah, I'm holding in there. How come you are not around as much as before?

I am always with you, Lexi.

No. You barely talk to me anymore.

Lexi, you've been vibrating at a really low frequency. It is you who is not talking to me.

Susannah, how can that be? I haven't done anything differently.

It is your emotions. Your emotions control your resonating frequency and vibration. When you feel bad, angry, sad, frustrated, or in pain, your energy level shifts and creates a lower vibration.

Well, I can't help that I am in pain. I was in a car accident and was severely hurt.

True, but why did you have a car accident?

What? How would I know? I guess God wanted me to.

Lexi, God never wants someone to be in pain.

Well, he must have wanted me to be in pain because I am. And, of course, I am sad. This is mom's funeral. Not to mention that my fiancé doesn't know who I am and is with another woman. I live in someone else's house because I can't imagine living in the place where all of us used to live. Oh my God, Susannah, you are right. I am messed up.

Susannah didn't answer.

"Lexi. Lexi. Hey, are you alright?" Neo said, shaking her slightly.

Turning to Neo in the pew, she just stared at him. *He would think I was crazy if I told him I talked to my dead sister. There is an old saying that you aren't crazy talking to yourself and that answering back is a bit risky, but when you start to have a full conversation is the real problem. Yep, he would have me in a white jacket in an instant.* "Ya, I just drifted off for a second. What did I miss?"

"Frank is asking you to come up and say something about your mom."

Lexi looked around, and everyone was staring at her. "I can't."

She could see Frank nodding and motioning with his hand for her to come on up to the front of the church.

She yelled, "I can't!" and wheeled herself down the aisle and out of the church.

Redington was sitting in the back row and went after her. Finding her near a bench, he sat down and said, "I felt Susannah."

Staring at him, she started to cry.

"What did you say to her to make her cry?" Neo asked as he put an arm around Lexi.

"Nothing that is any of your business."

"If it has to do with my fiancée, then it is my business," Neo snarled.

"Fiancée!" Redington and Lexi said at the same time.

"Alexandra, is it true?" Redington asked quietly.

Looking at Neo then at Redington, she said, "I thought he was going to ask on Valentine's Day, but we never went on our date." Then, looking at Neo, she said, "Fiancée?"

Getting down on one knee, Neo took out the velvet box and opened it. "Alexandra Elizabeth Constantine, will you marry me?"

Lexi was in shock from everything that was going on. Her head started to spin.

Alexandra, you need to take this call.

"Who are you?" she yelled.

Alexandra, you need to take this call.

"In God's name, who are you!"

Neo's face turned white. "What is happening? Lexi. Lexi. Can you hear me? Call 911. She needs an ambulance."

Redington took hold of Lexi's arms and said, "In the power invested in me, I banish the demon who is talking to you!"

Lexi blinked her eyes a couple of times, then said, "What happened? Where am I?" Seeing Redington, she said, "Redington, the voice is back."

"What in God's name is going on?" Neo yelled.

Redington looked at Neo and said, "Obviously, something that you would never understand." Then, picking up Lexi, he started walking toward his car.

"Put her down this instant!" Neo demanded.

Redington just kept on walking.

"Put her down! I am her doctor, and I order you to put her down."

Redington turned his head slightly and said, "I am her friend and a cop, and I overrule you."

"I am her fiancé, and I say put her down!"

"Not yet, you're not," he said as he placed Lexi in the passenger seat of his car, then called it in to his captain.

Lexi heard Redington say, "Sir, I have Lexi Constantine. I have reason to believe that she is in danger. I request you put a restraining order on her doctor. He is trying to say that she is crazy," then she passed out.

When Lexi awoke, she was on Redington's couch. "Red."

"Ya, I'm right here."

"The voice. That is what I was trying to tell you about."

"I know. What does it say?"

"Something about a call I need to take."

"That's it? That's all it says?"

"So far. Yes."

"Is the voice here now?" he asked.

Lexi looked around but couldn't sense anything. "No, I don't think so."

"I think I should call Isabella. She might know what to do," Redington said, trying to figure out how to help Lexi.

"That might be a good idea. Isabella knows about the stuff Tamara taught us. So, yes, call her. She would understand."

Lexi watched as Redington texted Isabella.

A few moments later, he said, "Isabella said she'll be over after her daily. Whatever that means."

"After her shoot. She is shooting a film here, in New York City."

"Okay. Well, Isabella said she'd come over after that."

Chapter 59

Aias stared at the pictures of both Shirdi Sai Baba and Bhagawan Sri Sathya Sai Baba sitting on the altar.

One of the chores left to Aias was to look after the dhuni. Dhuni is the sacred, perpetually burning fire that creates the holy ash called Udi, better known as Vibhuti. The fire burns 24/7/365 in a two-foot-by-two-foot hole crafted in the floor of a small temple inside of the gurukala.

That night, Aias's job was to make sure the fire didn't go out. He was to place a piece of wood on the fire every two hours.

While he waited, he decided to read the Brihad Jabala Upanishad, one of the ancient spiritual texts stored in the temple.

Vibhuti translates to, *vi* refers to something valuable beyond imagination, and *bhuti* refers to wealth or treasure.

The sacred vibhuti ash is usually placed on the forehead as a dot, but many also place some on their heart and tongue. It represents Bhasma, "ashes," because it burns away all sins; Bhasitam, "brightened" because it increases one's spiritual splendor; Ksharam, "destruction" since it removes danger; and Raksha, "protector" for it is an armor against the plotting of evil spirits.

Looking up for a moment at the burning fire, Aias then kept on reading the story about the power of vibhuti. Once upon a time, a devotee of the Lord had to pass through a known haunted woodland. Scared for his safety, he applied some ash from a burned tree and prayed for protection. Unbeknownst to him, this tree provided shelter for Sai Baba years earlier. Walking quickly through the forest, he almost stumbled into a large hole in the ground as he heard groans and shouts. Even though he was scared for his life, his curiosity got the better of him, and he peered in. The minute he did, all the groaning and screaming stopped.

Thinking his imagination got the better of him, he turned to walk on, but as soon as he took his first step, the shouting started again. So, he moved back and peeked in again, only to be met by absolute silence. He repeated this action several times, with the same result.

Thoroughly confused, he called down, "Hello! Anybody down there?"

No answer.

Deciding that the hole was the story behind the haunted forest, he decided to walk away from it for good this time.

As he did, he heard a voice, "Sir! Please do not go away! This is the hole that leads to hell. We are all suffering here. It is your presence that gives us relief."

Astonished, the man asked, "How is it that my presence gives you comfort? I am no one special."

"Sir, every time you look down into the hole, a sprinkle of ash falls inside from your forehead! The ash gives us great relief."

"Ash? What is so special about it that gives you relief?"

"It is vibhuti. You must have used some ash from the tree that Sai Baba blessed."

The man bent over the hole and rubbed his forehead, and said, "I gift you all that I have. But, for now, I am the one truly blessed. I have been given the knowledge of always passing through this forest knowing that I am forever safe."

Holy ash. Aias bilocated to a Catholic church and witnessed the sign of a cross being traced with repentance ash on a parishioner's forehead as the priest said, "Remember that you are dust, and to dust, you shall return." Aias heard someone in the church whisper to a child that the ashes are prepared by burning palm leaves from the previous year's Palm Sunday celebration.

As Aias opened his eyes, he realized the fire had almost gone out. Hurrying to place another log onto the fire, he blew the coals to ignite the wood, but it was not igniting. Trying to think fast, he decided to tear out the last page in the book and placed it on the cooling coals. Instantly, it caught fire and created enough flames to start the piece of wood on the fire. Relieved, he sat back and took a breath.

The boy who was to relieve Aias saw what had happened. "Aias, you burned a page from the sacred book. Therefore, you must go to the guru and confess what you have done."

Startled because he had not heard him come into the temple, Aias fumbled with the book. As he could only hold on to a single page, it tore, and the rest of the book fell into the fire, bursting into flames faster than the paper had. And in front of their eyes, the book turned into ash.

"Aias, look what you have done. You will be in so much trouble. I believe you will be kicked out of here."

Fearing for his expulsion, Aias held onto the piece of paper and willed all the words in the book to materialize. Like a phoenix rising from the ashes, the book rose from the fire and landed beside Aias's feet.

With eyes as big as pancakes, the boy bent down and dusted off the book, opened it, and shuffled through the pages. Even the last page was now back in the book. Bowing to Aias, the boy backed out of the temple and yelled, "He is here!"

Aias froze in place, not sure what to do.

Moments later, many boys, the guru, and Delish came out to see what the shouting was about.

"He is here!" yelled the boy again.

Delish came to the boy and said, "What are you yelling about?"

Pointing at Aias, the boy yelled, "He is here!"

Delish looked at the roaring fire and then at Aias and said, "Good, it was his job to look after the fire."

"The fire went out!"

Delish asked Aias, "Is that true?"

Aias bowed his head and said, "There were still warm coals."

Coming over to Aias, Delish said, "How did you start the fire again?"

The boy tattled and said, "He burned the ancient spiritual text!"

Looking to the boy and then back to Aias, he asked, "Is that true?"

Aias, returning to his senses, pointed to the book in the boy's hand and said, "I replaced it."

Taking the book from the boy, Delish looked through the book. Other than being covered in a little bit of ash, it looked as it should. "Aias, go to your room. And you, young man." Taking hold of the boy who tattled, he said, "You better have a good explanation for your outburst."

Chapter 60

$\mathcal{I}$sabella was having a hard time focusing on her lines. All she could think about was Redington's text.

Lexi hears voices. I need your expertise!

She knew it had to be bad if Redington, the non-believer of all this "weird stuff," was asking for help.

"Iss, darling, focus!" the director demanded.

Isabella tapped her thymus a couple of times, also known as the happiness point. She'd learned that from Tamara. Isabella knew that tapping the area of the thymus gland three times shifts a person's energy. She remembered Tamara saying that the word thymus comes from the Greek word, *thymos*, which means "life energy." In Chinese Medicine, the thymus gland controls the body's meridian system. Its role is in keeping a person's life-force energy vibrating at a higher frequency, and tapping the thymus gland can increase a person's strength and vitality. *I sure miss you, Tamara.* "Bill," Isabella said to her director. "I need a break. We have been working on this nonstop for weeks."

Looking at her, he said, "Do you know how much it costs me each day? We have to get this film finished." Looking at Isabella, he said, "Everyone, take five. Wait!" Looking at his watch, he said, "Might as well take lunch. Meet back here in an hour and a half." Looking at Isabella, he said, "Happy?"

She faked a smile. *A…hole.*

The film had been going well. It was sure to be a box-office hit.

Hurrying, Isabella texted Redington, On my way.

She used the company helicopter to fly her to Redington's. Shortly after, she was ringing up to his condo.

"Thanks for coming, Isabella. I didn't know who else to call," Red said as he let her in.

She walked past Redington and sat down beside Lexi, saying, "I needed a break anyway. Okay, I only have an hour so let's make this quick. Lexi, what is going on?"

"I keep hearing this creepy voice."

"What does it say exactly? Lexi, it is important to tell me the exact words."

"It says, 'Alexandra, you have to take this call.'"

"That's the exact words?"

"Oh, wait. No. It said, 'Alexandra, you need to take this call,'" Lexi repeated, changing the "have to" to "need to."

"You need to take this call?" Isabella repeated.

"Yes. That is what it keeps saying."

"When was the first time you heard it?" Isabella asked, trying to figure out what was going on.

"Right before my car accident."

"That was months ago," Isabella said. "Why didn't you tell me?"

"You were busy filming your movie. So, I didn't want to bother you."

"I am never too busy for you, Lexi. You should have called."

"I know."

Isabella thought for a moment. *What would Tamara do?* "Have you just heard it, or have you seen it too?"

"I heard it here, in Redington's place, but when I ran outside, I thought I saw the Devil."

"The Devil?"

"Yes, the Devil. And he asked me if I was okay."

"Lexi, the Devil asked if you were okay?" Isabella said, shocked that a dark entity would care how she was feeling.

Listening to the conversation, Redington started to pace.

Isabella had another thought. "What did Susannah say about the voice?"

"I didn't ask her. She hasn't been around lately."

"She hasn't been around lately?" Isabella repeated, feeling like a parrot.

"Well, she said it was me that wasn't vibrating at a high enough frequency to hear her."

"Oh, that makes more sense," Isabella replied.

"It does?" Redington asked.

Nodding, Isabella said, "Yes. Lexi has had a lot of negative drama lately."

"That's an understatement," Lexi said.

"Negative energy attracts negative energy," Isabella said to Redington.

"I thought two negatives equal a positive," Redington said innocently.

"I am assuming that you are serious, Red," Isabella said, unsure. "Only in math, not in energy."

"Note taken," Red said. "So, why does negative energy attract negative energy?"

"Think about it, Red. Take yourself, for instance. You know when you are feeling normal and when you are feeling sick, right?"

"For sure," he agreed.

"You also know when you are feeling better than normal."

"Is there such a thing as better than normal?" Redington asked, not believing what he'd just heard.

"Of course, there is. Imagine the feeling you experienced with your first romantic relationship. Maybe you fell head over heels or were completely swept away. New love is euphoric. Everything in life seems to be existing on cloud nine. It all boils down to dopamine."

"Dopamine? You're talking about the chemical your brain produces, right?" Redington asked, confirming that he was following what she was saying.

"Yes, the love chemical. Not only does dopamine increase in your system when you feel love, but so do your oxytocin levels, creating feelings of attachment, safety, and trust. In addition, lasting love is consistently linked to lower levels of stress, and happiness equals a healthier body, mind, and soul."

Redington rubbed his chin. "So, what I am hearing is that when you have love, you are healthier, and when you have stress, your body doesn't manufacture these chemicals?"

"Exactly. Lexi has had so much stress lately that her body isn't producing these essential chemicals, and so, she becomes more depressed, and then her body doesn't heal properly."

"But what does that have to do with the Devil?" Redington asked.

"It refers to personal demons. Unconscious thoughts have more power than a person realizes," Isabella said, knowing all too well how emotions can affect a person's behavior.

"So, the voice she is hearing isn't the Devil, but rather her own demons?" Redington asked, trying to make sure he was following Isabella's train of thought.

Isabella answered, "Well, I am not God, and spirits don't speak to me, but…"

"I thought that Erland speaks to you?"

"He does, but he is not a ghost. He is bilocating from Alfheim. His soul lives in a body, just not here on Earth."

"You do know how crazy that sounds, right?" Redington said.

"Hey, at one time, people believed the Earth was flat," Isabella said. *If he thinks that is crazy, just wait until he finds out the truth about all the spiritual gifts granted by Spirit*, she thought, remembering her son's gifts.

Lexi interrupted both of them by saying, "No matter what you two believe, I heard a real voice telling me to take the call."

Isabella and Redington looked at her.

Isabella's timer went off on her phone. "Oh, I've got to run. The show must go on. I'll call you guys tomorrow and tell you if I come up with any ideas."

Chapter 61

"You have learned about the chakras, and now it is time to learn about Nāḍī," Delish told the students once everyone was seated.

Aias was feeling a bit homesick today and missed his mom. She had been busy filming her new movie and was tired at night, so when he bilocated, she was usually sleeping since there was about a ten-hour difference between their time zones.

Aias had to concentrate as Delish started to talk. "Similar in action to what the Asians call meridians, in traditional Indian medicine we call them Nāḍī. The translation is tube, pipe, nerve, blood vessel, or pulse. No matter what name you call it, both spiritual knowledge and life-force energy flow through these channels to the physical body, the subtle body, and the causal body. There are seventy-two thousand nadis that channel prana energy to every cell. When these channels flow freely, we have vitality and health."

Listening to Delish, Aias forgot about being homesick.

"There are three principal nadis that run from the base of the spine to the head. They are the *Sushumna* in the center—which lies dormant until you open it, the *Ida* on the left—feminine, moon energy, and the *Pingala* on the right—masculine, solar energy. On the physical level, these two channels correspond with the sympathetic and parasympathetic nervous systems. As the energy travels upward, the Ida and Pingala switch sides at each chakra, like two intertwined snakes on the caduceus, then up over the crown chakra and back down, exiting the body through the nostrils," Delish informed the students.

Aias touched his nose, thinking about the energy escaping.

"See if you can tell which nostril is more open," Delish said to the boys. "Close one nostril while you breathe, and then the other, which one is more open?"

Aias used a finger and closed his right nostril. His left was a little plugged. Then he switched and closed his left nostril and found that his right was clear.

After a moment or two, Delish said, "When we are healthy, the breath switches nostrils regularly, about every ninety minutes. When we are ill, the time between switching is longer, maybe every few hours. Interestingly enough, it has been said that when death is near, the breath does not switch nostrils at all."

Aias stopped breathing for a second to test what happened, but the urge to breathe was too strong.

"A person is continually balancing between the Ida and Pingala energies. Ultimately the goal is to unblock these nadis to bring liberation. Unfortunately, most people live and die using only the Ida and Pingala energies, never experiencing the power of Sushumna. But once the prana energies enter into Sushumna, and the breath flows through both the nostrils, you will attain a new kind of balance, an inner balance that lets you dare to scale the peaks of consciousness."

Being a sponge for knowledge, Aias couldn't help himself and put up his hand.

"Yes, Aias."

"How do we achieve Sushumna?"

"First, you must master Ida and Pingala."

"How do we do that?" Aias asked.

"Hatha Yoga," Delish stated as a fact.

"Why do we want to practice yoga?" Aias asked.

"To invigorate the channel, to clear obstructions, and to allow the free flow of prana—life-force energy."

"That seems important," Aias said.

Delish continued with his lecture, "We are going to try a simple form of yoga. I want you all to spread out and to lie down as if you are in your beds."

Delish waited for the boys to find space, then said, "Turn so that you are lying on your right side. This position will clear your left nostril. In addition, it will activate the Ida energy channel and right hemisphere of the brain."

Aias put up a hand.

"Yes, Aias," Delish said, never losing patience.

"What does Hatha mean?"

"*Ha* means sun, and *tha* means moon. The whole purpose of Hatha yoga is to balance the Ida and Pingala channels."

"Why is balancing these two channels so important?" Aias asked, needing to know.

"Not only do they bring harmony, balance, health, and well-being, but you cannot achieve Sushumna unless these two channels are balanced and both nostrils are open at the same time."

"Yoga can achieve this?"

"Yes, yoga is vital in unblocking these two channels," Delish answered. "Now turn so that you are lying on your left side. This position will clear your right nostril. In addition, it will activate the Pingala energy channel and left hemisphere of the brain."

Aias put up a hand.

"Yes, Aias," Delish said.

"What blocks these two channels?"

Good question. "Usually stress, but nadis can also get blocked because of toxicity in the body, an unhealthy lifestyle, or physical and mental trauma."

Instead of putting up his hand, Aias just asked, "What happens to our bodies when these nadis are blocked?"

"When the Ida nadi is blocked, you might experience cold, depression, low mental energy, sluggish digestion, and a blocked left nostril. Whereas when the Pingala nadi is blocked, you might experience heat, a quick temper, irritation, itching body, dry skin or throat, excessive appetite, excessive physical or sexual energy, and a blocked right nostril."

Aias smiled at the words "sexual energy." He had heard some of the boys talking about it a few days ago.

Delish said, "Okay, everyone, sit up. We are going to practice alternate nostril breathing techniques. Sit comfortably with your spine erect and shoulders relaxed."

Delish watched as the boys went into the new position.

"Place your left hand on your left knee, palm up, and do Chin Mudra by gently touching the tips of your thumb and index finger together. At the same time, place the tip of the index finger and middle finger of your right hand in between your eyebrows."

Delish waited a second for the boys to follow.

"Now, your ring finger and little finger are going to control your left nostril, and the thumb will control your right nostril. Touch each side to get used to the movement."

Delish waited again for the boys to follow his instructions.

"Now, exhale completely and then press your thumb down on the right nostril closing it and start to breathe in and out gently through the left nostril. Keep your eyes closed throughout and continue taking long, deep, smooth breaths without any force or effort."

Delish waited five minutes, then said, "Remove your right thumb from the right nostril, and after your exhale, close the left nostril by gently pressing it with your ring and little fingers. Breathing in and out effortlessly from the right nostril."

Delish watched the boys again and waited five more minutes. "You have now completed the first round."

Aias asked, "How many rounds are there?"

"Usually nine, but no matter how many rounds you do, always end the last one by finishing with an exhale on your left side."

"Is what we just did Hatha yoga?" Aias asked.

Delish told all the boys, not just directing his answer at Aias, "It is the start to Hatha yoga. First, you need to understand breath before I can teach you yoga poses."

"Why are the poses important to learn in yoga?" Aias asked.

"After you understand breath, the poses are to help improve balance, flexibility, and strength. All three aspects are vital to longevity. Finally, each yoga class ends with a meditation to connect your body with your mind and soul."

"Yoga seems an essential part of health," Aias said.

"It is a yogi's way of life to achieve Sushumna and bring with it the kundalini energy."

"What is that?" Aias asked.

"Next class Aias, for now, practice what I have taught you, knowing that this simple breathing technique will unblock the Ida and Pingala channels, induce a better night's sleep, increase your oxygen intake, and improve your heart's health."

Chapter 62

"What do we get to do tonight?" Kesia asked Luna.

"We are meeting with the women of our coven. The high priestess is going to teach us about the divine feminine energy that exists in all of us."

"I wonder what that is?" Kesia asked, now interested even more than before.

As Kesia hopped into Luna's mom's car, Luna answered, "It's something about spiritual liberation."

Today's Esbat was held in a different location, in one of the other witches' backyards.

Outside under the stars, the high priestess was sitting on a white wicker chair—with a thick purple, crescent moon patterned cushion. Wrapped around her was a loose-weave chunky knit wool blanket so she wouldn't get cold,

which was doubtful since there were a few
outdoor patio heaters and a fire pit.

Kesia had a seat in a lounger and listened to
the high priestess.

"Traditionally, tantra comes from the esoteric
arms of Hinduism and Buddhism, but first, I
must tell you the most epic love story. It is about
Parvati, the goddess of fertility, love, beauty,
harmony, marriage, and children. The wife of
the Hindu god Shiva, and mother to Ganesha
and Kartikeya."

Kesia shifted on the lounger to get more
comfortable.

"Once upon a time, there lived many gods and
goddesses of the Hindu Pantheon. In particular,
there were three brothers, Brahma the creator,
Vishnu, the preserver, and Shiva, the god of
destruction who was broken-hearted from the
loss of his first wife, Sati, the avatar of Shakti."

"I adore a good love story," Kesia whispered
to Luna.

"You see, Shiva and Sati were married
without her father's blessing, and her father
disowned her and didn't invite them to a grand
party. So, to Shiva's disapproval, Sati went to
the party anyway, unwelcomed. Her father was
so furious that he humiliated her by mocking
Shiva in public. So, to be free of her father, Sati
set herself on fire and burned to death. Shiva's
wrath was like no other, and all were destroyed,

but the pain was unbearable, and so he removed himself from life."

"How sad," Kesia said out loud.

The high priestess kept on with her story, "One day, Brahma looked around the universe and realized that Shiva was not playing his part in the drama of everyday life. So, when Shiva was detained from life, Brahma went to the Divine Feminine and asked her for help because he needed his brother back to normal so that the cosmos would be in balance once again. So, the Divine Feminine, the MahaDevi—Mother Goddess—told Brahma that she would take the form of a woman that would entice even the likes of Shiva. So, the Divine Feminine became his first wife's reincarnation, Parvati, and eventually won Shiva's heart."

"Didn't see that one coming," Kesia whispered to Luna.

The high priestess smiled, hearing Kesia's words, but continued with her story as if she hadn't. "MahaDevi, the Divine Feminine, is the power of the universe. Another name she goes by is Shakti, which means power. It is the source of our creative power, spiritual gifts, and divine feminine energy. Through practices such as kundalini yoga, Hatha yoga, and tantra, we can access this power."

Kesia sat up straighter on the lounger. *Spiritual gifts.*

"Shakti is pure energy, untamed, unchecked, and chaotic. To awaken the kundalini, we are going to use a ritual. First, though, I want you to imagine that your root chakra is Parvati or Sati, you choose, and your brow chakra is Shiva. Sati loves Shiva and will do anything in her power to be with him again. So, she uses her inner power, her inner fire, and ascends toward him. As she rises, she must go through each chakra to reach pure consciousness, Lord Shiva himself."

The high priestess stood up and waved her hand, sprinkling some magic dust on the fire. The flames became a multitude of colors. Then, raising her arms to the moon, she called out, "I call upon the triple goddesses, the maiden, the mother, and the old crone. Come to our aid and awaken our inner fire. Oh, rise my mighty snake, rise, igniting our creative energy to join with pure consciousness."

Then she started to chant, "The *'I am'* energy is connected to my body, and the snake of the rising kundalini intertwines within me. Rise, my snake, rise! It is now in this witching hour of the hooded and holy to bloom your lotus petals. As the *'I am'* energy is rising, it also cleans and clears a sacred path. Rise, my snake, and ascend into the brilliance of your blossom. *'I feel'* as you rise, the bond of my goddess, my sisters, and my tribe. Thou have given me sisterhood, and as the *'I feel'* energy is rising, it also cleans and clears a sacred path. Rise, my snake, and ascend into the brilliance of your blossom. *'I do'* as you rise. It explodes inner confidence, capable of accomplishing anything. As the *'I do'* energy is rising, it also cleans and clears a sacred path. Rise, my snake, ascend into the brilliance of your blossom. *'I love'* expands my heart, and as so above, so below. As the *'I love'* energy is rising, it also cleans and clears a sacred path. Rise, my snake, ascend into the brilliance of your blossom. *'I speak'* with a straight tongue, for you have healed my forked tongue. Your glory now blesses my words. As the *'I speak'* energy is rising, it also cleans and clears a sacred path. Rise, my snake, ascend into the brilliance of your blossom. *'I see'* the truth. Be still, oh my soul! That the spell may dissolve as the wands are upraised, and the ages revolve. As the *'I see'* energy is rising, it also cleans and clears a sacred path. Rise, my snake, ascend into the brilliance of your blossom. Ah me! In the splendor of your ravening storm that encompasses thee and wraps thee in your whirl of form. Behold! In your beauty, how joyous thou art, oh snake that caresses the crown of my heart! Behold! We are one. How blessed am I to accomplish the *'I know.'* I awaken to the glory and power of Spirit! I thank you, triple goddesses, for assisting us in awakening our kundalini, our inner fire, our spiritual gifts."

Kesia wasn't sure what to expect, but she wasn't ready for what happened next. As the high priestess chanted, Kesia had her eyes closed and had gone into a light meditative state. She imagined that the three ladies were flowing softly and gently as they danced around a pole, going higher and higher. The pole being her spinal column, and the ladies, she assumed were the triple goddesses. Kesia could sense the kundalini energy rising through each of her chakras: the I am—root chakra, the I feel—sacral chakra, the I do—solar plexus chakra, the I love—heart chakra, the I speak—throat chakra, and the I see—brow chakra, but just before it reached the I know—crown chakra, it felt like a warm tingling feeling that ran from her core up through her body and blissfully exploded through her forehead. She had never felt anything so exhilarating in her life.

As Kesia left this evening's celebration with the invigorating feelings still lingering, energizing her, she felt enlightened and even closer to the Creator than she ever had before.

On the way home, Kesia asked Luna, "How do you think she made the fire change color?"

"Oh, that is easy. I'll email you the recipe."

A bit later, after arriving home, Kesia's phone tinged to alert her that she had a new text message.

She read it…

Here is the recipe for an amazing "Ooooh-aaaah" effect:

- *Potassium chloride: Makes a purple flame.*
- *Magnesium sulfate: Makes a white flame.*

- *Strontium chloride: Makes a red flame.*
- *Copper chloride: Makes a blue flame.*
- *Lithium chloride: Makes a pink flame.*
- *Copper sulfate: Makes a green flame.*
- *Sodium chloride: Makes an orange flame.*
- *Use iron filings for gold sparks.*
- *Sprinkle some sugar on your campfire for small sparks.*
- *A little bit of regular flour will create a flash flame.*
- *Use powdered coffee creamer for sparkly flashes.*
- *Use powdered aluminum or magnesium shavings for silver sparks.*

You can throw the chemicals into the fire for a short color burst, but if you want the color to last longer, do this...

How-To:

- *Safely, melt some candle wax in an old pot—double boiler or a large pot that the second pot can sit in. Place an inch or more of water in a large pot and bring to boil while the wax is melting in the second smaller pot. Have a fire extinguisher ready in case of a worst-case scenario. Wax is highly flammable.*

- *In a paper cup, fill it with a ¼ inch of your chosen chemical. Mixing chemicals will produce different colors.*
- *Pour the melted wax into the cup.*
- *Stir the mixture and make sure that all the chemicals are coated with wax.*
- *Let the mixture cool for at least 2-3 hours.*
- *When you are ready for the colored flames, you can either throw the entire cup into the fire or cut it into smaller pieces and toss them into the fire.*

I hope you enjoyed tonight's Esbat. I know I did.

Luv, Luna

P.S. By the way, some of the kundalini symptoms include:

- *A deep sense of purpose and destiny.*
- *The urge to make life changes.*
- *Experiencing a heightened awareness of intuition.*

You may go through:

- *Physical and emotional changes like sleep disturbances, anxiety, surges of energy, and shaking (all of these symptoms can be normal, as your body shifts to the new energy).*

- *Some people have a bad experience and feel like they had a bad drug trip, or even a psychotic break, depression, or even changes in their identity (Hopefully not in your case. If so, call me right away).*

P.P.S. Look up Kundalini Shakti or Kundalini Vidya.

Chapter 63

$\mathscr{D}$elish started the class by saying, "There is a myth about a place in the netherworld called Naga Lokas, which is filled with dazzling palaces, beautifully ornamented with precious gems. The Nagas, half-man half-snake demigods, now live there. Naga translation means serpent, and at one time, they lived on Earth. They could assume both forms, wholly human and wholly serpentine."

Now, the equivalent age of twenty-one, Aias's eyes went big as he heard the story. He had a question and put up his hand.

"Yes, Aias."

"What is the difference between the netherworld and the underworld?"

"Really, nothing. They are the same." Delish then continued his lesson, "When the Naga became too populous on earth, Brahma demoted the Nagas to the netherworld—Hell, any place of darkness, or eternal suffering—and commanded them to bite only the truly evil or those destined to die."

Aias tried to put his hand up, but Delish gave him a look and continued his story. "Before they left Earth, the Naga demigods mated with the indigenous people. Their offspring are called Nage and considered superhumans. The great temples of Angkor in Cambodia are said to have been built by Naga descendants. Interestingly, Nagas were ruled by queens, not kings."

Aias was too absorbed in the story to ask any more questions.

"You all are old enough to understand kundalini energy. The Sanskrit word, *kundalini*, means 'coiled snake,' and there is no Indian temple without the symbol of a serpent. *Kundalini* is the potential energy coiled up at the base of the spine in the base chakra. This energy is an invisible, dormant, holy power, and when awakened, it pierces through the other six chakras and activates them. Kundalini works to uncoil the snake," Delish said to the boys.

Aias put up his hand.

"Yes, Aias."

"Why is this energy represented by a snake?"

"The reason for this symbolic status is that when celestial beings enter our dimension of existence, it is believed that they take the form of a snake."

Asking his next question, Aias inquired, "Why a snake?"

"Because a snake sheds its skin through sloughing. On a spiritual level, a snake symbolizes rebirth, transformation, and immortality, and on a physical level, the snake symbolizes fertility, creative life-force energy, and healing."

"Is that why Lord Shiva is always shown with a serpent?" Aias asked.

"The snake represents the Ahamkara—ego—also known as pride. One must shed their *pride* to attain enlightenment."

Aias put his hand up again.

"Yes, Aias."

"Why does one have to shed their pride? Is pride not a good thing?"

"Pride is the quality of having an excessively high opinion of oneself or one's importance. The word to be noted is 'excessively.'"

"I still don't understand," Aias said honestly.

"Pride is considered to be a cosmic arrogance. I am pretty sure it was St. Augustine who said, 'It was pride that changed angels into devils; it is humility that makes men as angels.'"

"How will I know if I have too much pride?" Aias asked.

"People with pride are boastful, insincere, impatient, self-absorbed, conceited, believe that their way is the only way, and are always searching for recognition," Delish answered.

"What am I supposed to feel if not pride when I accomplish something?"

"Confidence."

"Confidence," Aias repeated.

"Yes, confidence does not need to feel anything. You do not need recognition or a pat on the back. As Yogis, our job is to surpass the mundane emotions that hold us back from enlightenment, but we are getting off-topic. Today's class is about working toward the highest perception, opening the brow chakra or third eye. The presence of the snake marks Shiva's forehead."

Aias tried to listen without putting his hand up.

Delish continued the class. "Kundalini is the ultimate life-force energy. It is the source of our creative power and spiritual gifts. In India, a yogi's fundamental goal is to cleanse and prepare their body, mind, and soul to safely experience a kundalini awakening."

Aias put his hand up.

"Yes, Aias."

"Is kundalini poisonous?"

Delish almost laughed but answered by saying, "As a very wise Swami said, 'Before awakening the kundalini, you must have purity of body, purity of the nadis, purity of mind, and purity of the intellect.'"

"So, it is poisonous," Aias blurted out.

"Not poisonous but without a master, the awakening of the kundalini can be very dangerous to attempt, for instead of entering the Sushumna nadi, it is likely to force itself into the Ida or the Pingala nadi, causing immense havoc in the body and mind. Moreover, such premature awakening is burdened with dangers of self-deception as well as the misuse of the spiritual gifts."

Aias put his hand up.

"Yes, Aias."

"Why do we want to wake the serpent?" Aias asked, now scared of this energy.

"For spiritual enlightenment," Delish answered.

"I don't understand why it is dangerous?"

"Once kundalini is activated, the energy doesn't slither up and around the spinal cord slowly through the chakras. Instead, it usually moves at lightning speed, not waiting for anything. So, if a person hasn't first cleansed their body, mind, and soul, and the energy hits a blockage, the powerful kundalini energy can rip through, leaving behind chaos and destruction."

"As in?" Aias challenged.

Delish thought for a second. "As in a dramatic spiritual transformation, an awakening that you weren't ready for. It can cause nerve problems and a burning sensation. It can cause mental breakdowns and insanity. And worst of all, it can cause the pursuit of more pleasure and status. So many people end up chasing the kundalini energy high, trying to feed their self-image—since it's an intoxicating, euphoric feeling. Remember though, *pride* as in delight belongs to the ego, the arch-enemy of spiritual practice."

"How are you going to teach us kundalini safely?" Aias asked, knowing that eventually, Delish was going to teach them.

"In the West, to gain enlightenment and spiritual development, it is through ritual, while we use meditation and yoga in the East."

Chapter 64

*T*errified of the voice, Lexi couldn't stay in Red's condo. She knew she couldn't go back and stay at Neo's parents' place after the incident at the funeral, so while she looked for a new place to live, she decided to rent a hotel room.

Once settled in the hotel, she was exhausted from the last few days and lay down on the bed to take a nap. Shortly after, she was dreaming that she was in an oasis. She could hear the birds singing and could feel the warmth of the wind blowing against her skin. She could see lush trees of all varieties and smell the glorious fragrance of many flowers. *This must be heaven?*

To her delight, in this fantasy, she lived joyfully in this blissful sanctuary with the man of her dreams, and where anything and everything that she could ever have desired was instantly provided. A heavenly paradise that is what she thought this place was.

As in any dream, time was distorted, and this dream was no different. It seemed that she and her lover had been living there for what seemed like an eternity.

Intuitively, she knew that she and her mate were there to take care of the land, and it was their job to make sure that all the animals had names.

All her days were blissful, until… as she was taking her daily walk, she came upon an animal that she had not met before under the forbidden tree. Talking to it as she did to all the animals to make them feel calmer, she said, "What shall we name you?"

Not expecting an answer, for no other animal had talked to her before, it said, "Snake."

Not afraid, for she knew that no harm could come to her in this paradise, she sat down and said, "Why would you want to be called that name? We could call you something nicer like Serpent or maybe Viper. Yes, Viper would be a good name."

"You can name me whatever you like. Viper is as good a name as any."

Hearing the snake speak, Lexi thought the sound came from behind the tree, so she got up to look and found a man. He looked similar to her partner but not identical. They had different colored hair and height. "Who are you, and why were you hiding?"

The man came out from behind the tree and said, "I thought that you would prefer that I pretend to be an animal, so I threw my voice like a ventriloquist and created the illusion that the snake could talk."

Lexi's partner ran up and said, "Devil."

Looking at her partner, she said, "No, I don't think the snake looks like a Devil. I like the name Viper." Looking at the new man, she said, "What name do you like?"

Lexi watched as the man picked the fruit from the tree and gave it to her. Ignoring her question, he said, "A gift for being so kind."

Before her partner could stop her, she took a bite and said, "Thank you. This is the most decadent fruit that I have ever tasted." Then, passing it to her partner, she said, "You must try this."

Being curious about what it tasted like but too scared, fearing that it might kill them, he had never taken a bite before today. Seeing that his mate had not died, he took a bite.

A moment later, Lexi's eyes started to blur, and everything looked different. Paradise looked different. What she knew and believed life to be, was no more. All of her childhood memories came flooding back. Her mom and dad were smiling at her, her older sister, Susannah, was tickling her and making her laugh. Her first kiss, her first everything, came flowing into her memory like a river after a storm.

When did it all change? When did I know that evil existed? It wasn't because of my recent car accident. No, it was way before that. It wasn't when my mom died. No, it was way before that. It wasn't when I found out that I couldn't have children. No, it was way before that. It wasn't when Edward left me for another woman. No, it was way before that. So, when did it all change? Think Lexi, think. It wasn't because of all the crazy, woo-woo adventures. No, it was way before that. Oh my God! I know exactly when it changed. It was right after Susannah died. That is when I found out that there was a Heaven and a Hell, and for that matter, all the in-between places. It all changed when my eyes opened, and the truth was told. Meaning that even though my eyes were open and I was conscious, I could not see the spiritual truth right in front of me. It was when I knew for a fact that I hadn't imagined all the metaphysical woo-woo stuff. That all the paranormal abilities were actually the spiritual gifts granted by Spirit.

Snapping out of the dream, Lexi knew why she was being punished. She had metaphorically taken a bite from the Tree of Knowledge, granting her *Omniscience*. Consuming the tree's fruit gave the eater, her, the knowledge of everything—and now evil was upon her.

Sitting up in her hotel bed, she focused her attention on the voice she had heard at

Redington's. *I am not afraid of you! What do you want?*

Alexandra, it's about time you took my call, but unfortunately, you are no longer ready. Your vitality is too low. You need to heal first, and then when you can handle what I have to say, contact me again.

Chapter 65

"What kind of magic do we get to learn today?" Kesia asked Luna.

"As you know, magic is usually performed at the smaller gatherings that we call Esbats, which coincide with the phases of the moon. So since today isn't an Esbat, we are going to practice individual spiritual development here at my place."

Kesia sat beside Luna on her bed and then asked, "How do we do that?"

"I am going to teach you the *I Forgives*."

"How is this going to develop my spiritualism?" Kesia asked, not understanding.

"Helping the world and others by doing rituals and spells is great, but you also have to look after yourself."

"I don't feel sick or in need of any help," Kesia told Luna.

"As you probably know, a body needs to heal physically, and a mind needs to heal emotionally or mentally, but did you know that a soul needs to heal spiritually?"

"No, but how is doing the 'I Forgives' going to help Lexi? She still is not walking and is hardly even talking to me. I want to help her, not me."

"Let me put it to you this way. To help someone else heal, you have to be at a higher vibration than they are."

"So, you are telling me that Lexi is at a higher vibration than I am?"

"Possibly. Doing the 'I Forgives' can't hurt anything, but learning how to do them will raise your vibratory rate."

Feeling like she was being made to do something that she didn't think she needed, yet wanting to learn more about the Wiccan ways, Kesia said, "Fine. How do I do it?"

"There are three phrases that you must say for your body, mind, and soul to shift your energy. I forgive *myself* for something, I forgive *someone else* for something, and I *allow someone to forgive me* for something."

"It's that simple?"

"Yes. Let's start with an obvious one. Repeat after me. I forgive Luna for making me do this stupid exercise."

Kesia looked at Luna suspiciously but repeated, "I forgive Luna for making me say what she just said."

"No. Try again. I forgive Luna for making me do this stupid exercise."

"I did."

"No, you changed the words."

"Fine. I forgive Luna for making me do this stupid exercise."

"Great. Now take a breath and keep your lips apart when you blow out. Imagine you are blowing the energy into a cosmic garbage can."

Kesia took a breath and blew.

"Great. Now, repeat, I forgive myself for making this exercise harder than it has to be."

"What? I am not."

Ignoring Kesia's tone of voice, Luna said again, "I forgive myself for making this exercise harder than it has to be."

"Oh, brother. Fine. I forgive myself for making this exercise harder than it has to be."

"Great. Don't forget to take a breath."

Kesia blew hard.

"Now, this time, say, I allow Luna to forgive me for making this exercise hard on her."

"I am sorry. I didn't mean to make you feel bad, Luna."

"Kesia, I know you will get this exercise right. Just copy what I said. I allow Luna to forgive me for making this exercise hard on her."

Kesia repeated word for word what Luna had just said.

"Great. You did one set of the 'I Forgives.'"

"I did? But I don't understand how it works," Kesia said honestly.

"Just remember there are three parts to the I Forgives: You must forgive your*self*, forgive *someone else*, and have that *person forgive you*?"

Trying to understand this spiritual exercise, Kesia repeated what Luna had just said, "I must forgive myself, other people, and have them forgive me."

"Yes. You got it."

"But how many 'I Forgives' do I have to say?"

"As many as needed. You'll know when you are done because you won't be able to think of anything else to say."

"That's it. That's all I have to do?"

"It is harder than you think. When the topic matters, you might choose to say, I give myself permission to forgive..."

"Okay, let me try one on my own."

"Sure," Luna said as she sat back and leaned on the wall.

Kesia thought of a topic to do the "I Forgives" on. "Okay, I got it. I forgive God for letting Lexi hurt herself."

"Good, now remember to take a breath and blow it into the imaginary cosmic garbage can."

"I forgive God for not letting our spells work on Lexi." Kesia took a breath. "I forgive Lexi for forgetting about me." Kesia took a breath. "I forgive my mom for—" Kesia couldn't finish. She just started to cry.

Luna waited a moment and then said, "Spiritual cleansing can be very freeing. Your subconscious mind knows what it needs to heal. For example, you started talking about Lexi, but you ended up forgiving your mom."

Kesia wiped her tears away. "I don't know why I said that. I don't have anything to forgive her for."

"You must, or you wouldn't have said it. Let me help you. Please, repeat after me. I forgive my mom for… just say whatever is the first thing that comes to your mind."

Kesia took a breath and said, "I forgive my mom for almost getting killed." Kesia took another breath. "I forgive my uncle for killing my friend." Kesia took a couple of breaths for that one. "I forgive my ancestors for creating drama around my tarot cards." Then, after taking another breath, she said, "I forgive myself for feeling responsible for Tamara's disappearance, Lexi's accident, and Edward becoming a walk-in."

Luna interrupted, "You have to take a breath with each one, individually."

"Oh, okay. I allow Tamara to forgive my family for the horror over the tarot cards." Kesia took a breath. "I forgive. No, I allow myself to forgive Julian for all the terrible things he did." Kesia took a bigger breath. "I forgive myself for being so young and not being able to stop the chaos." Again, Kesia took a breath. She felt much better getting the truth out of all the terrible emotions that were pent-up inside her.

Luna said, "Good job. Now practice this exercise at home. Do the 'I Forgives' every day until you have nothing left to forgive. And if you get bored with just saying the words add some tapping to the exercise."

"How do I do that?"

"While you are saying the 'I Forgives,' tap the side of your index finger, just below the nail."

"Either finger?"

"Yep, either one works. This spot is part of the Large Intestine Meridian and helps to release whatever it is you are working on while you are breathing out."

"Seems easy enough."

"Not everything in life has to be hard," Luna said as she was tapping the side of her index finger. *Right. A good one for me to release. Not everything in life has to be hard.*

Chapter 66

A Few Days Later

"How superstitious are you?" Luna asked Kesia.

"What do you mean? I don't think I am superstitious."

Not giving up, Luna asked, "What about your family? Do they believe in any superstitions?"

"Ah, I guess my mom does. I remember that she used to have a horseshoe nailed to her door."

"Do you know why horseshoes are considered good luck?" Luna questioned Kesia.

"To ward off evil spirits?" Kesia said, guessing the obvious.

"Actually, it was to ward off witches."

"That doesn't make much sense. I can't believe that witches are afraid of horses?" Kesia said, trying to figure out the connection.

"They must be."

"Why?"

"Because they ride broomsticks," Luna said, laughing at her own joke. "But on a serious note, make sure that your mom has the horseshoe open side up."

"Why?"

"Since she believes that horseshoes are magical, then this way the magic will not run out."

"Seriously?"

"Yes, this time, I am serious," Luna said. "Do you know why it is bad luck to walk under a ladder?"

"Because you might have something dropped on your head."

Luna smiled then said, "It is to avoid violating the Holy Trinity by walking through the triangle formed by the wall, the ground, and the leaning ladder."

Catching on to today's lesson, Kesia said, "Hmm, I didn't know that. Interesting. What is the folklore about black cats?"

"Ah, back in the day, Europeans believed that witches could turn themselves into black cats."

"What about a four-leaf clover?" Kesia asked.

"It is believed that Eve had taken one along when she and Adam were expelled from the Garden of Eden. There is also an old folk rhyme that goes like this: 'One leaf for fame, one for wealth, one for a faithful lover, and one to bring you glorious health are in a four-leaf clover.'"

"I like that. Okay, what about the unlucky number thirteen?" Kesia said, trying to find one that Luna didn't know the answer to.

"Thirteen is unlucky because there were thirteen people seated at the last supper, and two of them ended up dying shortly after."

Trying again, Kesia asked, "Why is it bad luck to break a mirror? And not just because it is expensive or dangerous?"

Luna thought for a second and then said, "Oh ya, because it is based on the belief that a mirror could foretell the future, and breaking it would deprive man of this ability."

"Oh, that is cool. I have never heard that answer before," Kesia said as she was thinking of another old wives' tale. "Oh, I got one. How about spilling salt? Why are you supposed to throw some over your shoulder?"

"That one is easy. Leonardo da Vinci's painting of the 'Last Supper' showed Judas— second from the right—knocking a salt container on its side with his arm. His left hand is starting to raise as if he was about to throw something over his shoulder."

"No kidding, now I have to look up the painting," Kesia said, taking out her phone.

A moment later, Kesia said, "Well, look at that, spilled salt. Who would have thought to look at the small details on the painting?"

"I know, right?"

"Luna, how do you think that all of these old beliefs came to be?"

"The high priestess talked about this a while back. She said that all folklore, including that about medicine, was helpful to the sick and injured and was created to prevent misfortune of any kind. She also said that the earliest physicians were priests and that they believed that God provides a remedy for all human illnesses. As did Shakespeare in Romeo and Juliet, when he wrote, 'O! Fickle is the powerful grace that lies in herbs, plants, stones, and their true qualities: For naught so vile that on the earth doth live, but to the earth some special good doth give.' Kesia, we Wiccans follow this belief as well."

Kesia thought for a moment about what Luna had just said. "Are you saying that Wiccans follow medical folklore?"

"Take the pandemic, for instance. An old folklore belief was that the cause of all illness lies in evil winds, evil spirits, the evil eye, or black magic. Kesia, think about chemical warfare. Wouldn't you say it could be considered black magic since it can travel from person to person as easily as the wind blows?"

"I never thought about it like that. I guess that anything evil could be considered black magic."

"And even though it is an educated scientist and not a witch who can produce these weapons, its creation could be considered magical to you and me."

"Let me get this straight. Wiccans use herbs, plants, and stones to perform magical spells, just like priests of old did to help a parishioner heal?"

"Not only that, but we chant charms or *spells*—which is a Teutonic word meaning *spoken*—just as many religions chant mantras, affirmations, or prayers to create a positive outcome. Spells and charms are to bring about the desired outcome or to prevent one," Luna said before she changed the topic. "Kesia, how much do you know about hypnosis?"

"Not much. Why?"

"Did you know that for many centuries, statesmen, clergy, professional people, and the military have recognized the potency of psychic influences?"

"No."

"An Austrian doctor and mystic, Franz Anton Mesmer, knew that a superstitious person was particularly susceptible to suggestion. The power of the subconscious mind is incredible. It has been proven that words spoken can create evidence-based outcomes."

Kesia said, "I remember reading about Dr. Masaru Emoto and his rice and water crystal experiments. Wow, he sure proved what the power of a word could do." *His experiments still amaze me.*

"Ya, I watched his YouTube videos, crazy. But see, this is what I am talking about, the power of words. Talking about all this makes me believe that you are truly ready to understand the power of spells and charms."

"I thought that you were already teaching me spells."

"No, I was just performing them in front of you."

"Oh, I can't wait," Kesia said excitedly. "This is almost as exciting as our graduation next week."

"I know, right. June has arrived so fast. It is incredible how quickly our senior year has gone by," Luna said, thinking about all the new mysteries that her future would hold.

Chapter 67

"Aias, have you said your goodbyes?" Delish asked as Aias walked toward the front gates of the gurukula.

Aias turned to look at the big banyan tree and said, "I am going to miss this place." Then, gripping Delish's upper arm, he said, "I am going to miss you the most, my friend."

"Aias, you have installed in me a new level of belief. I am so grateful that Acharya Shri Sharma invited you to attend our school." Then, holding out his hand, he said to Aias, "It has been a pleasure teaching you, my friend. Who would have ever guessed that a one-year-old child could come to us looking twelve and then ten months later leave us looking twenty-one?" Shaking his hand again, Delish said, "Good luck on all your new adventures."

Aias leaned in and hugged Delish. Then, letting go of him, he got into the taxi waiting to take him to the airport.

His mom, Isabella, had bought him a first-class airplane ticket for the flight to New York City.

Not long after sitting in his seat, the flight attendant asked if he would like an alcoholic beverage.

"No, thank you, water will be fine." To the world, he was twenty-one, and luckily with all his mother's money and connections, Isabella had new identification made for Aias that suited his perceived age. *I guess I will have to get used to the American ways and customs.*

Once the plane had taken off, Aias shut his eyes and relaxed. But as soon as he did, a vision of a beautiful teenage girl came into his mind. Somehow, she seemed familiar to him. In his vision, she was sitting on a bed with her head down and her hands held over her eyes, crying as her mother came into the room. He could hear their conversation as if he was there.

Aias heard the mother say, "It is not the end of the world. You can still go."

He heard the daughter say back, "And be embarrassed for being a loser? No, thank you. I'm not going!"

"Kesia, be reasonable," her mother said.

Kesia, that's why she seems familiar. I remember her from when I was a baby.

Aias listened as her mom said, "You are all dressed up and look so beautiful in your glittery teal gown. Please, change your mind and go to the prom."

Another girl entered the vision saying, "Come on, my coven sister. Let's go dance."

The girl who was crying looked at the new girl and said, "No."

That is when the mom left the room saying, "She's all yours."

"Kesia, there is no time like the present to teach you a new spell. Come on. I'm taking you back to my place."

"Luna, I don't think this is the time to be learning anything. I got dumped on the night of my prom."

Aias watched as the new girl tugged Kesia up and out of her house. Interested in the outcome, Aias watched the girls and their conversations as if he were watching TV.

As they left, his vision followed them.

At the new girl's home, in her bedroom, Aias heard Luna say, "No time like the present to start learning. The first thing you must know is that the words chanted during a spell usually rhyme. The words are like a poem and should flow. Like, roses are red, violets are blue, please make my friend happy and new."

Kesia grabbed for tissue and wiped her eyes. Then, smiling, she said, "Look, it worked. Not."

"Okay, how about this one? Abracadabra, alakazam, Kesia's make-up will be revised as fast as she can."

Kesia looked into the mirror on Luna's wall. Due to her tears, her mascara had run down her face. Aias watched as she took another tissue and wiped her face clean.

"See? That spell worked, too," Luna said, laughing.

Turning to her friend, Kesia said, "Luna, you don't understand. All my life, I have dreamed of dancing at my prom with a tall, handsome guy wearing a tux, and now I have nobody to dance with."

"Well, let's do a spell to attract a tall, handsome guy to sweep you off your feet."

"This should be good," Kesia said sarcastically.

"Let's start the chant with Merciful Goddess, unite Mars and Venus."

"Actually, that sounds good. What's next?" Kesia asked, getting into this spell thing.

"Hmm, well, we want a tall, dark, and handsome man for you, so let's put that in the chant."

Kesia giggled. "You could say bring me a tall glass of water."

"If you literally want a tall glass of water, then sure, but Spirit is very literal, so we can't use any urban expressions. Let's say, bring to me a young man similar to my prom dream, please. No. Scratch that. Let's say, bring to me a young man of delight."

"Okay, I get it." Kesia closed her eyes. "I have a good idea of what his physical appearance should look like."

"Good. Keep that in your mind. I think you said something about dancing with him."

"I did. Yes."

"Okay, let's say, let us dance to my heart's birthright."

"Fun. I like that," Kesia said with a smile.

"Now, we have to close the chant."

"How do we do that?" Kesia asked, trying to figure out the spell's formula.

"By summing up your intent. Let's say, bring to me this very night, my white knight. That is my will. So, mote it right."

"What does mote mean? I haven't heard that word before," Kesia asked.

"Mote means may or might."

"Is that the best word to use?"

"It is used a lot in spells. If you can think of a better one, I'll use it," Luna said, trying to think of another word to use.

Kesia looked up spells on Pinterest. "I guess that one is as good as any."

"I thought so. Let me say the whole chant out loud. Merciful Goddess, unite Venus and Mars. Bring to me a young man of delight. Let my prom dream become bright. Let us dance to my heart's birthright. Bring to me this very night, my white knight. That is my will. So, mote it right."

"I like it. Now, what do we do?"

"We say this chant while doing the spell. I just need to get a couple of things."

Opening his eyes, Aias decided that this was a perfect opportunity to help another soul. Looking down at his new watch that his mom had sent with the American clothes, he closed his eyes again—*eight more hours of flight, perfect.*

Chapter 68

Luna went into her closet and searched for a specific candle. "Have I told you what color of candle to use for different spells?"

Kesia walked over to the closet and said, "No."

"A **black** candle is mostly for banishing negativity, creating safety and protection, but also for vengeance, payback, pride, shapeshifting, revealing secrets, loss, grief support, illness, reverse hexes, curses, and justice. A **gray** candle is for imagination, visions, wisdom, psychic protection, patience, and obstacles. A **silver** candle is for the astral realm, ambition, fame, purity, communication with ancestors, and creativity. A **white** candle is for divination, purity, unity, peace, blessings, healing, innocence, and exorcisms. A **pink** candle is for romantic love, emotional and spiritual healing, faith, friendship, forgiveness, and self-healing. A **purple** candle is for spiritual power, intuition, wisdom, enhancing psychic ability, astral travel, breaking bad habits, bad karma, and warding off evil. A **blue** candle is for meditation, tranquility, serenity, inner peace, focus, forgiveness, good fortune, truth, loyalty, patience, trauma, and overcoming addiction. A **green** candle is for healing, harmony, luck, wealth, money, ambition, new beginnings, growth, and fertility. A **gold** candle is for abundance, happiness, awareness, knowledge, influence, divination, and power. A **yellow** candle is for learning, intelligence, memory, concentration, luxury, comfort, confidence, charm, and joy. An **orange** candle is for creativity, justice, legal matters, joy, ambition, opportunity, celebration, and sudden changes. A **red** candle is for strength, passion, lust, survival, career, independence, and courage. And lastly, a **brown** candle is for a house blessing or protection, pets, animals, earth, stability, balance, grounding, travel, rebirth, renewal, financial success, enhancing telepathic abilities, and locating a lost item."

"So, which one are you going to use for my spell?" Kesia asked.

"Hmm, candles are magical tools that work with the Fire Element and the Will Energy. I think we are going to use three. Pink for romance, purple for enhancing your psychic powers, and blue for your prom dream to come true."

Luna grabbed the three candles from a shelf and then placed them on a flat plate in the center of the pentacle drawn on her floor. "Okay, do you have your corsage?"

"No. My date would have given me one if I had a date," Kesia said, almost in tears again.

"Right. I had my mom pick me up one since I had decided to go alone. We can use mine."

"But won't that be your energy in the spell?"

"Good point. It might shift the intent. Okay, we won't use a flower." Something caught Luna's attention, and she looked at Kesia's hair. "Hey, you have baby's breath in your hair. Bend down, let me take a piece of that."

Kesia bent her head and let Luna take a small piece from her hair and watched as she placed it on a candle.

From a shelf, Luna took down a jar of mugwort. "We'll sprinkle a bit of this on each candle to help manifest your dream."

"Mugwort?" Kesia said.

"Yes, it is also good for increasing one's strength. Okay, we are almost finished. I just need you to pick an incense and a gemstone."

Holding out various sticks of incense to choose from, Luna said, "Close your eyes and let your intuition decide which one is the best for this spell."

"Any of these will work?"

"Yes. Trust your gut."

Kesia closed her eyes and picked a stick of incense.

"Great. Now do the same for a stone."

Again, Kesia closed her eyes and picked from a bowl of mixed stones.

Luna placed the incense stick into the hole of the holder, then lit the end and blew out the flame, letting the energy of the smoke rise from the stick. Then, she placed the stone in the center of the three candles. "Okay, we are ready. Have a seat on the floor next to the sacred circle."

Kesia sat cross-legged on the floor.

"Now, chant after me three times."

Kesia closed her eyes and repeated Luna's chant. "Merciful Goddess, unite Venus and Mars. Bring to me a young man of delight. Let my prom dream become bright. Let us dance to my heart's birthright. Bring to me this very night, my white knight. That is my will. So, mote it right." Then, slightly opening an eye and peaking at Luna, Kesia said, "Now what?"

Getting up off the floor, Luna said, "Now we go to the prom."

"That's it? That's all we have to do?"

"Now, we let the universe answer our request."

"But how do we know the spell worked?" Kesia said, worried that she might have done it wrong.

"You worry too much. You have to have faith."

"No, really, how do we know if it worked?"

Luna took a breath, motioned for Kesia to follow her downstairs, and said, as she walked out, "We know it worked because it comes true. Sometimes the spell isn't done until the flame burns out, or there is no more candle to burn. Sometimes I perform a spell in a new moon phase when I am manifesting and a full moon phase when I am discarding something, but we don't have time to wait for that."

A weird question came to Kesia. "Hey, what do you do with the spell after you are finished with it?"

"Good question. Safely disposing of the spell or ritual leftovers is a very important part of the spell. The leftovers will usually be herbs, melted wax, paper, jars, charms, fabric, ash, stones, or poppets."

"What is a poppet?"

"Many spells require a poppet. It is a handmade doll. In witchcraft, you can use it for casting spells on a person."

"How do you get a poppet? Do you buy them?"

"You can carve a root, use grain, corn shafts, paper, wax, a potato, clay, branches, or cloth stuffed with herbs. Anything that can be made to represent a body."

"Oh, thanks for explaining. Go on with the disposing of the items information you were sharing," Kesia said, interested in that, too.

"Anything biodegradable can be buried in the garden, crossroad, or in the forest. Make sure jars used to catch negative energy don't sit around in your garbage. Wait and throw them out on pickup day. Natural fabric can be buried, but synthetics must be cleansed then thrown into the garbage. Paper can be burned, and then the ash can be buried. If you use natural wax, like beeswax or soya, they can be buried, but not candle wax made from paraffin. Paraffin is bad for the environment. In this case, throw the wax into a fire. There, it will be completely burned away. Oh ya, stones can be cleaned by washing them and then letting them sit overnight in the moonlight."

"What do you do with a poppet when you are finished with the spell?" Kesia asked.

"That you can cleanse with the smoke of burning sage, and when ready for another spell, you can use it again."

Luna went into the living room and said to her mom, "Can you take a picture of us before we leave?"

Luna's mom took a few pictures for them.

"Also, mom, I have three candles burning upstairs, so don't blow them out. The spell I am doing is for Kesia."

Luna's mom nodded and said she'd check them in a bit.

Tugging on Kesia's arm, Luna said, "Come on, Kesia, or we'll miss our prom."

Chapter 69

As Luna opened her front door and stepped out onto the stoop, she turned and blew a kiss to her mom.

As she was taking too long, Kesia slid past and started down the stairs.

Without looking where she was going, Luna almost pushed Kesia down the stairs. "What in tarnation are you doing? You nearly wrecked our night with a visit to the hospital."

Luna looked at Kesia, whose mouth was wide open, then to where she was staring. Standing at the bottom of the steps was a tall, good-looking, dark-haired young man in a black tux holding two corsages, one teal matching Kesia's dress and the other black matching Luna's. "Well, damn, that was the fastest spell in history."

Luna bypassed Kesia and walked down the steps. Holding out her hand, she asked, "And you are?"

Bowing as if he was in the eighteenth century, the young man said, "Your lady's white knight."

Under her breath, Luna said, "Thank you, Goddess. No, really, who are you?" Luna asked again.

Coming down the stairs, Kesia said, "Aias?"

When he smiled, a shiver ran through Kesia.

"How did you guess?" Aias said.

"You look just like your dad."

Luna was confused. "You know this guy?"

"Yes. Well, kind of. I babysat him."

Luna laughed. "No, really, how do you know this guy?"

"It is a long story," Kesia said.

"Ladies, I believe we have a dance to get to. Shall we?" Aias put out both his arms for each to take hold of one. "Luna, will you drive? I haven't had enough practice yet."

As Luna nodded to Aias and opened her car for them all to hop in, she asked him, "How do you pronounce your name?"

"Say 'I as' fast. The first A is silent."

"'I as.' Okay, got it. Thanks."

Kesia and Luna felt like they were in a movie as they walked into the prom, dressed to the nines and one on each arm of this gorgeous man.

As they entered their school's auditorium, they were asked for their entry tickets.

Luna and Kesia gave theirs and knew that there was no way they could get Aias in without a ticket.

"It was fun while it lasted," Luna said, turning to Aias. "Thanks for trying."

Aias smiled and pulled out a ticket from his pocket.

"But how?" Luna whispered.

Kesia lightly punched Aias in the arm. "So, this was what you were learning in India?"

Luna was so confused. "Who did you say this guy was?"

Kesia turned to her and said, "Our white knight." Then, laughing, she added, "Man, Luna, you gotta have faith."

The rest of the night was magical.

Aias was the perfect date. He danced with both girls, got them beverages, created funny and memorable photos at the photo booth, and hooted when the king and queen were announced. But just before midnight, he said, "Ladies, I have to go. It has been my pleasure. Thank you so much for allowing me to escort you to this most wonderful event."

Just as he took his leave, Luna said, "But you have to go to the after-party."

"I wish I could, but my mom is picking me up at JFK, and I have to get off the plane."

Luna was perplexed. "What are you talking about?"

But before he could answer, he disappeared.

"Pinch me," Luna said to Kesia. "Did I just see him disappear?"

"It looks like it."

Luna turned to Kesia. "How are you not freaked out? A guy just disappeared in front of your eyes."

"Oh, that is nothing. You should see what his dad can do."

"Wait," Luna said, grabbing Kesia's arm. "I thought you didn't know anything about magic?"

"I never said that. I said I didn't know anything about Wicca."

"Holy cow! What else are you hiding from me?" Luna said as Kesia dragged her back onto the dance floor.

Kesia just smiled and started dancing.

Chapter 70

Lexi had taken an Uber to the grocery store.

As she picked some items and put them into her wheelchair basket, she saw a pregnant woman in a mini skirt and high heels. The lady reminded her of one of those pampered housewives you see on TV.

As Lexi maneuvered around the aisle, she almost bumped into a man. "Excuse me."

"Alexandra? What happened?" the man said.

Lexi looked at the man closer. "Edward. Oh my God. I didn't recognize you with your new look."

He had streaked his hair blond, and it was spiked and cut short on the sides. He also had an oversized diamond earring in his right ear. There was no way Lexi would have ever recognized him in his tight-fitting T-shirt and faded denim jeans that had rips in them on purpose.

"I had a car accident months ago."

"Oh, it must have been serious for you to be in a wheelchair?"

"It was."

Just as Edward was going to say something, the pregnant woman walked up to Edward and slid her arm through his, showing off a very large diamond wedding ring. "Babycakes, this is Alexandra, an acquaintance of mine. Alexandra, this is Candy, my wife." Touching his wife's tummy, he said, "And soon to be, baby girl." Then, smiling from ear to ear, he added, "We are expecting next month."

Almost choking on her words, Lexi answered, "I am so happy for the both of you."

Smiling, Candy said, "Thank you. We have started to set up the nursery in our new Manhattan condo. It looks onto Central Park."

Lexi forced a smile. "Well, congratulations again, but I must be going."

"Take care and get better soon," Edward said as he lovingly wrapped an arm around his pregnant wife.

Lexi couldn't get out of there fast enough. With tears at the brink of exploding, Lexi paid for her groceries and waited outside for her ride.

As she was waiting, Evangeline came walking up and said, "Lexi, fancy meeting you here."

Forcing a smile, so she wouldn't start crying, Lexi said, "Evangeline, so nice to see you."

"How have you been? I am so sorry that you and my brother didn't work out. I really enjoyed having you around."

"That is so nice of you to say. I enjoyed our time as well. How is your family?"

"Dad is great. Mom is a bit upset over Neo, though."

Lexi made an inquisitive face, then said, "Why is that?"

"Oh, I thought you would have heard by now. He went overseas for a year and is doing Doctors Without Borders."

"No, I hadn't heard. That is very humanitarian of him."

"It was a surprise to all of us. Your break-up hit him hard."

"I am sorry."

Evangeline shrugged. "It is what it is. No need to cry over spilled milk. Well, nice chatting with you Lexi, I must get what I came for. You know my mom when she is cooking. Time is wasting if she doesn't have all the ingredients."

Thankfully her ride drove up. Lexi smiled and said, "Nice seeing you, Evangeline. Say hi to everyone."

Bending down and kissing Lexi, Evangeline said, "Take care, Lexi."

Once in the Uber, Lexi tried to relax, but it was short-lived. Her cell phone rang.

"Hi, Isabella. How are you?"

"Good. It's been a while, and I thought I should catch up. How have you been?"

"I've seen better days. How's Aias?"

"Oh, he is in love."

"Really? When did that happen?"

"On the flight over from India."

Lexi laughed. "How did he have time to fall in love? Don't tell me it was the flight attendant?"

"Funny. No, it is someone you know."

Lexi scrunched her eyebrows. "Who?"

"Kesia."

"Wow! We are going to have to get together, so you can tell me the whole story."

"I would like that. That is part of why I am calling. I have another movie starting to film in a few days, and Aias doesn't want to come with me. Do you think he can stay with you?"

Lexi was a bit startled by the question and said, "Um, but I don't have a place. I am living in a hotel."

"That's great."

"It is?"

"Yes, because I just bought him a condo with three bedrooms. You can move in with him."

Lexi didn't know what to say. "I guess I could for a bit."

"Great. I'll set it all up. Talk to you soon. I gotta go. But hey, I almost forgot to ask. How are you doing about Redington's news? Oh, sorry, I gotta go. Talk to you soon."

Isabella had hung up, and Lexi was now wondering about Redington's news.

Calling Redington, his cell went to voice mail. "Sorry to have missed you. If this is an emergency, please call my precinct. They will forward me your message."

Lexi hung up her phone. "What the?"

Lexi tipped the Uber driver extra for helping her into the hotel's foyer.

Once in her room, she started to cry. *If there is a God, I need to know because, at this moment, I am beginning to doubt it. Life can't get any worse than today. I am jinxed. Ever since I heard that voice in Redington's condo, I have had one issue arise after another. I can't take anymore. You hear that, God. I can't take any more bad things happening to me!!!*

Chapter 71

"Kesia, it is time to learn about the moon cycles and spells," Luna said, even though she would rather be talking about Aias and what Kesia knew about magic.

Sitting on the floor in Luna's bedroom, Kesia said, "Great. I can't wait to hear about the moon."

"Before I get into the moon phases, what do you think a lunatic is?"

"That is a funny question to ask," Kesia said. "A crazy person."

"True. It refers to a person who has a severely disordered state of mind, usually someone who is mentally ill, dangerous, or very foolish. Lunatic can also be referred to as insane. Insanity—also known as madness or craziness— describes a gamut of behaviors that are also considered abnormal mental or behavioral patterns."

"Ya, I know what insane means. So, what is your point?" Kesia asked, wondering what this had to do with spells.

"I'm getting to it. Patience." Just as Luna was going to continue, Aias popped in.

"Hiya. What are you girls up to?"

Freaking out and grabbing at her heart, Luna screamed, "You almost scared me to death, Aias. You can't just pop in like that."

Kesia smiled at him. "I'm glad you did, though." Then, patting the floor beside her, insinuating for him to sit down next to her, she said, "Luna is teaching me about the moon phases."

Sitting on the floor beside Kesia, he said, "Fascinating," and looked at Luna so she could continue.

Taking a breath, Luna said, "As I was about to say, the moon's lunar cycle affects the behavior and physiology of humans and animals. Moon magic is not only a significant symbol of the Roman goddess of the hunt, Diana, but its continual lunar cycle can be used for many different purposes in a person's life."

Aias asked, "Is that why they say people go crazy during a full moon?"

Luna pointed at him and excitedly said, "Yes, every twenty-nine and a half days, we move through the moon's lunar cycle. The waxing and waning cycles affect our energy levels and moods."

Kesia put up her hand and asked, "I don't understand waxing and waning. What is that?"

Luna nodded. "Good question. You know what a new moon is, right?"

Both Kesia and Aias shook their heads.

"A new moon starts the lunar phase. It is when the Moon and the Sun have the same ecliptic longitude."

Both Kesia and Aias had blank stares on their faces.

Luna shook her head. "Don't feel bad. Most people don't know what a new moon looks like because the lunar disk is not visible to the unaided eye. During the first half of a lunar month, the amount of luminosity on the Moon increases. Astronomers call this a 'waxing moon.' Waxing is the period when the moon appears to be growing larger and larger in the sky. This entire period lasts about two weeks, give or take a few days."

"And what is a waning moon cycle?" Kesia asked.

"It is any time after a full moon, and before a new moon, the amount of luminosity on the moon is decreasing. It also lasts about two weeks."

"So, let me get this straight, there are four stages to a moon cycle?" Kesia asked.

"Well, there are many stages, but the four main ones are the new moon, the waxing moon, the full moon, and the waning moon."

"Okay, I'm following," Kesia said. "Can't see it, start to see it, see all of it, then it starts to disappear again."

"Basically, yes. Now the important part is that the cycles of the moon play an important role in what spell you should be doing."

Aias piped up, "Spells? You gals do spells? Why?"

Luna looked at him as if he had two heads. "Not all of us have mastered magic as you have. We need help from the Horned God and Mother Goddess."

"Wow, that is freaky," he said.

"Can I continue?" Luna asked.

"Yes, please do," Aias answered.

Shaking her head, Luna continued, "The new moon is the beginning of a new moon cycle. You will know a new moon because it is completely dark in the sky."

"Yep, we've got that much so far," Kesia said.

From old habits, Aias put his hand up and asked, "How is a new moon created?"

"From our perspective here on earth, the new moon happens when the sun and moon are exactly lined up together. Therefore, it is also known as the dark moon. The new moon lasts for about three days and is a great time of the month to set new intentions, making a fresh start, and cleansing negative energy."

"So, give me an example of a spell that I would use during this phase," Kesia said.

"Sure. This spell lasts for about three days. First, get some paper and a pen. Then choose one or two intentions you are passionate about and make sure your intentions are clear, concise, and specific—something that you want, wish, or desire to manifest in your life and write them down. Next, trust your gut and choose a candle color that suits your intent. Light the candle and ask the universe to shine a light on you during this new moon. Now, it is time to infuse your candle with your intention. Honor all four cardinal directions, north, east, south, and west as you light the candle. Then, staring at the flame, chant a spell, or just recite your intention, three times. As the flame is burning, your energy is merging with the universe in helping you to manifest your request."

"I like that. It is like writing an affirmation, but using the power of the moon to amp up the intention," Kesia said.

"Yes, using the power of the moon boosts your psychic energy," Luna added.

"Okay, now give me an example for a spell during a waxing moon."

Luna smiled at Kesia's enthusiasm. "Now that you set your intention during the new moon, these next two weeks, the waxing moon cycle, is all about growth, planning, and taking action. During these two weeks, you need to do the practical steps to create what you desire."

Aias said, "This sounds like what the mindset coaches are teaching nowadays. Using your subconscious mind to manifest your dreams."

Luna shrugged and said, "I doubt they use the power of the moon to manifest anything."

Aias added, "But could you imagine if they did?"

Kesia asked before their conversation got heated, "You still haven't given me any action steps. What do I do during this phase?"

Luna answered a bit defensively, "One action you can take is to use an oracle card deck. A moon deck is an awesome card deck to use, but any oracle card deck will do."

"What do you do with the deck?" Aias asked, having never seen one before.

Not sure if he was mocking her or not, Luna told him, "Take a breath and pick a random card, then meditate on the card's message."

Kesia added, "Oracle cards are different from tarot cards because you only pick one card and concentrate on that day's message. Whereas tarot uses many cards to tell a story."

"Oh, good to know," Aias said as he smiled at both of them.

Kesia melted a little more each time she saw his smile. Then, looking at Luna, she asked, "What about a spell during a full moon?"

"This cycle is the most beloved and magical phase of the moon and lasts for only three days. It signifies power, success, goals coming to completion, and a time to recharge any magical item. This is the time to focus and reflect. It is all about celebrating your progress. To celebrate your wins, no matter how big or small. It is the time to surrender and trust the universe."

"What spell should I do, though?" Kesia asked.

"It is not really a time for a spell, but you could say affirmations, such as, 'I'm proud of everything that I have achieved' or something like that. Or maybe, 'I am ready to manifest for my highest good.'"

"So, there is no ritual to do?" Kesia asked, a bit disappointed.

"Well, some of my coven sisters like to do this during a full moon. They use a jar filled with moon water."

Aias asked, "How do you get moon water?"

Luna giggled, thinking that it was apparent. "You let water sit in a jar during any moon-lit night."

"Oh, that seems too obvious," he said, thinking now how stupid his question was.

Luna continued, "For the ritual, light a candle and sit under the moon. Close your eyes and lift your face to its luminance essence. Soak in the moon's magical energy. This ritual works best if you have something silver, like a silver coin.

Hold the item up to the light of the moon and concentrate on your desire, and then when your instincts tell you to, drop the silver item into the water and wait until the ripples run smooth. Next, allow the reflection of the moon to hit the water. Then, gaze at the silver through the refection and repeat your original new moon intention. Lastly, leave the silver in the moon water until the next full moon or until your dream manifests."

"Oh, that one seems fun. I will have to try that ritual," said Kesia. "Okay, we did new moon, waxing moon, and full moon. What about the waning moon?"

"The waning moon cycle is for the next two weeks. This is where you discharge ideas, patterns, behaviors, situations, and even people who no longer serve your highest good. This phase is all about releasing negative energy. This is the time to make space for that wish, want, or desire that you are creating from the new moon, by releasing whatever it is that no longer serves you or holds you back from achieving your intention."

Aias said, "Wicca doesn't seem that scary. I am not sure what all the hype is about. It sounds like you are all about self-care and creating a better world."

"I know, right? Just because witches love to do spells, that makes us bad in the eyes of many. It's too bad that they judge before they know what they are judging," Luna said, defending her beliefs.

Kesia added, "What I'm starting to think is that all cultures have their beliefs, and an apple is an apple no matter what you call it." Kesia started to laugh.

"What's so funny?" Luna asked.

"It reminds me of a Facebook picture I saw the other day."

"What was it?" Luna inquired.

"It showed a brown egg, a white egg, a colored Easter egg, and all were cracked open."

"I don't get it," Luna said. "What is so funny about that?"

Kesia laughed again. "That no matter how different the outside is, the inside is all the same. Meaning, no matter what name you call a similar idea, concept, or thought, it is all the same. Wicca is just another religious name for a similar outcome for peace on earth. Instead of prayer beads, they use spells. Instead of holy water, they use moon water. Instead of singing a hymn, they chant. Instead of calling the higher power God, they call it the Horned God or mother goddess. What's so funny is that it's all the same."

Aias added, "If they only knew what the energy of judging others does to their karma, they wouldn't be looking outward. They'd be looking inward." Aias's energy shifted. "Ah, I'm needed elsewhere. Talk to you girls soon.

Thanks for today." Then he disappeared as quickly as he had shown up.

"I hate it when he does that," Luna said.

"I think it's sexy," Kesia said dreamily.

Chapter 72

What the heck am I doing? I should have told Isabella no. Thinking about Isabella brought back their conversation about Redington. Lexi still hadn't talked to him. *Now is as good as time as any.*

Deciding to call his precinct, she found out that he was promoted and was on an assignment. They wouldn't tell her when he would return but said, "If you are important to him, then he will contact you."

Great, I cannot walk, no job, no family, no husband, no baby, and now no friends. "Great! Life is just freaking great!" Lexi yelled. *And now I agreed to babysit a baby who looks like a teenager. I must have lost my mind along with everything else.* Frustrated with life, Lexi yelled, "Ahhhh." *Susannah, are you there?*

No answer.

Lexi started to cry. *I can't go on like this. Life is too hard. I never signed up for this.*

Looking up, she yelled at God, "I don't understand the lesson. Why? Why are you making my life so miserable?"

The light on Lexi's cell phone flashed, and Lexi looked to see what it was. It was a prayer. *Heavenly Saint Raphael, hear my call. I beg you to assist me during this crisis, my time of need. You are the medicine of God. Please, hear my plea. I humbly ask that you heal my body, mind, and soul. Through your divine grace, heal my eyes to see, my ears to hear, my voice to speak, my tongue to taste, my heart to feel, and my soul to believe. Make me whole once again. Amen.*

Lexi couldn't believe the coincidence of its timing. She had to read it again.

Lexi's phone rang, scaring her.

"Hello?" she said, not knowing who was on the other end.

"Hi Lexi, this is Aias, Isabella's son. How are you doing?"

"Aias, you sound so grown up."

"Well, I'm twenty-one, so I guess I better be."

"Wow, twenty-one. Your mom never mentioned that. I don't understand why you need a babysitter?"

Aias laughed. "You know my mom. She tries to look after everyone. I think she thinks we will be good for each other. You'll keep me out of trouble and all that."

"Great, but who will keep me out of trouble?"

"Oh, I am sure that won't be a problem."

Not sure if that was an insult, Lexi said, "I might surprise you."

Changing the subject, Aias asked, "So, when should I have supper prepared?"

"Supper? You cook?"

"Hey, they don't just teach mystical things in India. We learned practical stuff as well. Actually, I am a great cook."

"Well, then. I guess I will be over at seven. Will that be okay?"

"That will be perfect. See you soon."

"Thanks for calling, Aias. That was really sweet of you."

"See you soon, Lexi. And bring your appetite."

After hanging up, she thought, *He sounded so grown up. I wonder why Isabella wants me to go and stay with him.*

Lexi finished packing her things.

After she had everything packed, she called down to the front desk to send someone up who could bring her things down for her.

Waiting, she reread the Archangel Raphael prayer. *I wonder what healing the soul means. Is it referring to physical healing or spiritual healing? And how does one heal a soul anyways?*

Lexi contemplated this thought as she traveled in the elevator and even after paying her hotel bill. She was still thinking about it in the taxi.

Healing of a soul. I know that my soul is part of me that lives even after I die. So, how come a soul might need healing? Is it damaged? Did someone else damage it, or did the soul damage itself? What part of the soul needs healing? All of it? Or maybe only parts of it need healing? Are there even parts to a soul? I have all these questions.

Lexi did what Kesia liked to do and looked up "healing a soul" on her phone. Lexi read that to *heal a soul,* one needed to spiritually awaken—to believe—to consciously understand this life's purpose and lessons.

She then read something that took her breath away. She read that *soul healing* is needed when one feels disconnected from the source, from God. When one feels alone, and that life is not worth living anymore. Healing the soul is not about healing the body or even the mind. It is about reconnecting one's belief to a higher power. She read that when trauma, loss, major stress is inflicted in one's life, one's energy level diminishes, and an assortment of negative emotions create a spiral of more negativity. When one's emotions become out of control, one attracts more negative energy. Unfortunately, this negative energy affects the soul and creates dis-harmony. The more dis-harmony, the further one feels from God.

Lexi took a breath. *That is exactly what I am feeling, alone.*

She kept reading. It said that one needs to find their inner consciousness, their God power, that the road to healing starts with a single step, a step toward the source. This step is not something you can get from an outside source, but rather something you must do from within. Inside, a spiritual connection is required. YOU MUST BELIEVE!

That is all she could read before her cab dropped her off at Aias's.

Chapter 73

"Luna, I think I'm in love," Kesia said shortly after Aias had left.

"What makes you think that?"

"This feeling I get when he smiles or when he enters a room. He takes my breath away. I feel a heightened sense of euphoria. I…"

"Okay, I get it. You're in love. Do you think he feels the same way?" Luna asked.

"What if he doesn't?" Kesia said, worried. "Is there a love spell we can do?"

"Are you sure you want that? I mean, what if it is not meant to be? Then what? You just amplified the energy, and it is not that easy to reverse a spell once it is set in motion. So, you better be sure, Kesia."

"I'm sure. Let's do it. What do we need?"

Luna got a red pen, some paper, and an envelope. Giving them to Kesia, she said, "Start to write out all the qualities you require in your soulmate."

As Kesia started to write, Luna grabbed a pink candle, red lipstick, and some perfume. Lastly, she took down a jar filled with dried rose petals.

Placing them all on the floor next to the sacred circle, she waited for Kesia to finish writing out her soul mate's list of qualities.

After Kesia finished writing everything she could think of, she passed the paper to Luna.

"No, you keep it. Here, spray some of this perfume on yourself and then rub some onto the paper."

Kesia did as Luna instructed.

"Now, fold the paper and place it into the envelope."

Kesia folded the paper and placed it into the envelope.

"Now, with your right hand, take some of these rose petals."

Kesia did as instructed.

"Envision yourself in love while you squeeze the rose petals. Send that love energy into the petals. Then, place the petals into the envelope."

Kesia closed her eyes and squeezed the petals, envisioning herself in love. Then she dropped the petals into the envelope.

"Seal the envelope."

Kesia licked the envelope and sealed it.

"Here, apply this lipstick and then kiss the envelope."

Kesia smiled and happily applied the red lipstick. Then, taking the envelope lovingly, she kissed it as if it were her true love that she was kissing.

"Now, place this in a safe place and never open the envelope. If you do, the spell will be broken."

"What do we do with the pink candle?" Kesia asked.

"Light it, my dear," Luna said as she passed a lighter to Kesia.

Kesia took the lighter and lit the candle. "Now what?"

Luna started to chant, "If your love is pure and your intentions are too, may your true love come to you."

Next, Luna passed Kesia another piece of paper. "Here, write out your true love's name and your name, and encircle them with a heart when you are done."

Luna waited until Kesia was finished, then said, "Now, close your eyes and think about the two of you together. Focus on that thought. Visualize your love and how happy you are."

Luna waited a few moments, then said, "Repeat this incantation, 'Our fate is destined. We are to be, so mote it be.'"

Kesia repeated the chant three times.

"Now, stare at the candle flame for five minutes and imagine that it is you and your true love dancing."

Kesia stared at the flame.

Luna sat back and waited until the five minutes were up. "Okay, take a breath and let it be."

Kesia took a breath and then said, "Let's go."

"Go where?"

"To my true love," Kesia said, dancing around the room.

Chapter 74

The two-hour drive felt like an instant to Kesia. She was so excited to see Aias in the flesh, not just as bilocation.

"Are you sure he will be happy to see us?" Luna said as she drove them to New York City.

"I believe he will be. Plus, we did the spell, and I am sure he is my soulmate."

As Luna parked in the visitors' parking area of Aias's condo building, she admitted, "I am so not ready to find my soulmate. I have so much to do before I settle down with one person."

As they walked to the front entrance, Kesia ran over to a lady struggling with her luggage. "Lexi!" Hugging her, Kesia said, "What are you doing here?"

Surprised to see Kesia, Lexi said, "I am staying with Aias. What are you doing here? Isn't it a school night?"

Kesia said, smiling, "We graduated last week. I am free!" and started to dance around.

Lexi smiled. "Congratulations. Who is your friend?"

"Oh, sorry. This is Luna. A good friend from school."

Lexi put out a hand but almost dropped her luggage. "Hi, I'm Lexi."

As she grabbed Lexi's luggage, Luna said, "Nice to meet you."

"Thanks," Lexi said as Luna took her bag.

Kesia was so excited to see Lexi. She hugged her again. "I am sorry you are still in the wheelchair. Luna and I have been trying to cast a spell to help you heal, but obviously, it hasn't worked."

Lexi smiled. "Spells can be dangerous. You should have asked me first."

Luna said, "We only do spells that can empower someone."

Lexi looked at her and said, "That may be so, but what if I didn't want to heal? Or maybe, my energy is protected, and you are wasting your time?"

As she pushed the button to call Aias to let them in, Kesia asked, "What do you mean that your energy is protected?"

Before she could answer, there was a "Hello, Lexi, come on up" and a buzz to alert her to open the door.

They all went into the building and right into an open elevator.

Lexi answered Kesia's question while the elevator went up. "Ever since we went through the fairy door…"

Interrupting, Luna said, surprised, "Fairy door?"

Kesia turned to Luna and said, "It's a long story." Then, turning back to Lexi, she said, "Continue."

"Ever since then, I have put up a protection bubble to keep away evil, bad spirits, or angry elves."

"Angry elves?" Luna said, even more surprised.

Without looking, Kesia said again, "Long story. No wonder our spells are not working on you."

Suddenly, an alarm went off, and the elevator stopped, trapping the three of them inside.

"What the?" Lexi said as her wheelchair almost tipped over. "For heaven's sake. I can't take any more of this chaos!"

Surprised at Lexi's reaction, Luna said, "Calm down, I am sure it is something simple, and we will be on our way in a moment."

Lexi started to cry. Then went into hysterical screaming. As she began to fling her arms around, she shouted, "God, this is not okay! I have had enough! I can't handle anymore." Then she started to cry uncontrollably.

Luna stared at Lexi, then at Kesia. "Do something," she whispered to Kesia.

"Like what?"

"I don't know, anything."

Kesia softly said, "Lexi, what is going on? I can help. Just tell me what is happening. Why are you so angry?"

Lexi could hardly catch her breath to answer.

"Take a deep breath," Kesia said.

But Lexi was past hearing her and started to scream again.

"Do something. She's your friend," Luna shouted.

Kesia closed her eyes and prayed. "Lexi, I am going to do a tarot card reading for you."

"How is that going to help?" Luna asked.

"It can't hurt."

Kesia pulled out one of her tarot decks and shuffled them. The cards, two of swords and the page of swords fell to the ground. Picking them up, Kesia said, "Lexi, the two of swords shows me that you feel like you cannot see your future and that you are on guard. The rocks in the picture tell me that you have a couple of obstacles to overcome. But on a good note, the water is quite calm, and you are sitting freely. Lexi, what this is telling me is that all you have to do is put down the swords and take off the blindfold and walk away."

Luna stared at the card. "You got all that by the cards?"

"Yes," Kesia said, realizing that she had never done a spread in front of Luna. They had been too busy learning Wicca.

"Lit."

Lexi looked at the cards and tried to catch her breath.

Kesia continued, "It might not seem like it, but there is a man that can help you… Luna, look. It's the white knight." Shivers ran down her body as she said it.

"You think that Aias can help her?" Luna asked.

"Let me see." Kesia pulled another card. "It is the six of swords. Lexi, all three cards are swords. Swords mean to take action. Lexi, you need to go on a trip."

"You think the six of swords means she needs to go on a trip? It looks like it is a scary trip. Look, the swords are stuck in the small wooden boat," Luna said anxiously.

Ignoring Luna, Kesia said, "Lexi, look. See? You will be going with a man and children."

Lexi looked at the card but still couldn't say anything due to having trouble catching her breath.

"This card tells me that it is a bit unorthodox, and it won't be perfect sailing, but it will be worth the effort."

"Who?" Lexi forced out.

Kesia looked at Luna. "Did you understand that?"

"I think she said 'who.'"

Lexi nodded and was able to take a breath.

Looking at the card, Kesia got shivers. Before she answered, she pulled another card—the three of cups. "It looks like you're also going with two girls. Whoever you go with, it will be a celebration."

Lexi whispered between breaths, "Where?"

Kesia pulled another card—ace of cups. "It is a new beginning, especially for your emotions. By the looks of it, I would say somewhere spiritual."

Luna asked, "How do you know that?"

Kesia pointed to the dove, cross, chalice, and lastly, the lotus flowers."

"Ah, I get it. These are all symbols you are reading," Luna said, starting to understand the cards.

"Yes, and there are a lot of spiritual symbols here."

"When?" Lexi said a bit clearer.

Kesia pulled another card—two of pentacles. "It's a toss-up. See the big waves in the back. I think it would be best to go when the water is calmer."

Luna looked at the card closer. "Hmm, I wouldn't have even thought to look at that part of the picture."

Kesia pulled another card to see what it showed—queen of pentacles. Kesia got shivers again. "Lexi, I think you need to meditate and talk to Tamara."

"Tamara? But you know she is in hiding."

"Try anyway. By the looks of it, we are not getting out of this elevator any time soon."

Kesia sat down on the elevator floor and motioned for Luna to do the same. She started the meditation by saying, "Lexi, take a breath as deep as you can and let it out slowly."

Kesia shuffled all the cards and then pulled another card while asking what to say in the meditation—the hanged man. "As you take a breath, think about being upside down, hanging lazily from a tree branch. You notice while you are hanging, you have a moment of enlightenment."

Kesia pulled another card—queen of pentacles. "You all of a sudden know how to contact Tamara."

Kesia pulled another card—three of cups. "You rejoice in the reunion."

The next card Kesia pulled was the death card. Taking a breath, Kesia said, "She has been reborn. She is not the Tamara that you used to know. She now is blessed and carries with her the knowledge of the underworld. She is not afraid of death, for she knows that each day a new light arises."

Kesia pulled two more cards—the lovers and the queen of wands. "Your future holds love and power. Your words are heard, and you will be granted your wishes. Spirit has listened to your call. Now take a breath, and in your mind, talk to Tamara. Tell her what you are feeling. Tell her your wishes. Tell her anything and everything that your heart wants to share."

Kesia watched as Lexi took a breath.

Tamara, wherever you are, please hear me. I have missed you so. I feel so alone in the world. So, lost. Everything that I knew before seems lost. Everything I wished for before seems lost. I don't know what to live for anymore. Life doesn't seem worth living. Would you please help me? Would you please tell me that my life is worth living? That there is something in my future to live for? Would you please give me a sign? Would you please help me help myself? I have fallen, and I don't know how to get up again. I am afraid that I am losing my faith. I am afraid that I don't believe in magic anymore. That all the spiritual growth I attained has been forgotten. I can't hear Susannah, God, or for that matter, any spiritual being. I can't take the silence. I wish for my life to go back to how it was. I wish to have friends, family, someone to love, someone to love me, and to have crazy adventures that can't be explained by science. Crazy adventures that expand my spiritual beliefs. I want to believe again. I want to sense Spirit again.

Before Lexi could think of anything else to say, Aias popped into the elevator saying, "Well, supper is getting cold."

Kesia laughed and said, "Really? That is all you came here to say?"

Aias smiled, and Kesia melted.

Luna stood up and demanded, "Aias, get us out of here!"

"First, you all have to calm your energy. You are making the electricity in this place go wild."

Luna screamed, "Aias, get us out of here!"

Aias disappeared.

Lexi asked, "His mom told me he could bilocate, but it is something else to see it in person."

"Tell me about it," Luna said. "He scares me every time."

Moments later, the elevator started to ascend, and the doors opened on Aias's floor.

He was there to greet them. "Nothing like making an entrance. Come on, let's eat. I'm starved."

They all followed him into his condo.

Chapter 75

Lexi was relieved to finally be in Aias's condo after the elevator fiasco. She liked how Isabella had decorated it with a young man in mind.

Aias showed Lexi to her room.

Lexi smiled, knowing that Isabella always thought of everything. It was beautiful.

As she freshened up, she heard Kesia ask, "Why weren't you surprised that we were with Lexi in the elevator?"

His answer surprised Lexi. "I already knew you were coming."

As Lexi wheeled into the dining area where the other three were sitting, Kesia said, "How would you know that?"

Aias smiled and said, "While I was at school in India, I was taught how to see the future."

Luna said, "You mean to predict the future?"

"No, predictions don't always come true. I can see the future."

"You can see the future?" Luna repeated.

"Yes."

Smart-aleck like, Luna said, "What is in my future then?"

Aias snapped his fingers. Her head fell forward, and she was out like a light. He had put her into a trance state.

"What did you do to her?" Kesia said as she got up to make sure Luna was still breathing.

"She wanted to see her future, so she is dreaming it."

A moment later, Luna opened her eyes. "Holy catfish! That was wild."

"What did you see?" Kesia said excitedly.

"It was kind of like that old movie where the guy astral traveled and experienced how life would be without him in it."

"It's *A Wonderful Life*?" Kesia said.

"Maybe. It was so lit. Aias, what else did you learn?" Luna asked.

"So much."

Kesia looked at Lexi, who was struggling to reach for the water jug to fill her glass. "Aias, I remember in India when we were by the water, that you could turn the water to other colors."

"I was a baby, I don't remember that, but I can still turn water to other colors." He touched the jug, and it turned a hue of pink.

"Lit!" Luna said.

"Taste it," Aias said.

"Why? Shouldn't it still taste like water?" Luna asked, pouring herself and Lexi a glass.

"Pink lemonade! How did you do that?" Luna almost screamed.

"I think it, and then it becomes," Aias answered her.

"Show me more. What else can you do?" Luna asked, so intrigued with his magic.

"So far, I can materialize items, bilocate, and see the future."

"You forgot one," Kesia said.

"I don't think so," Aias answered.

"Did you forget that you can heal?" Kesia said.

"Ya. But I don't know how I do that one, so I don't count it."

Luna asked, "Who have you healed? Or a better question what ailments have you healed?"

"Lots of different conditions. I don't remember them all."

"Which one was the coolest?" Luna asked, resting her elbows on the table, wanting to know the answer.

Aias thought for a moment. "I guess the blind man seeing again was pretty awesome."

"But you don't know how you do it?" Luna asked.

"No. It just seems to happen."

Luna asked another question. "Can you do it from a distance, or is it always in person?"

He thought for a moment. "So far, it is always in person."

"Do you wave your hand or something?" Luna asked, trying to figure out what he did.

Aias laughed. "No."

"Hey, don't laugh at me, I don't know."

"I wasn't laughing at you. The thought of waving my hands around made me laugh." Aias waved his hands theatrically around to make his point.

The girls started to laugh. Even Lexi laughed at the sight of him pretending to do a magic trick or something with his hands.

"Enough about me. Kesia, how are you doing with learning those spells?"

As she took a bite of the pizza Aias had ordered, Kesia nodded. "Ya, good. Luna is a great teacher."

Luna smiled and said, "Thank you, Kesia. I love that we can learn together."

Kesia smiled at her.

Aias got up and cleared the empty plates from the table. As he passed by Lexi, he paused and placed a hand on her shoulder, saying, "You have been so quiet tonight. Everything alright?"

As he touched her, Lexi felt a surge of energy run through her body. "Ya, I'm just tired, is all."

"Well, the girls can help you if you want a hot bath."

"That would be nice but way too much trouble, but I do think I am going to retire.

Thanks for the pizza. I'm glad that you learned how to cook in India," Lexi jested.

Aias grinned ear to ear. "Well, I didn't want the supper I made to be ruined."

Luna laughed, catching that he could see that they would be stuck in the elevator. "Good one."

Lexi smiled and wheeled into her room. Closing the door, she took a deep breath and moved onto the bed. As she undressed, she thought, *Lord, what am I doing here?*

Moving the blankets aside so she could lie under them, she heard Kesia yell, "Help! Aias! Lexi! Luna's choking!"

Not even thinking, Lexi threw the blankets to the side and hopped out of bed, running toward the door and down the hallway.

When she arrived in the dining room, she was greeted by three smiling faces.

Halting, Lexi said, "What is going on here? Why did you lie that Luna was choking?" Then, holding her heart, she said, "You scared me half to death."

The three smiles got bigger.

"What are you three smiling at? It isn't funny to trick a person like that," Lexi said almost angrily.

The smiles got even bigger.

Lexi turned around and stomped back down the hall and then stopped in her tracks. Then, screaming, she ran back and said, "Oh my God! I can walk!"

Kesia stood up and clapped her hands, then grabbed Lexi and started to dance around.

"But how?" Lexi said, stopping to stare at all of them.

"My guess is that it was when Aias touched your shoulder," Kesia said. "I am sorry that I had to scare you, but I had to test my theory."

Lexi sat down on a chair in the dining room, then stood back up and danced around. "Oh my God, it doesn't hurt." She bent over and touched her toes. "Holy moly." Tears started to run down her face. Then, coming over to Aias, hugging him, she said, "You are a miracle. Thank you."

"You're welcome, but I am still not sure how it works."

"Who cares?" Luna said. "You healed her!"

"I may have healed her body, but it is up to her to heal her soul."

Lexi took a breath and said, "That may take a bit, but you have sparked something in me that has been missing for some time."

Turning to head back to her room, Lexi said, "Night, you three. Don't stay up too late."

After going to the bathroom, Lexi lay back down in the bed and closed her eyes. *Thank you for hearing my prayer. I don't know how to repay you, Lord, but I will do my best.*

Within moments she was in a dream state. She was wearing an orange robe, and her head was shaved. She could hear chanting coming from down the hall.

Walking toward the voices, she noticed she was wearing sandals.

As she entered the room, she saw many monks wearing robes of red or orange, kneeling on red cushions, and chanting toward a giant buddha statue.

As she sat down in a lotus position on the mat, she noticed Tamara beside her. *Where are we, Tamara?*

You are visiting me at a Tibetan Buddhist Monastery on the outskirts of Kathmandu, Nepal.

Are you happy here, Tamara?

Yes.

Are you coming back to the USA?

No.

Never?

Never. I have found my place in life.

I miss you, Tamara.

I have always been with you. So, there is no need to miss me.

I miss seeing you.

Lexi, all you have to do is close your eyes, and I am there.

It sounds easier than it is. I have tried, but I couldn't find you.

You found me now.

Yes. Thankfully. Tamara, I don't know what to do next with my life.

Follow your heart.

My heart has been broken. I don't trust it.

Trust in God. God knows your life path and purpose. Trust that your angels will help you along the way.

Did you know I couldn't walk?

I know that the human body, when stressed, has a hard time healing. The stress hormone, cortisol, can cause havoc in a person's body. It can cause all kinds of dis-eases, even tumors.

I was so scared.

You were so scared. You're not anymore.

True.

Tamara, can I come and visit you?

Soon, but not yet. Your destiny right now is to help those three kids.

How can I help them?

By being you. Only you can help them on the next part of their journey.

I have no special gifts or powers. So, how can I ever help them?

Your power lies in your belief.

I don't know if I believe anymore.

You believe. You just had a bump in the road.

A bump in the road, more like I hit a land mine, and it exploded.

You'll heal from this trauma and the loss in your life. Time heals all ailments.

Tamara, do you know how to heal a soul?

With "belief." Lexi, the fact is, all a soul needs to do is believe.

I used to believe. I want to believe, but there was so much pain. I lost my faith.

And now you have a chance to get it back. God never gave up on you.

It sure felt like it.

No, Lexi, God is patient and allows a soul to heal, learn, and grow on its own timing. You had to go through what you did so that you could do what was required next of you.

What is that?

That is between you and God. Only you know what is in your heart. Follow your heart, and you will find peace again.

I miss talking to you, Tamara.

Bright light energy beamed on Lexi, and she felt illuminated.

In the following dream, Lexi was with Susannah, her mom, and her dad.

Oh my God! I thought you had all left me. I felt so alone.

Lexi, we are here with you, in your heart. We will always be part of you.

Susannah, I so missed your voice in my head.

I know, but when the human soul is depressed, the energy frequency is not high enough for you to hear me.

I pray that I never have to go through that pain again. I pray that I can always hear you.

And so it will be, Lexi.

I saw Tamara. She said that I must help Aias, Kesia, and Luna. Do you know what she was talking about?

All I can tell you is that you are going on a pilgrimage.
A pilgrimage. That sounds interesting.
Am I going to Europe to follow our family's ancestry?
No
Am I going to Europe?
No.
Can't you tell me where I am going?
No.
But you know?
Yes.
Am I going for me?
No.
So, I am going for one of the kids?
Yes.
Which one?
All of them.
Oh.
When do we leave?
Soon.
Is it going to be an adventure?
Yes, like none you have taken so far.
Hmm. Sounds interesting.
Is it an essential part of my life's path?
Yes.
Will I learn anything from this new adventure?
More than you could ever imagine.
Come on, give me a hint, Susannah.
Before Susannah could answer, Lexi's dream changed again.

Lexi was standing in a dark hallway. She instantly recognized the hallway. She was in Redington's condo. "Red? Are you home?"

No answer.

Lexi walked through his place and saw a note on the kitchen counter.

Picking it up, she read, *"Hey Alexandra, I hope you are doing well. I don't know how to tell you this, but I have loved you from the moment I laid eyes on you. You are the most incredible person I have ever met. You have a spark of life like no other. You are caring, heartfelt, dependable, sexy, and did I write sexy? Well, I meant it. I wish you all the best with Neo. But truthfully, I wish it was me. We would have made an incredible couple. Well, enough about my desires. I do wish you all the best.*
PS. Since I knew there was no chance for us, I decided to get as far away as I could from you and joined the FBI, and now I am undercover.
PPS. I love you!"

Lexi couldn't believe what she was reading. *He loves me.*

Then the voice was back … *Alexandra, you need to take this call.*

Lexi froze in place. *Who are you? And what call am I supposed to take?*

I am you. I am your soul talking to you. I am the part of you that knows deep down the call that I am talking about.

No. I don't know what call you are talking about! Do you mean a phone call?

Now that would be silly since we can talk in your mind.

Then what call are you talking about?

The one you are ready to take.

How do you know I am ready to take this call?

Because you believe you are.

Lexi took a breath and opened her eyes, ending the dream. Picking up her phone, she searched for the meaning of the word "calling."

A strong inner impulse toward a particular course of action, especially when accompanied by conviction of divine influence.

As shivers ran through her body, she knew exactly what the call meant. She intuitively knew that the call meant she was ready to learn the next spiritual gift—the Gift of Miracles!

Acknowledgments

As many of you know, my mom, aunt, grandmother, and husband Bata read my manuscript before I let my dear friend and mentor Diane read it. Then, it is off to the editor.

What a blessing it has been to find Ana!
Ana Joldes and House of Fables.
Thank you from the bottom of my heart. Your edits are gratefully accepted. I know my angels guided me to you. Again, thank you.

I would also like to thank all the amazing people who tell their stories or place their knowledge on the internet. What a marvelous tool and endless supply of research one can find there!

Companion Books

Secrets of a Healer Series:
Magic of
Aromatherapy, Adv. Aromatherapy, Massage,
Muscle Testing, Reiki, Reflexology,
Hypnotherapy, and Esthetics

The Author

Constance Santego is a Master Educator, Author, and Holistic Spiritual Coach. She is known for bridging the body, mind, and soul consciousness to create your dreams into reality. Her passion is teaching self-empowerment through the many ways of improving yourself: emotionally, spiritually, mentally, and physically.

MY GOAL
To provide healing, coaching, and training that motivates, inspires, and transforms enlightened souls— doing this through developing *The Nine Spiritual Gifts* you were born with: Knowledge, Wisdom, Faith, Healing, Miracles, Prophecy, Distinguishing Spirits, and Tongues.

Constance continually strives to advance her knowledge and is currently in the process of attaining her Ph.D. and DOCTORATE in Natural and Integrative Medicine.

Also Available

Play the game Ikona and test
your Virtues and Sins
For additional information on
Constance Santego's wide range of
Motivational Products, Coaching Sessions,
Spiritual Retreats,
Live Events and Educational Programs
Go to
www.ConstanceSantego.ca

Follow me on:
Instagram – Constance_Santego &
Facebook – constancesantegoo
YouTube Channel – Constance Santego
Subscribe and receive free information &
Meditations

452   Constance Santego